TERROR COPS

TERROR COPS

FIGHTING TERRORISM ON BRITAIN'S STREETS

HARRY KEEBLE with KRIS HOLLINGTON

POCKET
BOOKS

LONDON • SYDNEY • NEW YORK • TORONTO

First published in Great Britain by Pocket Books, 2010
An imprint of Simon & Schuster
A CBS COMPANY

1 3 5 7 9 10 8 6 4 2

Simon & Schuster UK Ltd
1st Floor
222 Gray's Inn Road
London WC1X 8HB

www.simonandschuster.co.uk

Simon & Schuster Australia
Sydney

PICTURE CREDITS
Getty: 1, 2, 3, 5, 6, 7, 10, 11, 12, 13, 14
Political Pictures: 4
PA Photos: 8, 22
Corbis: 9
Reuters: 16, 17, 19, 25
National News: 18
Metropolitan Police: 20
London Media: 21

A CIP catalogue record for this book
is available from the British Library.

ISBN: 978-0-85720-061-7

Typeset by M Rules
Printed in the UK by CPI Cox & Wyman, Reading, Berkshire RG1 8EX

This book is dedicated to the courageous
men and women of the British Army fighting
in Afghanistan. To 'TC' of Southern Command,
who epitomizes all that was excellent in Special
Branch. To S-squad and the SO15
Surveillance Support Team

CONTENTS

NOTE TO THE READER

It is important to ensure that the details of many individuals encountered through my work are not presented so that those individuals could be identified. Consequently, names have been changed and details altered where necessary. Cases on public record are reported in their original detail.

Some covert activities, code names and operational names detailed in this book have been disguised to protect UK national security. The reader should be left in no doubt that every case is based on real events, however, and that the feelings and emotions described in these accounts are an accurate record of what it is like to work for Special Branch surveillance.

ACKNOWLEDGEMENTS

I would like to take this opportunity to salute the bravery and courage of 'Ivor', C2 and C12 on 22nd July 2005.

My appreciation goes out to M15 for their professionalism in the field and for being so much fun to work with.

Kerri Sharp at Simon & Schuster is more than deserving of an honourable mention after steering *Terror Cops* through a complicated editorial process.

And, as always, much gratitude goes to Andrew Lowrie for his encouragement, vision and wise words:
www.andrewlowrie.co.uk

ONE

ACTION BEATS REACTION

'Awight, mate, got a light?'

Oh, good grief, not now.

It was 3 a.m. and I was walking the streets of the East End of London, operational but alone with a loaded Glock 17 on my hip, hidden by my coat.

This wasn't the best time to cross the paths of three hooded young black men who, clearly not realizing I was a cop, looked like they were about to mug me. They'd emerged suddenly from a side alley and – thanks to the way Londoners have to cram their cars along the street – there was no escape without vaulting over a car bonnet Starsky and Hutch-style. There was still a slight gap between the three men and the cars through which I could pass, but only just.

I put my head down and kept walking.

'Oi!' the tallest of them said, stepping out and blocking the gap. 'I asked you if you had a light. You deaf?'

Shit.

★

I was a detective sergeant in S-squad, a specialist surveillance unit that was part of SO15 – the code name for the brand-new Counter Terrorism Command, which had been formed just a few months earlier. Typically, S-squad would be charged with capturing intelligence and evidence on an address or suspect. My task, as a front-line covert officer, was to manage the reconnaissance of target addresses – which included the fitting of secret cameras and other technical 'assets'.

I also briefed the surveillance teams that followed suspect terrorists and the armed officers who would eventually raid the property on things to look out for: physical obstacles that might hamper surveillance, any comings and goings, what the environment was like, who was inside the target premises and whether they were still awake, and so on.

This could take place over months (lifestyle surveillance) or just a few hours after an 'executive action' (a decision made by the police and MI5 to arrest terror suspects). S-squad often had to scramble to join the hunt in an instant. Sometimes things went wrong, or the suspected terrorists would change their plans, or we received intelligence that suggested they were about to act and a massive op involving hundreds of officers would try to sweep them all up in sixty minutes.

We often wouldn't know the full story, not only because time was short, but also because these operations are complex and classified and therefore work on the 'need to know' principle. As long as we knew enough to do our job then that was fine by me.

That was precisely the case here. This was a fast-moving operation, a reaction to mounting intel from the Security Service, MI5. MI5 are civilians, they do not have the power of arrest for fear of becoming like a British version of the

Gestapo, hence the need for our involvement. We bridge the gap.

The intelligence told us that our suspects were involved in terror training, had access to weapons and were actively looking to carry out missions of their own. We were warned that it was highly likely that they were armed. The overall mission remained the same as ever: prevent an atrocity and catch the terrorists responsible without any harm to the public. No pressure there, then.

The order to arrest had sparked a huge operation. Running these rapidly developing scenarios in an inner city inevitably leaves us open to many tricky situations and it was no different here. A few hours earlier we'd been ready to deploy from our forward form-up point, which is where we go through the plan one last time. We also check that everyone's comms (communication systems) are working and that the pair of unlucky sods who are going to spend the rest of the night in the OP (observation point) vans are fully prepared for a long deployment – they'd have plenty of empty bottles on hand.

We'd found a discreet place in the back of a church car park, out of public sight, when a marked police car rolled up. The area car driver flipped on the spotlight, blinding us, and lowered the window. 'What are you doing here?'

'SCD7 mate, Flying Squad,' I said, producing my ID. I didn't want them to know that armed anti-terror officers were on the ground in their area. There was no need to advertise our presence. That's not because I don't trust other cops, quite the opposite in fact. But they might quite rightly warn the rest of their team via their radios that they shouldn't bother us. If there was a local officer sitting in a car at traffic lights with his window down in the street then it was possible that the wrong person would overhear the loud, sharp and clear transmission. We weren't taking any chances. Too much was at stake.

The teams also needed to know as much as possible about the houses that were next to our target. We had to do as much as possible to protect neighbours who were going to get a wake-up call they would never forget. These operations are deafeningly loud: much shouting of police dressed in ballistic armour and wielding guns, the booting in of the door, the use of flash bangs (non-lethal stun grenades) – not many people can sleep through that.

The last thing we wanted was for innocent people to be caught up in our operation. We were particularly concerned for the elderly. As well as being vulnerable or on their own, they tend to be light sleepers. There was only so much we could do; if they were living next door, we often couldn't give them any warning. Kids might be traumatized and may well scream and cry, but at least we wouldn't give them a heart attack.

We'd soon put an invisible net around the suspects' house, deploying various covert assets from SO15 and MI5 – one of which was me. I had plenty to keep me busy but I was well used to checking out properties prior to storming them. I'd cut my teeth raiding over a hundred crack houses in the neighbouring borough of Haringey.

The drugs problems were evident here, too, just a couple of miles from the 2012 Olympic Park at Stratford. This area was going through a period of regeneration in the run-up to the Olympics but it was still early days and there was little positive change to see – especially in the early hours of the morning.

Although all seemed quiet, my trained eyes spotted a couple of properties that could have been crack houses. The lights were on, sheets rather than curtains covered the windows, and the gardens were full of rubbish.

I checked my watch. Thirty minutes to the raid. I felt a knot of apprehension and excitement in my stomach. I knew exactly how the officers who were about to storm the property felt. I'd been there myself many times and had experienced everything from the horror of crashing full-tilt into the wrong address to getting into a full-on bone-breaking fist-fight with a house full of crack heads and prostitutes. I'd recovered guns and ammo, piles of crack and other drugs and nicked plenty of nasty characters. My new role was quite a change. Now I hunted from the shadows.

As we were going in armed, this raid would be a 'dig-out' – officers from SO19 (the Met's specialist firearms command) would announce the fact, very loudly, that they were carrying guns and that everyone inside the property should exit with their hands on their heads.

If this drew no response then either SO19 would go in themselves or the Method of Entry Team would force entry. These priceless units are actually made up of civilians who specialize in finding speedy ways into buildings they themselves will never enter. They're known as the 'Ghostbusters' or 'Ghosties' because they sometimes burn their way through doors using oxy-acetylene torches strapped to their backs, so they look like the characters in the film.

Their main weapon is the enforcer, a two-handled thirty-kilo hydraulic cylinder that packs a quarter-ton punch. Usually it takes just one or two strikes to obliterate even the sturdiest door. Another favourite is the Door-Breaker. This great piece of kit is a hydraulic ram that rips a door from the frame. It makes a deep, powerful hum, which during a dawn raid is especially terrifying for the occupants. In extreme situations, a firearms team will load pump-action shotguns with Hatton rounds. These fire a burst of compacted lead powder, which disintegrates anything it hits – including door hinges. As soon as they had the door open, they would stand back.

In this case, as we were worried they might be armed, the occupants would be given a final chance before we released 'the hounds' – a team of super-smart and incredibly powerful dogs trained to ignore gunshots. These animals lived for the moment when they'd be able to hunt down and disable a suspected gunman.

I felt a real buzz from the sheer power of the police in these kinds of circumstances. There was no way anyone could resist all that – but there were still huge risks.

With surprise raids on crack houses we used to smash the door in and charge into the darkness, never knowing exactly what we would find on the other side or how much resistance we would encounter. Of course there was always the concern that there might be some crazed drug addict waiting for us in the hallway with a shotgun. If we thought this was possible then we'd simply call in armed officers and do a dig-out.

Raiding a house full of suicide bombers is an entirely different ballgame. They're ready to die and won't hesitate to take as many innocent people with them as possible. There may even be boobytraps, such as tripwires or switches on door handles.

In a similar raid in Madrid a couple of years earlier, a terrorist cell had blown themselves up, taking one Special Operations officer with them and injuring fifteen more. Madrid was the worst kind of wake up call to law-enforcement agencies around the world.

In this line of work, we were always playing for the highest stakes.

'Oi! I asked you if you had a light?'

I shrugged, shoe gazing. I didn't want to meet their challenge by making eye contact.

'Sorry, I don't.'

My escape route was gone. To my left, a line of parked cars, to my right rows of tightly terraced houses. Three lads in my path. Trapped.

Should I run? I wondered. It's always an option, but here it's complicated by the fact that I'm wearing bulky clothing, am on a mission and am carrying. Besides, these guys look light on their feet. Nope, I'm not going anywhere, I concluded.

Deciding whether someone is dangerous or not is a fine art. Anyone who walks down a city street late at night makes these decisions instantly. How well we make them is another matter. In that moment I sized them up and decided that they were certainly suspicious and quite possibly dangerous.

One was short, of average build, in his twenties, wearing a tracksuit, while another was much taller, dressed in loose-fitting black hoodie, low-hung jeans and baseball cap. He couldn't have been more than nineteen. The third was all in dark clothing. I am sure that after whatever shady event they were planning had been carried out, all the tops would be swapped and kitchen and Stanley knives chucked into the hedges of East London where they'd lie with all the others.

This was a crime-ridden neighbourhood, one of London's roughest areas. Just how many reasons were there for three young men to be standing in a side street, just off the high road at 3 a.m.? Taking a breath of fresh air? I didn't think so.

This was bandit country, so-called because the police weren't welcome here. I kept walking towards them, hoping the fact that I didn't look like I was a worthwhile target would save me from any grief. I was sporting an old army coat, a cheap pair of jeans, tatty-looking boots and unwashed hair, which looked in desperate need of a cut.

The kid started reaching round into the back of his jeans with his right hand.

Shit.

My gun was a real complicating factor. Any contact has to be reported. If these men tried to mug me, I couldn't just wave my Glock at them, tell them to bugger off and expect to walk away as if nothing had happened. They wouldn't exactly stay quiet after I'd gone.

Everything slowed down. I brought my right hand up under my coat while looking at their chests, still not making eye contact. My peripheral vision went into overdrive, consciously trying to take in all their movements until the hand reappeared and all my concentration would be instinctively drawn to the weapon.

If they mugged me, there was a good chance they'd find or see my gun. I couldn't let them take it. Weapon retention is massively important. If someone tries to take a policeman's weapon, then the officer can lawfully shoot them to prevent this from happening.

Heaven forbid I should fire and wound or kill one of them and they turned out to be unarmed. No matter what the situation, even if the resulting inquiry concluded it was just a horrible accident, an inevitable by-product of the fact that police officers sometimes have to make life or death decisions in conditions of uncertainty, the local community would never forgive or forget. They'd say it was an open-and-shut case of racism.

By now my hand was over my Glock, my thumb silently flipping open the retaining strap. The three lads didn't react to this. I could not now beat a 'shank' though. I would be able to get a shot off quick, but not in time. My left arm was ready to come across my body to hopefully take the blade. My right hand was now ready to draw.

I knew that even if I missed the loud bang would probably be enough to scare them off, but it would also create havoc. In a few minutes the sirens would start up all over the borough and the operation would be in serious trouble.

Time slowed further as his hand started to come up. I went from seeing the whole picture to only seeing the man's arm and upper body. His black Ice Cube T-shirt, his thin stubble, his red eyes, blue baseball cap, the shoulders hunching. Everything else just disappeared. My breathing slowed. I would fire from the hip. The quickest way to get a shot off. If I didn't get stabbed that would enable me to get my stance correct, my arms out and looking down the barrel of the gun. I had no worries about a safety catch: the seventeen-round Glock doesn't have one as such, it's always ready to go. No British police officer to date has ever emptied their magazine.

During training the instructor had told us: 'This course is not for kicks. What you learn here will prepare you for the day when you stand and face another human being and end their life.'

I was in no hurry for that day to arrive. Even so, if it was going to happen, then it was most likely going to be in this spot of East London. I knew from our background briefing on this area that there had been five shootings in six weeks; the last was a 24-year-old-man who'd been shot in the knee as he sat drinking in a pub.

Before that a man in his late twenties had taken a bullet in the head as part of a gang's revenge attack. Murder detectives later learned that this was a case of mistaken identity. The killer was still at large.

Although we're taught that action beats reaction, my own experience of these streets combined with the overriding desire not to compromise the operation, meant that I held my nerve and kept the Glock holstered but ready.

Numerous intelligence agencies, from Pakistan's Inter Services Intelligence (ISI) department to the UK's Government Communication Headquarters, not to mention MI5 and the CIA, had brought us to this point. I had no intention of becoming infamous the world over for screwing up a major job like this.

His hand came into view; he was holding a cigarette packet. A bloody cigarette packet!

Fucking hell, I thought in relief, he *actually* wants a light!

Time gradually returned to normal. My breathing slowed, my hand slipped away from the gun.

'If you ain't got one, bruv, just say so.'

Phew. I shook my head, smiled apologetically and walked on, my adrenaline still pumping hard.

I had sized up a situation and, with twenty years experience behind me, I'd got it wrong. A wave of guilt broke over me.

On my little drugs squad, the majority of my officers had been black. I think it was the first proactive unit in the country to have more black officers than white. It wasn't by design; I'd simply chosen the best men and women for the job.

They'd once returned from a visit to the flagship Edmonton

police station in a state of extreme annoyance after the three of them, all walking along together, had been challenged and asked for ID while *inside* the police station. I remember them laughing as they described the extreme embarrassment of their challenger who then spent the next few minutes apologizing and babbling, while opening door after door for them.

Whatever the case, I thought to myself as I marched on towards the target address, sometimes life would be a lot easier if we didn't have to carry a bloody gun.

TWO

INTO THE WORLD OF SECRETS

Six months earlier I was standing in the office of Detective Inspector Terry Caudle. Terry had his head down, looking at his notes and my file, giving me a moment to admire all the diplomas and awards that covered the wall behind his desk.

Closer inspection, however, revealed some surprises among the official service awards. One was a twenty-five-metre swimming certificate; there were others for a variety of childhood athletic achievements and a handful for book reading awarded by long-gone grammar schools.

I stifled a grin. Well, at least he's got a sense of humour, I thought.

The view from Terry's office took in the National Gallery, Thames House (MI5) and the Houses of Parliament. If he leaned forward in his chair he'd be able to see the London Eye. He shared the room with three other DIs. In any other police department, as a DI he would have had his own office. In Special Branch and the world of counter-terrorism in general, rank shrinks. An inspector is god in a county force, but not here.

Special Branch's role was to counter the threat of political violence and subversion. Formed in 1883, it was the oldest unit of its kind in the world. Within Special Branch, a specialist protective unit known as A-squad was charged with protecting high-profile politicians and civil servants.

B-squad tackled Irish Republican terrorism and had been massively scaled down in the wake of the Good Friday Agreement. The numbers of terror-related incidents in Ireland remain high, however, and often go unreported in the mainland press.

C-squad dealt with domestic extremism and animal rights. The emergence of the far right on the edge of mainstream politics has kept them busy in recent years.

D-squad dealt with the national functions of Special Branch.

P-squad dealt with the ports, like Heathrow and Dover. These officers are acutely aware that, thanks to the Terrorism Act 2000, they have more powers than any other police officer and use them maturely and wisely.[1]

I had signed up for S-squad, which contained all of Special Branch's surveillance units (including photo and technical support divisions), one of which was the newly formed Surveillance Support Team (SST), created in October 2006, which I had been assigned to. Until then, the SST had been in a much smaller form called the Planning Team. Terry was the boss of the SST and the Grey surveillance team. The Greys were 'people-followers', elite armed surveillance officers who followed targets wherever and however they went.

The SST was at the forefront of any new covert operation – they were the spearhead unit responsible for reconnaissance and planned the placement of technical and human surveillance assets. They worked very closely with all of the other surveillance teams as well as the Met's covert photographers. So when a suspected terrorist left a property, for example, it was up to us to ID them to the people-followers.

Many in the SST went on to join the people-followers. It was a great way to learn the tradecraft of surveillance. For any major counter-terrorist operation, the SST would be right in the front line – and that's just how I liked it.

My decision to join the police fifteen years earlier was as much a surprise to me as it was for my parents. I was studying for my A levels when one day, in between lectures, I spotted in the bin a pamphlet on joining the police. Something made me stop, reach into the rubbish and pull it out.

The idea suddenly seemed appealing. Breaking the speed limit to get to dangerous and exciting incidents, getting into fights and being able to bust the heads of violent criminals with the full power of the law behind me – fighting crime seemed like a worthy job and a lot of fun.

I first became a special constable and found myself on the street in police uniform, including baton and handcuffs – an eighteen-year-old who didn't know the first thing about the law. It was brilliant. I signed up looking for excitement and the job didn't let me down. In fact I got too much excitement right from day one.

I arrived at Stoke Newington police station in 1992 as a fresh-faced uniformed constable just as a massive corruption scandal broke. A total of forty-four officers from my station had been placed under investigation. To say the community hated and distrusted the police was a massive understatement. As allegations of officers dealing in drugs and beating innocent people half to death in the cells flew around the neighbourhood, I stepped out to patrol the mean streets of Stokie.

It proved to be an eye-opening time, to say the least. My colleagues and I were always suffering from some injury sustained in the course of our duties and I soon learned how to fight.

This was excellent preparation for what was to come four and a half years later when I moved to Haringey as a sergeant in charge of the borough's drug squad. As far as I was concerned, drugs – crack in particular – were the number one source of crime in London and I wanted to do something about it.

Working in Haringey made Stokie feel like a walk in the park. My five-man team and I decided that the only way to return the streets to the community was to fight a war against crack. Our mission: to eliminate all one hundred crack houses in our borough in one year. It should have been impossible. But we did it; we literally smashed our way through a hundred crack dens. As a direct result, black-on-black killings in Haringey were halted for the following twelve months.

I'd been disturbed by the number of children we'd rescued from crack houses and the problems with child protection in general. Victoria Climbié had been tortured to death just a few doors away from where I'd been raiding crack houses. So, instead of accepting an offer to head up part of a major new glamorous drugs task force, I transferred to Hackney's Child Protection Unit where I stayed for four years, bringing dozens of child abusers to justice for the most horrific crimes imaginable. I travelled everywhere from Jamaica to Africa in the hunt for the monsters that abuse innocent children.

In July 2005, I was in a swish conference room at the

brand-new Emirates Stadium in Highbury, North London, home to Arsenal Football Club, to promote the work of child protection and to try to convince more officers to join us. When it was time to give my presentation, I went through all the major cases I'd worked on. I spoke with enthusiasm about rescuing children, and the elation I'd felt on more than one occasion at preventing another Climbié.

Afterwards, our stand had been swamped with interested detectives and I was soon running low on business cards. As I continued to sell my job, I noticed that people's attention was being drawn elsewhere. I tailed off in mid-conversation and looked around. Everyone was staring at the giant plasma TV screens. Sky News was on. The ticker tape flashed across the screen 'BREAKING NEWS: Four explosions in London. Four suicide bombers on the loose.'

We'd been hit again. The second attack in only three weeks. Was this the beginning of a new sustained campaign? How many more attacks might there be? I looked around the conference room and out through the window into the stadium. Imagine them attacking here, if Arsenal were playing at home. Tens of thousands of people; whole families, young and old. I couldn't bear the thought.

People were already calling their loved ones when the most senior officer present called for everyone's attention. 'I am sure you are all aware of the seriousness of the situation we're currently facing,' he said gravely. 'I'm calling on volunteers who can be deployed from here if the need arises.'

I felt no little pride when the whole floor stepped forward as one, without a second's hesitation. Officers from across the force, of all ranks and departments, were united with the same simple thought in that instant; we were ready to do whatever was necessary to defend London and protect the public. After all, no matter where our careers had taken us, this was the core reason for signing up for the police in the first place.

In the event we were not needed that day but a seed had been sown, reinforced by the then Met Chief, Sir Ian Blair. 'This is a campaign we are facing – not a one-off event,' he told reporters. 'The second attack on July 21 should not be taken as some indication of weakening of the capability or the resolve of those responsible. This is not the B-team. These are not amateurs. They made a mistake. They made one mistake. We are very, very lucky. The carnage that would have occurred had those bombs gone off would have at least been the equivalent to those on July 7.'

Over the following few days, Sir Ian said there were many 'tired faces' at Scotland Yard. A thousand officers were involved in the inquiry but the extent of the threat meant the Yard's resources would need to be extended. 'We will have to strengthen in the next year the firearms capability of the Metropolitan Police,' he said. 'We have to give people rest.'

Sir Ian had issued a call to arms and I felt as though it were my duty to respond. Many Londoners lost friends and relatives on 7/7 – and to have this followed by another attempt just two weeks later, well, it was just impossible for me to ignore.

So that's how I found myself, just a few months later, in the offices of the world-famous Special Branch.

Terry looked up from my file.

'Twenty-three years I've been doing this,' he said to me in his soft-spoken northern accent. 'I've seen it all. And you know what I've learned?'

'No, sir,' I said.

'Don't call me that,' he barked. 'It's Terry.'

Looking me directly in the eye, he continued, 'Keep your eyes open and mouth shut.'

'Yes, si— Terry,' I replied and, in keeping with this advice, I decided not to add any comment.

Although this informality was appreciated, I could see Terry was clearly not a man to mess about. His reputation as a rock-solid detective inspector was second to none but if anyone crossed him or screwed up an operation, then his wrath was a terrible thing to behold.

'This job is the crown jewels of British law enforcement. I guarantee it's unlike anything else you've experienced. This is a whole other kind of policing. You will be sent on the best courses, courses that will change you as an officer and as a person. You will work on some truly amazing and crucially important operations – but much is expected of you in return.

'To start with, Special Branch is cultured, sophisticated. Our officers have to be able to talk to any ambassador, diplomat, minister or spy from any country about almost anything. This takes a little getting used to but I'm sure you'll pick it up in due course. It's vital that in your work you understand the communities within which you'll be operating and I expect you to do your homework. Also, one of the first things to bear in mind is that AQ [al-Qaeda] is not a unified body. They have no definitive political aim, no controlling leadership; even the ideologies between different AQ cells often differ. The only thing that unites them, apart from their worship of Osama bin Laden, is their wish to carry out terrorist acts against innocent people.'

He went on: 'The British army are the best in the world at "hearts and minds" and they have their work cut out in

Afghanistan. Out there, one day a man can be a starving farmer, the next he might be earning ten dollars a day fighting the Coalition. Fighting AQ is not like fighting a uniformed cohesive army. That is why you have to understand communities. It's vital. Believe me, it'll help you when you're out on a job in East London at all times of the day and night.

'More importantly, there's the danger. The "good old days" of the IRA are long gone,' Terry said. 'An IRA active service unit would always be armed and ready, but AQ-inspired terrorists are different. The people we spend most of our time hunting these days are prepared to lose their lives at any moment. Your missions *will* be life-threatening.'

I found this concept quite hard to get to grips with. I had signed up for the 'War on Terror' and I thought it was a case of 'Just go and get the bad guys, let them have it', but it was clear from what Terry was saying that I was going to have to be able to deal with a much more complex reality.

My own experience in fighting terrorism was virtually nil. I'd encountered the IRA once in my career in 1996 when I was still a keen and green PC based in Stoke Newington. I was sitting in the top Portakabin in a stack of three piled up at the back of the station, completing about the twentieth form out of twenty-eight that needed to be filled out when processing a prisoner, when I heard a 'Boom'. The whole cabin rattled worryingly.

I looked across at my mate and we nodded in agreement. 'I suspect that was a bomb,' he said, stating the obvious.

That night I was sent with other officers from Stokie to guard part of the outer cordon of where the explosion had occurred, right by the docks. As we passed the newsagents

near the site of the blast, we were told that the two dark
bloodstains on the concrete floor belonged to the shop worker,
one of two fatalities. The half-tonne bomb, which had demol-
ished a six-storey building, had been detonated on a Sunday.
Had this happened during the week then hundreds of City
workers might have been killed while thousands more would
have been cut to pieces by flying glass.

I ended up with a deserved rollicking from an inspector
after a press photographer managed to slip past the cordon by
jumping onto a nearby barge. I soon had him back but not
quickly enough. My skipper had hurt his ankle, causing him to
limp (he had to walk around and around the cordon while we
manned the points), and he was understandably in the foulest
of moods.

It was a freezing February and the hours dragged inter-
minably by. Looking for something with which we could
amuse ourselves, I discovered that one of the girls on the team
had a mobile phone (they were still a new-fangled invention in
those days). She made a note of the number of a payphone on
the corner that was far enough away from us not to cause suspicion, yet still gave us a good view. Every time someone
walked around the corner, we rang the phone. Most ignored
it but for some reason we got our skipper every time he passed
by. He would hobble over with increasing speed, only for the
ringing to stop just as he went for the receiver.

'You'll work with Box, of course,' Terry continued, nodding
towards Thames House, 'and they'll teach you a thing or two.'

'Box' was the nickname for MI5, so-called because its
wartime postal address was Box 500.

'Their motto is *Regnum Defende*, "Defend the Realm", and

I'd go along with that except to add *Servo Populus* – "Protect the People". That's why they don't have the power of arrest. Their constitution, if you can call it that, puts Queen and country before the people living in it.'

MI5 was a highly professional – but sometimes tricky – department to work with but Terry was a shrewd DI. His twenty-plus years of Special Branch experience meant he knew exactly when they were trying to pull a fast one or keep intel from him. He was always able to ask them the right questions before Box called with a 'simple request' at 4 p.m. on Friday and disappeared to their country cottages for the weekend.

We had another nickname for MI5, apart from Box, which was grossly unfair, but very funny. No, it's not 'Spooks'. Sometimes, we cheekily called them 'The Toads, from Toad Hall (Thames House)'.

Special Branch, SO12, was being brought to an end and Terry was convinced this was a mistake. It was about to be merged with SO13, the Anti-Terrorist Branch, to form the new Counter Terrorism Command, SO15. I was one of the very last policemen to ever become a Special Branch officer. New recruits simply join SO15.

SO13 was Britain's anti-terrorist investigation police, which included explosives experts. They were kept on 24/7 stand-by to respond to any domestic or international terrorist incident and worked closely alongside SO19 (the Specialist Firearm Command branch which includes everything gun-related from officers in armed response vehicles to counter-snipers).

Special Branch (SB) officers sometimes referred to their colleagues from the anti-terrorist branch as 'bellies', in the belief that they drank too much beer and carried too much weight, or as 'jingle-janglers' as they were famed for their cheap suits and bad jewellery: gold bracelets, signet rings and medallions. I have to admit that I'm in no position to criticize them for their dress sense – and there are a few Special Branch officers who have no right to criticize the girth of SO13 men.

They called us 'The Bwarnch', the posh lads. SB officers drank red wine and appreciated fine dining. Many were, and still are, members of London clubs. SO13, on the other hand, preferred the Masons.

As far as SB was concerned, SO13 officers were well meaning but unintelligent. They might do a good job every now and again, but this wasn't to be expected. Of course, this was hardly fair but as far as policing went, the difference between these two departments came down to this: Special Branch were a tight-knit unit with a proud history and strong identity, and worked closely with the Security Service. Their role was in intelligence. SO13 were more open and worked closely with other police departments in old-fashioned policing – collecting evidence – and they did it very well. SB worked as a firewall between SO13 and MI5. SO13 would often refer to any SO12 officer who had annoyed them as a 'Branch anchor'; accordingly, sometimes SO12 would have to admit the occasional 'Branch eccentric'.

The formation of SO15 was to bring together these two very different (some would say incompatible) cultures and backgrounds – which meant that one thing was certain: I could expect to see plenty of fireworks during and after the merger. I decided that Terry's advice was indeed the best policy. Eyes open, mouth shut.

Many of Terry's colleagues were outraged by the move; the merger would kill the much-treasured identity of the legendary Special Branch (at the time of writing, SO15, which came into being at the end of 2006, still doesn't have an emblem or badge, unlike many other Specialist Operations Units).[2]

The merger was orchestrated by Assistant Commissioner Andy Hayman, the Met's head of Specialist Operations, and supported by Commissioner Sir Ian Blair who had been appointed to the top job after promising he would streamline the Met, which also meant cutting budgets. Sir Ian was all about restructuring and modernizing the Met. Of course, nearly all of these cuts went out the window or were eaten up by our counter-terrorism efforts after 7 July 2005.

Terry looked at my file. I'd gone through something known as Security Vetting. This involves financial and other checks on your background. If you pass it gives you unsupervised access to secret material and supervised access to top-secret material. I was yet to complete my Developed Vetting, the most thorough background examination there is, including criminal checks on all relatives as well as financial, MI5, social and psychological checks. DV cleared you at top secret level. This was updated every five years and lasts for ten.

It used to be that all SB officers were DV-cleared before they could start. However, due to the shortage of officers to work on counter-terrorist operations, as well as the impending merger, things were about to change.

'They're thinking of scaling this down, you know,' Terry said, prodding my SC (security clearance) and impending DV clearance file. 'If that really does happen, it will be a mistake that we'll pay for.' However, like many things that are banded around, thankfully, this was as far as it got.

'Well, that's about it for my "welcome aboard" speech, Harry. Now let's meet your team.'

THREE

THE TERROR COPS

We bumped into David in the corridor outside Terry's office. A 48-year-old former lecturer, David had found his way into Special Branch after he became bored of his chosen profession. He was the head of S-squad's Red surveillance team and classic Special Branch stock: privately educated and with a Master's degree. He wore the classic SB uniform. In the 1980s this was a Barbour jacket and outfits befitting a country gentleman.

The modern dress of SB tends to feature casual trousers, open-necked shirts (unless they felt like wearing the SB tie), brown brogues and a jacket. Although these days officers are expected to wear a jacket and tie, you still see the occasional dicky bow, and if you're really lucky, a trilby.

David shook my hand warmly. 'Welcome aboard, dear boy,' he said in a plummy Leslie Phillips-style accent straight out of the 1950s comedy film *I Was Monty's Double*. 'You're joining us at a very interesting time. Anything you want to know, just ask. OK, old chap?'

He gave me a wink. I could see that behind his warm hand-shake lay decades of experience in tackling terrorists, someone who understood his enemy's methods well.

David, along with many other Branch officers, was an out-and-out intellectual; so much so that I struggled to keep up sometimes. He had an analytical mind and was always mentally dissecting situations. I felt most of these chaps were overqual-ified for their rank (I certainly felt underqualified in their presence) and I was grateful to have them as role models. David was a very valuable resource and I would learn a great deal from him.

The warm welcome was repeated throughout the depart-ment over the next few days as people came up to introduce themselves. This was unusual for the police, a profession in which people aren't usually so forthcoming. It seemed to me that everyone in this department oozed confidence and charm – they were expert and natural socializers who could talk as easily and expertly about the issues that drove apart com-munities on the Shankill Road or in the tribal areas of Kashmir.

Next up was George. In his early thirties, he was an impec-cably groomed and unflappable ex-army officer. He was the Surveillance Support Team's voice of reason. Whenever dis-cussions became 'heated' he'd use his broad shoulders to nudge the warring parties apart before placating them with his soft Yorkshire accent. His favourite phrase, oft repeated to me over the coming months, was: 'Play to people's strengths, old man.' His army skills were invaluable and always employed to plan and execute his strategy on any operation.

Other ex-army lads included Raj, a quiet, self-assured, straight-backed and professional fellow, a fearless and dedicated worker. He was a lively, happy soul and gladly took new people like me under his wing. An Asian, he'd been a squaddie in the 1980s. That couldn't have been easy. He had my instant respect and admiration.

Being in the army was excellent preparation for the Branch, as soldiers had some important parts of the necessary skill-set – they were used to handling firearms, were able to remain cool under fire and, by default, were used to the idea that their enemy wanted them dead, plain and simple. They were able to take orders but make quick decisions on their own and could react to rapidly changing situations when they had to.

Then I got a bit of a shock.

'Awight, geez?' Danny was an East End boy in his late twenties; he had an unashamedly risqué sense of humour and was just the sort of bloke who would charge a machine-gun post armed with a pencil if ordered to do so – he was 100 per cent unquestioningly loyal to the job. Although he often played the fool and committed more than his fair share of gaffes, he was smart, streetwise, witty and any dull meeting was brightened by his presence. Danny's keenness to make a difference was a constant source of inspiration. He was also a very trendy dresser and never grew tired of poking fun at my 'designer label' Tesco value range of outfits. Although he was by no means your usual Special Branch stock, the department prided itself on recruiting genuine one-off individuals, people who were self-assured and were happy to operate independently.

A young Asian lad called Asad offered me a bone-crushing handshake. Asad was a rock and could sit in an OP van for thirty hours straight with no complaint. He was totally devoted to his work and volunteered for the worst jobs without hesitation and never complained about the hours or conditions. He just got on with it.

'I'd love to stay and chat,' Asad said as he got up. 'But I've got a shift on the monitors.'

'Thank God it's us and not someone from accounts any more,' a female voice called across from the other side of the room. I turned to see a very tall and attractive young woman. She gave me a friendly wave.

'Meet Theresa,' Terry said, 'she's referring to the recent "reorganization" of Special Branch. The first Branch unit to fall under the streamlining sword was E-squad.'

Theresa was a straight-talking ex-services girl. I soon discovered she was a very good leader and knew I could count on her for excellent advice.

E-squad was made up of a hundred officers, each of whom specialized in the security services of one particular country, from America to Zimbabwe. They provided the Met with up-to-the-minute written assessments on each country so we knew all there was to know, saving us precious time in any situation that involved a foreign nation. So, when a Russian assassin struck, for example, we knew who we should be looking for and where we might find them – as well as who would be best placed to assist us.

When they weren't doing this, the officers of E-squad manned our operations room in the Yard and acted as live intel monitors during any Branch operation. They answered the phones and kept an eye on the audio and visual intelligence coming in from all the surveillance teams placed in a complex net around the target.

Part of this involved listening in to the radio channels of every surveillance team and typing out their latest communications, which were put up on plasmas that line one side of the room, so those running the operation knew exactly what was happening when and where.

It was a high-pressure role. Even though an enormous amount of information arrived every second, the guys from E-squad had to be 100 per cent accurate. After all, lives were at stake.

'They were abolished overnight,' Terry said, 'and were replaced with a trained-up section of our admin staff. They were drafted in as and when they were needed to staff the ops room.'

It's quite a step up to suddenly find yourself working as a monitor on a counter-terrorism operation, dealing with ever-changing intel, after having dealt with the Met's finances all day.

'Great in terms of career development, but maybe a bridge too far,' Terry said. 'And while they may have just about coped, it didn't exactly seem fair to drag them into such a high-profile role.'

'Those chaps and chapesses were really dedicated,' David added. 'But listening to surveillance chat is not something that's learned overnight.'

'Yes, well,' Terry said with a sigh, 'sometimes they struggled to understand the language, codes and subtleties of communication as well as police procedures. And as they weren't doing it day in day out, they were sometimes too slow, but that wasn't their fault.'

Theresa chuckled. 'I still can't believe the guy who came up with this system was given a £500 bonus.'

'That's just a rumour, Theresa, thank you very much,' Terry said severely. 'And you know what I think about rumours.'

Thank goodness this system was quickly reformed and now S-squad officers are back doing the job.

'Be warned, there are certain financial realities we all have to face,' Terry told me. 'Chasing terrorists is very expensive, every large op costs millions to run and the top brass will always be looking for money-saving ideas. The Met is taking the Special Branch bike apart and it's our duty to help them put it back together once they realize they need to ride it again.'

A-squad had already been dismantled. The men and women who protected our top politicians and civil servants had been absorbed into the Specialist Protection Command, which looked after the Royal Family and VIPs. Although this made sense the politicians still liked to refer to their guards as from Special Branch as it was such a well-known and much-admired 'brand'. After all, you had to be very important indeed to require the protection of the Branch.

On the other side of the large office, Terry introduced me to Jenny, a dynamic and resourceful detective constable in her twenties. Although she was very pretty and feminine she was also extremely robust and took no nonsense. She turned out to be one of the best covert officers I ever met. Originally from North London, she had no hint of this in her pristine Special Branch accent. She had the wonderful habit of calling even the butchest riot squad officer 'flower'.

Next to her was Mary, a really experienced, tenacious and good-looking investigator in her mid-thirties who'd joined the Branch from the murder squad, looking for a 'fresh experience'. Our resources would become stretched to the limit over the coming months, and Mary would end up leading the team for a number of weeks. For a DC to step into the shoes of a sergeant without any formal promotion process is a rare thing indeed and a real tribute to her capability.

Not all officers came with a wealth of experience. Marion was in her mid-twenties and had about three years' police service and an Oxford degree. Special Branch also wanted those with the most potential as well as those with experience and hard-won skills.

By the end of my first day, the team had completely bowled me over with their friendly and open natures. Joining a tight-knit specialist unit was always a bit of a gamble. All too often, the 'newbie' would have to make countless cups of tea and be cut out of conversations until those that held most sway in the department finally decided they could be trusted.

I got 100 per cent openness from day one and was immediately made part of the S-squad family. I think it had something to do with the fact that the stakes were very different from most other police departments who very often hunted criminals after the fact. Here, we were engaged in dangerous, life-threatening work to stop the terrorists before they struck, as George was keen to point out over lunch.

'Times have changed since the days of the IRA. Of course, they were very dangerous – but they were sometimes fun to watch. You'd follow them down the pub, drink a few pints and watch them chat up some women.'

'Bit different in a mosque, is it?' I said.

He grinned. 'Too right. Not nearly as interesting. We can end up going there five times a day and we're relegated to being sat outside, no fun in that. We can't exactly follow our suspects in and eavesdrop and then we have to play an impossible game of "Where's Wally?" when they come out of a mosque with a thousand other people.'

'Their goal remains the same, though.'

'Yes and no. The difference here of course is that they're prepared to blow themselves up and are determined to kill as many people as possible in the process. They're fanatics.'

'So what's on at the moment?'

'Something quite spectacular. I can tell you're chomping on the bit to get out on a job.'

But before that could happen, I had to get my gun.

FOUR

ARMED POLICE!

'Watch your fronts!'

I automatically drew my Glock, pushed myself back down in my seat, pointed it at the centre of the windscreen, held it steady and squeezed the trigger. The 140-decibel metallic crack was as loud as a fighter plane taking off but I hadn't heard a thing. I was already focusing on the large hole that was now in the car windscreen. Taking aim, knowing that the glass had deflected my first bullet from its target, I aimed through the hole and fired again. It passed through without leaving a mark and hit home.

I made my Glock safe, returned it to my holster and looked up at my instructor, feeling pretty pleased with myself. My first role-playing exercise with live rounds and everything had gone just the way it should.

'Try to aim a little higher next time,' the instructor said flatly. These sods were total perfectionists and it would have taken a miracle for me to impress them enough for them to admit it.

I'd asked for gun training as soon as possible. It wasn't compulsory, but the way I saw it, this was an integral part of working in SO12.

Although the idea of routine arming often crops up, it's very unlikely to ever come into force. Few SO12 operations were armed and although those in favour would argue that fast-moving operations can develop into situations where guns could be used, most officers would prefer not to take them out as a matter of course. Being armed means that operations have to be run differently. Also, as I would go on to discover, being armed could also lead to 'complications'.

Not carrying guns also meant that briefings were shorter. If we're using guns then a long warning statement has to be read out to the whole team (some briefings for armed operations are now recorded, so there's no reason to mishear or misinterpret an order or guideline) and it also meant that I didn't have to send two officers on a time-consuming trip to collect our guns from the armoury (and then put them back again at the end of the day).

To get my permit, I'd been sent on a three-week training course at Milton firearms centre with its set of ranges, a 'virtual reality' training room of sorts, as well as a purpose-built village where instructors ran 'live' missions. There were twelve of us on the course; half were from SO12, the other half were from SCD11 (crime surveillance). The rivalry between the two units was intense and a lot of fun – it drove us to try to achieve the precision the instructors were after and we all became firm friends.

After we had finished shooting through car windows we handed in our live ammo in return for 'simunitions'. Simunition rounds are paint pellets that can be fired through police and military service weapons. They fire and sound like the real thing but are simply fancy paintballs that hurt like hell.

We also used blank cartridges; these were not like normal blanks as they contained very little gunpowder and just cracked. Few people realize that firing a normal blank at someone at close range can be fatal; apart from wounds caused by casing fragments, the hot gas released by the exploding gunpowder can travel fast enough to shatter bone. The instructors used normal blanks in their shotguns when they played villains, however, and this kept us on our toes.

The scenarios were always extremely well run and felt as though they were real; we went through attacks on vehicles, hostage situations, 'dig-outs' as well as home, office and ware-house raids. Often we were simply told to sit in a car or stand on a corner. The instructor would say something like 'Wait for something to happen.' This may not sound very real, but it certainly felt like it. You are nervous and anxious. You want to get it right, the pressure builds, you want to make the right decisions as soon as something happens. It's extremely stressful.

'OK, the mission is this,' the burly instructor told our twelve-strong team. 'A constable has gained entry to that house . . .' He pointed to an empty house in the 'village'. 'He's been shot and is bleeding to death. There's no time to wait for the SWAT team. You need to make an emergency entry and get him out in one piece, bearing in mind that there's a lone armed suspect inside.'

After a moment's pause where we looked blankly back at him, he leaned forward, opened his arms, palms up and yelled: 'Well, what are you waiting for?! Are you gonna let him bleed to death?'

We formed up on the pavement outside the house. I

volunteered to boot in the door, something I missed doing from my days spent raiding crack houses. I also decided to duck as soon as I stepped into the hallway. If the gunman had already shot a cop, then he'd nothing left to lose, he would be going down for a long time. He's not going to worry about shooting more cops.

I gave the nod to my colleagues either side of the door, then took a run at it, raising my size eleven in the time-honoured fashion and, with great satisfaction, stomped the door open so hard that its hinges broke. Then I dived straight down the corridor and turned left into the first room. Empty.

'CLEAR!' I yelled as the team entered the house. Once the ground floor was secured I made my way upstairs. As I turned at the top, I saw him. The killer was in front of me, at the end of the hallway, two guns poking out of the top of his jeans. What the hell was this, Gunfight at the OK Corral?

He started to lower his hands. 'Don't touch the gun!' I yelled. Any lower and I'd have to shoot. He dropped his hands and I fired, hitting him in the chest. Game over.

Or so I thought.

As I walked towards the 'dead' killer I saw a shadow of movement in the doorway and another man stepped out holding a gun and firing, hitting me in the shoulder and the chest as I fired back repeatedly.

'Well, that could have gone better, couldn't it?' the instructor asked afterwards. 'How many rounds did you fire?'

It was a simple question but I wasn't sure.

'Come on! It's easy, isn't it? How many?'

Very few people give an accurate record of the number of rounds fired after a shooting. People tend to underestimate and, although your belief might be genuine, at an inquest you'll seem like a liar, as if you're trying to cover something up – and that could lead to a murder charge. We are told that if asked we should say that we fired 'a number of shots'.

We each took turns playing armed suspects in a variety of scenarios. When it was my turn, I was armed, sitting in a car. I climbed out with my hands on my head, the gun in my belt, walking backwards towards the arresting officers.

Now, even though this is just role-playing, when you're actually doing it, it feels like it's close to reality; the adrenaline courses through your body with all the shouting and gun-waving of the arresting officers. The simunition really bloody hurts so you really don't want to get hit – but I had an idea that I might be able to get a couple of shots off before they could shoot me.

As the team screamed at me to keep walking back towards them I lowered my hands slightly so they were in front of my face before whipping round, grabbing my gun, raising and firing it.

It was amazing. Time slowed. I could see everything. All the officers in front of me were clear as a bell. I could see their fingers on triggers but they were too late. I got off two good shots before they managed to fire; one of them had struck an officer in the shoulder. I kept firing as the first round hit the car behind me, the one after that hit my chest – the pain made me stagger backwards.

During the post-mortem the instructor said to the officers who'd shot me: 'What happened here should scare you. That was a good way to get killed. You should have got into cover.'

As fun as this was, I really wanted to do well. As a detective sergeant in SO12, I had to be able to deploy the right resources at the right time and this would sometimes include sending out detective constables with guns – I needed to understand the tactics and the pressures that armed officers faced. That way I'd feel better qualified to make those kinds of decisions and would be able to run an armed operation as effectively as possible.

As strange as this may seem, it's still possible to become a Bronze Firearms Commander (normally a sergeant leading a team of armed officers on a live mission on the ground) without being firearms trained. Silver and Gold Commanders are normally away from the front line of any operations, either at a building like Scotland Yard or in a command vehicle.

The weapon of choice for Special Branch was the Glock 17, arguably the world's most reliable firearm. Bury them in ground for a year, pull them out and they'll fire first time, no problem. Criminals' guns tend to be extremely unreliable, partly because they're poorly maintained but very often because they're old decommissioned firearms that have been reactivated by amateurs working from their front room with little knowledge or craftsmanship. Criminals also tend to be rubbish shots, but that's not much of a consolation – or something to be relied upon.

There's a lot more to firearms training than knowing how to fire the thing. There are *very* strict safety drills. It's a huge amount of responsibility; it's almost like a strange new person has entered your life – you have to learn how to hold it, clean it, strip it and put it away safely.

There are a surprising number of 'negligent discharges' ('accidental' discharges don't exist), especially during training. We were lining up at one of the ranges when I heard an ambulance siren in the 'village'. An officer was placing his gun in its holster when it caught on the toggle of his fleece jacket and he fired a round into his leg. Ouch.

Gunshot wounds are a real mess to sort out. As a bullet enters the body it creates a vacuum, drawing in dirt behind it. After the bullet has been dug out, the leg – as was the case with the chap on the range – has to be opened up and cleaned. Recovery is a drawn-out and horribly gruelling process; bullet wounds are nothing like they're portrayed in Hollywood.

Clothing can be a real problem; I managed to catch my T-shirt on my Glock as I re-holstered while on the range and had to call the instructor over to untangle it. I wasn't taking any chances after the earlier incident.

Most negligent discharges happen when the weapon is being put back in the armoury. We used Kevlar bags when dismantling so if they did go off the bullet would (in theory) be stopped by the bag.

Police bullets contain less charge, so they won't pass through the body. This is so that innocent people are not shot by a bullet that has passed through a criminal. The last thing you want is to shoot a man in the chest only to find that a child was standing behind them and you've hit them too.

In the 1970s it used to be (unofficial) Special Branch policy to always make sure you had a spare round on you in case of a negligent discharge, so there would be no awkward explanations or form-filling (as long as the stray bullet didn't hit anyone). I can assure you that this 'policy' has been defunct for many years. Churchill's Special Branch bodyguard was unable to use this 'policy' when it happened to him during the war as his negligent discharge went into his leg. That would have been much harder to square up.

There used to be a bar on the ground floor of New Scotland Yard called 'The Tank'. According to legend, there were two bullet holes left by a detective sergeant from Special

Branch in the ceiling who'd decided to treat the place like a Wild West saloon. The bar was done away with by Sir Paul Condon shortly after he became commissioner in 1993 and replaced with a gym.

The three-week course was very stressful; we were under continual assessment. We were told that if an officer did something deemed to be dangerous, such as firing too many rounds too wildly or too readily, they would be kicked off immediately. If we saw bad practice (someone fooling around or joking about gunplay), we were instructed to report them and they would be sent home. Fortunately, with everyone on high alert, we had no problems.

One of the instructors who'd had the misfortune to be shot said it felt like having a hot poker shoved through his leg and held there. 'But just because you're shot that doesn't rule you out of the game,' he told us. 'You can still make decisions and take action. Don't just sit there panicking and worrying about dying. Refuse to give up, let the shock come and remove some of the pain and then deal with the situation. Sometimes, if your adrenaline's gone through the roof, you won't even feel it.

'I once shot an armed robber twice. He was flat on the ground, surrendering, and we got the cuffs on. He complained that they were hurting his wrists. It was only when someone pointed out to him that he was bleeding from two holes in his side that he realized he'd been shot twice. So never, ever give up.'

Some officers found it much more nerve-racking than they expected; I certainly did. Some found it hard to pull the trigger knowing they were shooting to kill. Not wanting to kill someone is only natural and it's possible that this feeling could prevent an armed officer from doing his or her job. An important part of the training course was to identify those officers who were unsuited to carrying firearms.

Although the psychological effects of shooting someone was discussed during training, in my experience, most officers don't think long and hard about whether they can take a life. None of us would have been there if we thought we couldn't cope with this possibility, but until it happens you can never be sure. If you're placed in a position where you have to make a decision to save your own life or that of a member of the public then you shouldn't have a problem about using deadly force.

Those who struggled were given extra tuition but there came a point when some were sent away on other courses because they simply weren't able to pass. I don't think it's anything to be ashamed of; some people are great drivers, some are natural undercover officers and some are natural shooters. I managed to successfully complete the course somewhere in the bottom half of my group.

Training didn't finish with the end of the course. Like everyone else who passed, I would be retested every eight weeks and was expected to develop, improve and learn new skills, such as shooting from the hip or firing in low light. Every six months I'd attend an intense 'tactical refresher' course to really put everything I'd learned to the test.

The goal was to get us to where we didn't have to stop to think about what to do at the moment of engagement, and react more automatically. Do you walk towards the suspect? Do you remove their gun? When do you fire? All of these questions have different answers depending on the situation; hence the constant training.

Naturally, you're expected to succeed but if you fail you don't necessarily lose your weapon automatically; a red line is drawn on your blue gun permit. Too many of these and you'll eventually be stood down from weapons duty.

Once I'd passed the course I was presented with my very own Glock 17, which was stored in the Special Branch armoury at New Scotland Yard. It only ever leaves the armoury when we're authorized for a specific operation (so, no, we're not allowed to take it home).

I'd be collecting it soon enough, however. And while I'd been in training and going through vetting, the newly formed Surveillance Support Team were already right in the thick of the action.

FIVE

FLIES ON THE WALL

A long bank of huge plasma screens blocks the view over London from 1600 (Counter Terrorism Command's control room). Each one shows intel from various feeds, how many are active simply depends upon the size of the operation. *Sky News* is usually on one of them; it's a useful way to keep an eye on a rapidly developing situation. Monitors are sat in the front row in front of the screens; behind them are the less urgent, non-video linked investigators who check timetables, monitor traffic, look up numbers, people's records and so on. There's always a detective sergeant in the room to oversee the entire operation on behalf of the senior investigating officer (SIO). On one side of the banks of monitors sits the surveillance coordinator, along with other specialists who can operate the IT remotely, among other things.

When things begin to develop, 1600 gets very busy with several officers of varying senior ranks sitting in, unable to tear themselves away from seeing events for themselves first-hand.

'Have the feeds been working OK?' the surveillance co-coordinator asked.

'Sweet as a nut, old bean,' the monitor replied proudly. 'Have a look for yourself.'

He shoved a DVD into his computer and the pictures came up on one of the plasmas. Staring at these screens was like peering into another world. The images, recorded in East London, now being viewed in 1600, were crystal clear.

Everyone watched the two men at work in the kitchen.

'Talk about Big Brother,' someone piped up.

Putting on a Geordie accent, the operator launched into a fine impersonation of the BB announcer. 'Abdul is in the lownge making a bawmb, while Ali goes to the di-aree room to talk aboot dyin'.'

Everyone began to laugh. 'You Muppet,' someone from the back row said. 'Now I won't be able to watch this without that running commentary going through my head.'

Every profession develops its own sense of humour; it's only natural. Barristers joke about criminals, doctors about their patients and cops about criminals and terrorists. Perhaps it wasn't the best taste in humour but it helped keep us going – especially after everyone had been on duty for sixteen hours or more and had spent most of them either running after and watching dangerous lunatics travel around London buying their bomb-making equipment or watching every second of their (otherwise boring) lives unfold.

This intel didn't just provide valuable intelligence for the SIO, it was also a great 'trigger' in that overheard discussions could be passed on to the surveillance teams, giving them a heads-up as to what the bad guys were up to.

So, if they were deciding to buy a 'special ingredient', for example, from a specific location, this could be passed on to the team so they could have someone waiting for them at the purchase point with a long-range camera. More evidence in our bag.

What many people don't realize is that some of the men operating in this twisted extremist world aren't the good little boys you might assume. Before I arrived at SO12, I thought that the terrorists genuinely believed in an extreme version of their religion and lived as very strict Muslims. Thanks to our surveillance I learned this was not always the case. Some of them violated the basic principles of their religion; some of them drank and had more than one girlfriend, for example. Our Muslim officers within S-squad (of which there were quite a few) were disgusted both by the extremism and the violations of Islam.

The primary targets in Operation Overt, the men being watched on the plasmas were ringleader Abdulla Ahmed Ali, twenty-eight, Tanvir Hussain, twenty-eight, and Assad Sarwar, twenty-nine.

Ali's decision to become a terrorist came about after he delivered aid on behalf of the Islamic Medical Association to displaced Afghans living in refugee camps on the Pakistan–Afghanistan border in 2003. These camps had already existed since the Russian occupation in 1979, but the already poor conditions quickly worsened in the wake of the American-led invasion in 2001. Tens of thousands of Afghans poured across the border. According to the United Nations High Commissioner for Refugees (UNHCR), there were about 5 million Afghan refugees in Pakistan by the end of 2001. Ali was appalled and angered by the horrific state of the camps which, despite the best efforts of various aid agencies, lacked food, shelter, clean water and medicine. He wasn't alone.

The Taliban roamed the camps in Chaman, Quetta, Peshawar and Karachi, recruiting the old guard as well as young men angered by the invasion. They handed out leaflets with pictures of American soldiers frisking burqa-wearing women. 'You are seeing the picture of a dirty Jewish infidel searching the body of a Muslim woman,' the flyer read. 'If a Muslim does not display his feelings by defending his faith and honour, then he is not a Muslim nor an Afghan.'

The local tribes, sympathetic to the Taliban's cause, provided shelter and assistance to the fighters, while local militants who were affiliated with the Afghan Taliban government before 9/11, including Abdullah Mehsud and Baitullah Mehsud (who would go on to influence and provide assistance to UK-based terrorists) began to organize local Taliban groups across Waziristan, a mountainous tribal region bordering Afghanistan. Having gathered several hundred local Wazirs, they began to launch cross-border attacks in 2003 on American and NATO forces in Afghanistan with the support of veteran mujahideen commanders and Arab al-Qaeda fighters.

Ali's anger was compounded by the failure of the 2003 mass protest back in the UK against the Iraq war. This turned him once and for all against the West so he joined the radical Islamists calling for attacks on Britain.

The three men took S-squad on a property hunt round East London; the team had followed them like secretive Kirsties and Phils until they finally settled on a flat in Walthamstow, East London, which they paid for in cash.

Ali had told the estate agents he was in a hurry to move because he'd split up from his wife and needed a new place to live as soon as possible.

We needed to watch the flat 24/7. Understandably, we had

to have damn good reasons to explain why we were intruding into someone's life at this level, so the onus was on us to make it clear that we had enough intel to make such an intrusion worthwhile.

On average the Home Secretary would receive about 1,400 warrants from us and other agencies such as Customs and the Secret Intelligence Service every year. When David Blunkett was in the hot seat, we'd send him an audio recording of the warrant to help speed things along for him.

I was rapidly learning that in the world of counter-terrorism, things moved very quickly indeed, especially when a serious live operation was on. In no time at all the occupants in the flat were better protected than 10 Downing Street, with 24-hour armed guards, their own secret escort, and detectives back in 1600 monitoring their every move. Whenever they left the house, they were followed by S-squad and other surveillance teams who trailed them all over London and beyond. Police surveillance can be boring as hell, sitting in cars for hours at a time getting deep-vein thrombosis followed by groin strain caused by a sudden burst of activity. Not on Operation Overt.

It seemed as though our targets were always on the move, and so S-squad were right behind them, following every single step they took.

Following just one person around the clock is truly intensive work. You need a number of surveillance teams backed up by plenty of support officers and a fully staffed twenty-four-hour Operations Room. The many demands for our services meant we often suffered from a shortage of officers, and that meant lots of very long shifts.

One of the things that puzzled many about the men we were following was that they seemed so, well – *normal*. David was the team's scholar and knew more about the history and psychology of terrorism than anyone else – although Terry still outranked him on knowledge gained from two and a half decades in the field.

'Many terrorists live like Westerners. The 9/11 nineteen were utterly convincingly Western, as were the London bombers.'

'I never could understand why a man who worked with primary school children was among them.'

'Exactly. They played cricket for God's sake, you can't get more civilized than that. They were beardless, well educated and wore the latest Western fashions. But it's not exactly down to hatred. Very often it was their parents or grandparents that first came to the West and they've grown up influenced by two worlds while never quite belonging to either. I believe that there's something missing from our society for these young men and women.'

'Such as?'

'I wish I knew. Something is missing that fails to provide them with enough meaning and direction in their lives, something that fringe Islamist organizations are able to provide them with. Perhaps it has something to do with the fact that they're caught in between generations. What we see in these young terrorists is a mix of influences – the British way of life and a warped interpretation of Islam that reviles the West and all it stands for.

'Some of them like the idea of martyrdom for the immortality it brings, a twisted version of glory, an eternal infamy. Have you seen Mohammad Sidique Khan's suicide video?'

I nodded. Khan was the 7/7 bomber who exploded his device on the Edgware Road train, killing six innocent people. He had previously worked in a primary school in Leeds as a 'learning mentor' with children of immigrant families that had just arrived in Britain.

'It's a speech all about him, not about collective Islamic beliefs; he's totally self-absorbed. He says "I" about twenty times in less than two minutes. At the end he tries to put himself on a par with "the prophets, the messengers, the martyrs and today's heroes like our beloved Sheikh Osama bin Laden", by saying he has prayed to Allah to "raise" himself to their level.

'People like Khan violate more basic principles of Islam than anyone else. They have watched on the Internet, like millions of others, young Muslims committing atrocities, from the suicide bombers in Iraq and Afghanistan – young men who smile, wave goodbye then blow themselves up, all on camera – to the 9/11 hijackers, the greatest "heroes" of all. These are the inspirational videos that encourage new recruits – they actually see it happen in all its glory, they see how these young men are venerated, the lasting unforgettable impact they have made and they want to become part of it – and to go one better.

'They believe that by committing an atrocity, Allah will forgive them for everything, from the way they've dressed to their crimes of mass murder. There's little anyone can do to persuade them otherwise in the months and years in the run-up to the moment they push the button on their detonator.'

Every person they met was photographed and, if there was a 'significant meet', S-squad and the other teams were on hand to film it.

Everyone was, of course, very interested in the group's Internet activity. Abdulla Ahmed Ali got everyone's attention by spending hours researching airline timetables for transatlantic flights.

Meanwhile, Assad Sarwar took S-squad shopping. Wherever he went, whatever he bought, we watched, recorded and then bought the same things as him, all in the name of what we call 'Product' – things that would later become courtroom exhibits. Assad bought latex gloves, glue, drills, clamps and syringes.

'The problem is that individually you could ask what's so suspicious about that?' David said. 'Any one of us could have bought just the same things the other day. We have to wait until they have bought enough to mean something for a jury to be convinced.'

Sarwar was clearly the quartermaster. This term was common in the days of the IRA, and was used to describe the men who found and sent supplies to the active service units.

We still needed to find out the other parts of what they were planning – where, when and what kind of device they were trying to build – was it conventional, biological or chemical? We also wanted to know who taught them how to put together whatever it was they were making – the answer to that question lay many thousands of miles away.

SIX

LITTLE BRITAIN

Unmanned Airborne Vehicles, more commonly known as 'drones', are remotely piloted planes that are used to launch guided missiles on targets that are too dull, dirty or dangerous for manned aircraft.

The American government runs two drone programmes. The military's version, which is publicly acknowledged, operates in the recognized war zones of Afghanistan and Iraq. As such, it is an extension of conventional warfare. The CIA's programme is aimed at terror suspects around the world, including countries where American troops are not based.

The CIA quite rightly declines to provide any information to the public about where it operates, how it selects targets, who is in charge, or how many people have been killed. But they do tell us when they've hit a significant target – such as Qaed Salim Sinan al-Harethi, a suspect in the 2000 bombing of the USS *Cole*. Al-Harethi was killed when the car in which he and five other passengers were travelling, on a desert road in Yemen in November 2002, was vaporized by a Hellfire missile.

Such assassinations, although risky, can put paid to terrorist operations in the immediate region, saving countless lives, and so these targets are pursued relentlessly. America has an unofficial agreement with Pakistan that allows them to strike using drones within their border region, as long as the Americans have solid intelligence and especially if the Pakistanis won't or can't take firm action. Pakistan prefers to keep this understanding unofficial so that it can publicly protest against such strikes when they go wrong and innocent lives of its citizens are lost.

The Predator programme is described by many in the intelligence world as America's single most effective weapon against al-Qaeda. Counter-terrorism officials credit drones with having killed more than a dozen senior al-Qaeda leaders and their allies in recent years, eliminating more than half of the CIA's twenty most wanted 'high value' targets. The list includes Nazimuddin Zalalov, a former lieutenant of Osama bin Laden; Ilyas Kashmiri, al-Qaeda's chief of paramilitary operations in Pakistan; Saad bin Laden, Osama's eldest son; Abu Sulayman al-Jazairi, an Algerian al-Qaeda planner who is believed to have helped to train operatives for attacks in Europe and the United States; and Osama al-Kini and Sheikh Ahmed Salim Swedan, al-Qaeda operatives who are thought to have played central roles in the 1998 bombings of American embassies in East Africa.[3]

Sadly, while the missiles are shockingly accurate, the intelligence that leads to them being fired is sometimes off the mark.

In January 2006, just as S-squad was joining the hunt in Walthamstow, Pakistani-intelligence field agents were tracking a group of men who had crossed the border from Afghanistan into Bajaur, a small tribal region that borders Afghanistan's Kunar province. Among them were top al-Qaeda figures, including the once British-based Rashid Rauf.

Rauf, then twenty-five, was born in 1981 in Mirpur and British-raised.[4] He had lived in the UK ever since his father migrated to Birmingham in the early 1980s where he founded a successful bakery business. Rauf fled the country after his 54-year-old uncle was stabbed to death in 2002. The local Murder Squad had wanted Rauf to 'help them with their enquiries', but he was on a plane to Peshawar before you could say 'I have a warrant for your arrest'.

A short time later, Rauf, who adopted the name 'Khalid', was well established in Pakistan and lived in a multi-bedroomed technicolour mansion surrounded by several acres of empty land in one of Mirpur's more prosperous districts.

Mirpur, sixty-eight miles south-east of Islamabad in Pakistan, is known affectionately as 'Little Britain'. Its residents speak with thick British regional accents, which shouldn't be a surprise, seeing as the area has been exporting its young workers for more than a century, thanks to the acute post-war shortage of labour in England's Midlands factories. Ask any of the 370,000 locals from any age group and they'll tell you that everyone in their town has been to the UK at some point, whether to visit or work, or in the search of an education.

Ties to the ancestral villages remain strong, and every year Mirpur is inundated by a reverse flow of visiting family members. The large influx of second- and third-generation Pakistani immigrants coming from Britain every summer to visit relatives would certainly provide a good cover story for any radical elements looking to huddle with terrorist chiefs in Pakistan.

Mirpur has also been aptly described as a place of 'cultural confusion'. Multi-tiered mansions of pink marble and stucco line dirt paths; expensive cars wind through potholed streets and park in front of the British Airways office in the town centre. It's an industrial area with a new and growing interest in tourism, thanks mainly to the hordes of expats visiting from the UK.

An indication of just how closely Mirpur is linked to the UK is the fact that it's a friendship city with many English cities, including Birmingham and Bradford – as well as the London borough of Waltham Forest, the borough in which our targets now lived.

Mirpur was also the melting pot where Britain became more vulnerable to terrorist attacks. As the war in Afghanistan got under way in the latter part of 2001, al-Qaeda fighters flooded across the Afghan border and into Pakistan where they found themselves in a country with extremely close and long-standing ties to the UK, an area to which disaffected British youths of Pakistani origin, angered by the impact of British foreign policy on Muslims in Iraq, frequently journeyed.

Over 400,000 visits averaging forty-one days in length are made to Pakistan from the UK every year. It was simply impossible for the security services to track every possible al-Qaeda recruit.

As Rauf settled in, he married into the area's premier terrorist family – a relative of Maulana Masood Azhar, the head and founder of Jaish-e-Mohammed, a Pakistani Islamist militant group linked to al-Qaeda.

This group is opposed to Indian rule of the disputed region of Kashmir, and thought to have been behind the 2004 assassination attempt on President Pervez Musharraf as well as several other terror attacks. Azhar founded the group after he was released from an Indian prison in December 1999 in exchange for 155 passengers from a hijacked Indian airliner.

Another prisoner released as part of the same deal was Ahmad Omar Saeed Sheikh, a militant close to Jaish-e-Mohammed who'd been raised and schooled in Wanstead, Waltham Forest, before being radicalized at the London School of Economics. Omar had been jailed for the kidnap of three British men and an American in India. He was later convicted of the kidnap and beheading of the American journalist Daniel Pearl.[5]

It was thought that Ayman al-Zawahiri, second in command to Osama bin Laden, as well as his son-in-law bomb-maker Abu Ubaida al-Masri were travelling with Rauf. Abu Ubaida al-Masri, 'the Egyptian', who was missing two fingers, had pioneered the use of bombs made from everyday ingredients, based on a technique first developed in Palestinian refugee camps.

At Bajaur the group split into two and forked. The agents were forced to choose and so followed the group that led them to the small dusty settlement of Damadola. Their targets took shelter in a small compound of three houses on the edge of the town.

Their position was relayed via the American Army Central Command in Florida back to officials at the CIA headquarters in Langley. The men in their air-conditioned control room were able to watch the scene via cameras that beamed live footage from the unmanned MQ-1L Predator drone that zipped towards Damadola.

Even though it held an altitude of two miles, the resolution from the Predator's infrared cameras was so sharp that they could clearly make out the limbs of their targets as they walked back and forth among the houses. This was followed by a crystal-clear picture of the resultant fireball from the two AGM-114 Hellfire missiles that destroyed them.

Tragically, the Pakistani agents had decided to follow the wrong group. Thirteen people were killed in the attack; as far as we know none of them were al-Qaeda. Our targets lived to plot another day.

It was an important miss. Not long after this strike, one of Operation Overt's primary targets, Abdulla Ahmed Ali, boarded a plane at Heathrow bound for Pakistan. He was on his way to meet the 'British' man, Rashid Rauf.

SEVEN

WHAT TERRORISTS REALLY TALK ABOUT

HEATHROW AIRPORT, JUNE 2006

When Abdulla Ahmed Ali returned to Heathrow from Pakistan, a surveillance team was waiting for him.

At this time, we had no idea who Rashid Rauf was; as usual, S-squad didn't need the full picture so we didn't get it; at this stage we were far too busy to care what was going on in Pakistan.

Some of S-squad's surveillance officers had been tailing Assad Sarwar through the streets of Walthamstow when:

'Graham with the eyeball. T-One has just taken a bottle out of his bag and binned it next to the bus stop outside the front doors of Leyton leisure centre.'

A lucky DC went in and, doing his best impression of a hungry tramp, extracted Target One's piece of rubbish.

It was a bottle of hydrogen peroxide.

'I don't think he wants to dye his hair,' he said into his covert mic.

Hydrogen peroxide is also used as a propellant. This crucial piece of evidence gave all the teams working on the operation a terrific boost.

One major problem in such a massive operation as this was dealing with all the surveillance teams from different police and other specialist units. They came from all over the UK to help and 1600 was soon creaking at the seams.

The real challenge came when the suspects all met up. Imagine what happens when half a dozen people, all with teams behind them, have a get-together in a cafe. If they were all going to a meet over a coffee, we couldn't let someone from each team go in, otherwise the place would be packed full of undercover officers ordering cappuccinos. This required careful coordination between all the units.

The dedicated surveillance teams had great fun spotting each other as they crowded into East London. Every day there were observation vans, cars, motorbikes and footies who were parked up, driving or walking round each other's plots, each watching their specified target while trying to stay out of each other's way.

Avoiding any serious toe-treading or show-outs was a major priority. A compromise would be disastrous as the targets would immediately be on the phone to one other. As it turned out, the targets didn't have a clue about all this activity going on around them, and this was a real credit to the skill of those involved.

Meanwhile, we received intelligence that Ali had brought back a load of batteries and a massive bag of Tang soft drink powder with him from Pakistan. The Tang, batteries and hydrogen peroxide were added to the bizarre and ever-growing product list and passed on to our specialist Met police boffins.

It didn't take them long to put it together. When the report came back to our office, it made sobering reading. Hydrogen peroxide and Tang (among several other things they'd purchased), when mixed and treated in a certain way, produces hexamethylene triperoxide diamine (HMTD), a highly explosive organic compound. It's inexpensive and easy to synthesize, although extremely hazardous to make — another reason to train in the remote desert areas of Pakistan and why many al-Qaeda operatives are lacking fingers. It's volatile and reacts to metals, shock, heat and friction. It only takes a small amount to blow a hole in the side of a plane, for example.

HMTD was known as an al-Qaeda favourite, ever since Ahmed Ressam aka 'Benni Norris' or the 'Millennium Bomber' had attempted to use it to bomb Los Angeles International Airport on New Year's Eve, 1999. This had been part of al-Qaeda's foiled millennium plots aimed at targets in the United States and Jordan. Ahmed Ressam was caught after a suspicious Customs officer, acting on a hunch, ordered a second search of his car when he tried to enter America via Canada. They found enough explosives to take the roof off the airport hidden under his spare tyre.[6]

We also thought it had been used by the 7/7 bombers, although we couldn't be 100 per cent certain. All I knew was that some evil bastard in Pakistan was providing these young brainwashed Muslims with the means and support to commit atrocities. I could only hope that the ISI was as motivated as we were in doing all they could to take them down.

Ali, code-named 'Lion Roar', did his best to avoid surveillance by holding his meetings in open spaces, often playing tennis in Walthamstow, where we couldn't get close enough to hear. But it wasn't enough. It never is.

Soon, the Met and MI5 had created one of the largest, most expensive and most complex police operations since the Second World War.

The 'Walthamstow cell', which remained S-squad's priority, went on to make chilling but ludicrous suicide videos in which they promised death would 'rain' from the skies. They laughed and joked with each other as they kept fluffing their lines.

On 6 August the stakes were raised still higher as we followed Ali into an Internet cafe in Walthamstow. Looking over his shoulder, one officer saw him looking up flight times.

Of course, we made sure we got hold of everything.

He'd written down the details of seven flights, all bound for the United States. All of them took off within two and a half hours of each other, which meant they were going for a simultaneous mid-flight detonation.

Thousands of people – more than 9/11.

Three days later, when Umar Islam, a West Indian man who'd recently converted to Islam, visited the flat he asked Ali: 'What's the time frame anyway?'

'A couple of weeks,' Ali said as he coached his co-conspirator through the making of a suicide video. They also talked about taking their children with them.

'Martyrdom operations upon martyrdom operations will keep on raining on these *kuffars* [infidels],' Islam was heard saying as they made the video.

MI5 then came up with intel which suggested that they were probably about to attempt a dry run.

Most likely. And that's the rub. It's the same sort of situation that the Flying Squad always end up facing when they receive advance warning of a bank robbery. Nicking the robbers as they arrive in the car, before they go into the bank, gives them the opportunity to whine in front of a jury that the balaclava was for night fishing, that they didn't know the car was stolen and they had no idea how a gun ended up in the boot and/or the glove compartment. Arresting them immediately after the robbery guarantees a very lengthy conviction but traumatizes and arguably endangers the public.

The ideal time to arrest the terrorists would be immediately after their dry run. Filming them as they moved into position at various airports would really help to convince a jury that they weren't planning anything else but mass murder. We didn't want to give them the chance to claim that their aim was to cause panic by placing bombs in isolated areas where they wouldn't kill anyone. The worry was the longer we left it, the closer they would get to completing their goal – and if our intel was wrong – well, it didn't bear thinking about.

Those in charge of 1600 proved they had nerves of steel by deciding to wait and let them attempt their dry run.

But that's exactly when the Americans decided to call it.

EIGHT

SPRINGING THE TRAP

Before 9/11 there'd been quite a bit of old-school rivalry between the intelligence departments of Britain and the United States. But, since that terrible day, all intel and technology has been pooled unquestioningly; help is given with little query. It didn't matter how we got into this situation or what circumstances had brought us here, we were in it together. We only wanted to maintain a perfect score in the deadly game we played with the terrorists.

Every counter-terrorist operation was automatically a multi-agency effort. Much like the Met, MI5 and MI6, the CIA had been in a state of upheaval ever since 9/11, as they shifted their weighty focus from the old USSR to the Middle East. This is no mean feat. Decent intelligence networks take years to set up and develop. You can't just say 'Oh well, we'll switch everything to the Middle East now' and have it all up and running in a few weeks.

As ever, the Americans got to see plenty of our intel for Operation Overt in case it tied in with something they were working on – and vice versa. We were always able to ask for help from American Special Ops, the CIA and other agencies already embedded in foreign lands. Having that option was simply priceless.

When the United States, Britain and Pakistan shared intel about Rashid Rauf/Khalid, it was soon clear to us all that he was the ringleader. Everything was coming together beautifully.

The problem was, while we Brits remained calm, the Cousins were getting twitchy. Our counter-terrorist units had spent decades following the IRA's active service units as they planned major attacks on the mainland. The Americans were only five years into their 'War on Terror' and were understandably struggling to hold off demanding an end to Overt.

Although we said we had everything under control, Overt was pushing S-squad and other crime teams to their limits. The number of subjects of interest had risen steadily until we were following over twenty people across the country. A considerable amount of the Met's resources was being sucked up in the ever-growing vortex.

The slightest movement from any suspects caused our huge, budget-busting, anti-terror network to go into overdrive. Teams were constantly sweeping up all kinds of evidence; requests were made for CCTV footage, bins were being searched and a variety of bugs and devices were being installed. The results were being downloaded, bagged, studied, forensicated and filed in preparation for what we hoped would be an epic and triumphant trial. To run a huge operation like this under the nervous eyes of the Americans took plenty of courage from our bosses. What if we lost a target, what if we were compromised, what if we got the date or location wrong?

Everyone was just about managing to hold their nerve – until American President George W. Bush was told that the bombers were only 'a couple of weeks' from striking. The president – rightly fearing that a terrorist attack designed to kill more people than 9/11 was close to being carried out – decided he wasn't prepared to wait any longer. In the interests of protecting innocent people, he requested that Pakistan arrest Rashid Rauf.

Although we protested (that it was too soon and we wanted more evidence), the Americans had had enough.

Pakistan came down on the side of the United States – President Pervez Musharraf was still keen to win points. Besides, the last thing he wanted was for the world to point the finger of blame at Pakistan for allowing al-Qaeda to use their country to plan the world's most devastating terrorist attack.

On 9 August 2006, Rauf was travelling on a bus in the Pakistani city of Bahawalpur when it was forced to a halt by an unmarked van.

Before Rauf had time to move, armed men in mufti were on the bus. Thinking he was being kidnapped by bandits, he cried out for help, only realizing the truth when he was bundled into the back of the van and driven straight to the nearest police station. He was officially detained under the Security of Pakistan Act before being carted off to the notorious Adiala Jail.[7]

Packed into cells designed to hold 1,996 were 5,800 criminals from all over the world. Being a 'very important terrorist' however, Rauf was shackled to the wall of his very own private hell.

Before Rauf had even stepped through the gates of Adiala, British Home Secretary John Reid was already being briefed by Peter Clarke, head of the Counter Terrorism Command. 'I'll have them all in custody by the morning,' Clarke said.[8]

This promise wasn't as rash as it sounded. It wasn't as if we didn't know where they all were.

Even though this was a race against time, it was all quiet and professional, no panic, no shouting, no fuss. Internally of course, adrenaline was riding high. After months of work by thousands of people across the planet and tens of millions of pounds, the operation was about to be brought to an end. It had to be done clean and quick – as much evidence as possible had to be secured and preserved.

The main concern was if the suspects found out about Rauf's arrest. Bad news travels fast and it would only be a matter of time before word reached Ali and his gang. Although the ISI had kept the arrest as low key as possible by picking him up away from home, Rauf's wife would soon know something was wrong. Plus, the Walthamstow cell may have had a prearranged time to contact Rauf, and if he wasn't there or didn't answer his emails then there was a good chance they'd grow suspicious and make a few calls to Pakistan.

If that happened, they'd soon realize it was all about to come unglued for them and would possibly take their liquid bombs on the Underground or some other public place. They might also booby-trap the bomb factory or 'do a Madrid' and blow themselves up when we tried to arrest them.

Needless to say, the techies had their eyes and ears glued to their headphones as intel came in through cameras and bugs. Every piece of intelligence had S-squad on their toes in case the dreaded news had arrived. Within three hours of Rauf's arrest, armed teams across the country were in position. Operation Overt was about to reach its premature crescendo.

Although there were twenty-four people to arrest, S-squad's focus remained the three ringleaders: Abdulla Ahmed Ali, Tanvir Hussain and Assad Sarwar. A unit was due to pick up Sarwar near his family home in High Wycombe.

Waltham Forest Town Hall, a grand white rectangular building, is surrounded by playing fields. As it was still summer, the sky stayed light well into the evening. Children rode their bikes around the large fountain while parents stretched out on the grass. By 9.30 p.m. however, the time that Ali and Hussain had arranged to meet in an adjoining car park, most people had gone home.

As the two terrorists sat on the wall of the car park, Ali handed over a collection of the latest edits of their suicide videos.

'STRIKE! STRIKE! STRIKE!'

In the blink of an eye, dozens of armed officers appeared as if from nowhere, causing the two men to jump out of their skins. They were taken quickly, with no problems at all.

Marked vehicles shot out from side streets and cordoned off the roads as Ali and Hussain were prepped for questioning. Soon they would be isolated in a clean room where they'd be told to strip while standing on a large square of white paper. Any evidence that fell while they undressed would be captured. Their clothes would be placed in special breathable evidence bags and sealed. Apparently their faces made quite a picture when they were shown the razor-sharp Big Brother footage of them at home making their *Blue Peter* bombs.

Sarwar's home yielded important material including more suicide videos hidden in the garage and computer memory sticks with alternative targets including nuclear power stations, oil and gas terminals, as well as the Canary Wharf skyscrapers.

During the post-arrest searches we identified a number of key email exchanges. In July Ali sent the following email to 'Khalid' (we soon found out that this was Rashid Rauf): 'I got all my bits and bobs, I'm just waiting for lights. They should be here in a couple of days.'

He was talking about detonators.

A reply from Khalid in Pakistan on 13 July said: 'Your friend can go to his rapping contest anywhere. Make sure he goes on the bus service that's most popular over there.'

The rapping contest was the attack, the bus service the aeroplanes. They also called Khalid 'Paps' in some emails, suggesting perhaps a mentor figure, someone who was running the show.

They also talked about batteries, Tang and 'HP' (hydrogen peroxide) and American cities – New York, Miami, Philadelphia, Washington DC, Dallas, Chicago and Los Angeles.

We later identified that on 3 August Ali had written in an email: 'By the way, I've set up my mobile shop now. Now I only need to sort out an opening time.' The following day he sent an email to Khalid saying: 'I've done my prep. All I have to do is sort out opening timetable and bookings. That should take a couple of days.' This showed us just how close they'd come to realizing their plans.

It was a massive operation: while twenty-four people were being questioned in interview rooms up and down the country, forty-six properties and twenty vehicles were being searched – as was a huge swathe of woodland in High Wycombe, where it was thought the would-be bombers had tested and stashed some of their explosive mixture. Meanwhile, airports around the world were thrown into chaos as John Reid made an emergency statement detailing a ban on liquids on planes.

It took a further three years and two trials to convict the three ringleaders who all pleaded not guilty. Ali claimed that they were planning to record an Internet documentary which highlighted injustices against Muslims in Iraq, Afghanistan and Lebanon. He said he'd thought about setting off a small, explosive device at the Houses of Parliament or in one of Heathrow's terminals as a publicity stunt and that the martyrdom videos were a hoax to make their documentary more shocking.

Their story didn't fool anyone. They were sentenced to life; Ali must serve a minimum of forty years, Sarwar thirty-six years and Tanvir Hussain thirty-two years.[9]

The message was clear – try to plot an attack against the UK and we will stop it no matter how big the bill.

In total, the investigations and trial cost close to £100 million. But we had saved the lives of up to 5,000 passengers. It was likely that as many again on the ground would have died if detonations had taken place over cities. If the attack had gone ahead, it would have been three times more deadly than 9/11.

And what would we have given to prevent that?

In the immediate aftermath of the arrests, MI5 had a lot of questions for Rashid Rauf and several leads still needed investigating by many specialist police departments. Rauf's phone records revealed a number of calls to contacts in Germany and South Africa.

Although there are no formal extradition treaties with Pakistan, ISI officials told the press: 'He [Rauf] can be extradited, once we get the maximum out of him.'

I could only suppose that this would not be a pleasant process for Rauf. The ISI's frequent use of torture has been documented time and again over many years. Although MI5 travelled to Pakistan to have words with Rauf, the UK quickly abandoned plans to extradite and prosecute him as soon as they realized he might allege that he'd been tortured by his captors. Questioning him or bringing him back for trial could have made the UK complicit in any alleged torture. Besides, his defence would have been able to argue that any information he'd given to the authorities had been offered in the forlorn hope that his suffering would end.

Rauf appeared in a Pakistani courtroom several months later alongside a jihadist from the north of England, and Mohammed Siddique, a Pakistani who had been extradited from South Africa. Rauf told his Pakistani lawyer, Hashmat Ali Habib, and his relatives that he had been beaten, given electric shocks, and held in a cell so small his knees touched the ceiling when he lay on his back.[10]

Then, in December 2007, the unbelievable happened.

The West Midlands Murder Squad still wanted to charge Rauf with the murder of his uncle. If he'd had any sense Rauf would have embraced Britain's extradition request with open arms – a British jail would be a welcome break from the horrors of Adiala.

After a brief appearance in court related to the extradition, some junior officers had allowed Rauf to pray in a local mosque. His handcuffs were removed so he could pray freely. When the guards re-entered the mosque to check on the prisoner after having lunch, they discovered that Rauf had escaped through another door.

His escape was met with disbelief in Pakistan and in Britain. Rauf's lawyer and family said they believed he had in fact been taken into secret security-service custody.

Terry's experience told him all he needed to know about this one. 'I don't think we'll be hearing from Rauf again – not alive anyway.'

Sure enough, a few months later Islamabad announced that Rauf been killed in a missile strike from an unmanned American drone flying over North Waziristan – a claim that was unfortunately impossible to verify.[11]

Almost all of the Met's massive resources had been bundled together to crack this case – which meant that as soon as the arrests had been made it was time for us to leave the remainder of Operation Overt to the forensics departments and then the Crown Prosecution Service while we got to work on other threats.

John Reid told the world that we had another twenty-four plots to worry about – and these were just the ones that we knew of. These were dangerous times, he said, and the nation had never expected as much from its police and security services as it did now.

And that's when I walked through the doors of Tintagel House on the South Bank of the Thames as a fresh-faced member of S-squad.

NINE

MY FIRST HIT

At 8.30 a.m. I left Old Street Tube and marched towards Shoreditch police station in Shepherdess Walk, a heavy black bag slung over my shoulder. It was time for my first bi-monthly firearms test since getting my ticket and I was heading for the basement firing range. I wasn't the best shot but I was certainly hoping to keep my card free of red lines.

I passed the ancient Eagle pub in Shepherdess Walk, entered the drab 1960s police building and took the lift to the subter-ranean shooting range. The red light above the door was off, meaning it was safe to enter. The door made a sucking noise as I heaved it open – just like opening an airlock. The venti-lation on the range is more powerful than normal to draw the pungent smell of nitro-glycerine out of the air.

A couple of guys from the Grey surveillance team were already there and kitting up. I removed my ballistic vest, gog-gles and ear-protectors from my bag and got ready.

The door hissed open behind me. 'All right, old boy?' It was George.

We were there for accuracy tests and that meant target practice, which also meant that George, a former army officer and a fine marksman, was about to show me up.

No matter how experienced you become, you have to listen to the safety briefing given by one of the on-site instructors – every single time. Although the routine is about as exciting as the in-flight demos given by cabin crew, you never tire of hearing it; you can't help but focus when live ammo is involved.

After we'd gone through the briefing we shoved in our earplugs, put on our earmuffs and got down to it.

'Five sections, ten rounds per section,' the instructor had told us. 'Each section will be set at a different distance. I'm sure you're aware that the required hit rate is eighty per cent. Good luck, gentlemen.'

Anything below 80 per cent and you're red-lined. I steadied myself, let the tension leave my body and we were off. Soon, despite the powerful air-con, the smell of gunpowder was thick in the air as we fired our way through fifty rounds. After each section, the cardboard targets whirred back towards us. George's patterns were always neat little circles while mine looked more like a kid's join-the-dots drawing. Still, at least they were on target.

The instructors stood by and debriefed us after each section. 'Try not to snatch the trigger,' he told me. I was firing too quickly. I forced myself to slow down a touch. Shooting – much like surveillance – is a long learning curve; you're constantly building on your skills. George sailed through with 98 per cent while I scraped past with 84 per cent.

When we emerged from the basement, our phones latched onto a signal and simultaneously beeped into life. We exchanged looks. This could mean nothing, but as far as I was concerned simultaneous ringing usually signified something important. In 2002, when the Bali bombs took the lives of nearly two hundred people, I was with thirty other cops, all half-cut midway through a police 'lunch' in a trendy Islington bar. Suddenly, every phone and pager in the room was ringing and beeping – and the room fell silent and sober as we answered.

I was also on the scene not long after the 1999 Paddington rail crash that left 31 dead and 520 injured. I spent the morning listening to the eerie sound of dozens of mobile phones ringing over and over in the mangled carriages until their batteries finally failed.

In this case we received the same message. Mobile phones aren't secure so we weren't presented with any details, we were just told to get our arses back to Tintagel House at light speed.

My first armed operation was about to begin.

'Come on, Harry,' George said cheerfully, 'I've brought an S-squad car – ten times faster than a speeding Tube train.'

We chucked our bags in the boot of the souped-up car and George drove towards the electronic gates. As they slowly opened, George lowered the window and stuck the blue light on the roof. Always a nice moment; in this case it was the start of our flight from one side of central London to the other.

The mid-morning traffic melted away before us as George turned on the 'noise' and we shot down the Embankment, past the Palace of Westminster, left at Box, over the bridge and then it was lights off as we neared the office. We discreetly drove into the secure car park (which we affectionately refer to as the 'flight deck'), just seven minutes later.

George was 'duty detective sergeant' so I would automatically become his assistant. This was a system that we'd devised ourselves. There were four DS's and we worked out a rota among ourselves where we had a week each as 'Duty DS'. This meant that we would all take it in turns to be in charge and work 'under' each other.

'Sounds like a Marxist dream,' Terry said when we first presented the idea. It worked very well indeed.

So, on this operation I would be George's lackey. We passed through the many layers of security and strode straight into the detective inspector's office for a briefing from Terry.

'We have intelligence that there is going to be a weapons purchase tonight. The subjects are armed and will be buying detonators. We know where, but not when.' Terry checked his watch. 'It's now ten a.m. You may think we have a lot of time, but we don't.'

Fantastic. All the admin nonsense I'd been quietly dreading could go out the window and I could get on with some real police work. The day was going to be long but it would fly by. We had a few hours to put together a major op on a gang of unknowns, armed and dangerous.

Terry outlined the general plan. 'The subjects – codenamed "Scarface" and "The Technician" – are currently under control.'

This meant they both had teams following them already.

'The handover will be in a car park in Edmonton, North London. You're going to set an invisible net around them. They will not escape.'

Although I assumed these were terrorists, we weren't given any more information but operating on a need-to-know basis.

'Harry,' George said, 'you can do the recce.'

'Got it. Raj, with me,' and we were off to North London in a covert vehicle.

Edmonton had seen more than its fair share of gun crime in recent years. A seventeen-year-old local girl who'd just completed her A levels had been shot dead after an argument in a nightclub a few weeks earlier and there had been another five violent murders of teenagers in the last seven months alone. The murder weapons included guns, knives and, in one case, a brick.

We took a walk through the car park to get a feel for the 'plot'. I needed to know the immediate area backwards so that I could brief the surveillance teams, as well as the officers from SO19 who would put in the 'hit'. After an hour spent absorbing the position of streetlights, alleyways, one-way systems, zebra crossings and road junctions, I had a plan. We put OP vans in the streets to the front and back of the car park. That way we'd be able to film whichever way they faced when they did the deal.

In our operations we have a range of vehicles at our disposal and this includes hire cars. Hire cars can only be driven as per normal members of the public, so they have limited uses. If an officer who is working very late takes one home, and is called back urgently, then they can only 'pootle' along at 30 mph.

Legend has it that in the wake of the July 2005 bombings, the Met hired so many cars because so many officers were mobilized, that we lost track of one of them. It was discovered a couple of years later in a police station's basement car park with what was quite probably the biggest hire-car bill for a single vehicle in history. Oops. I could understand how it was all too easy to lose track when you're hiring dozens and dozens of generic hire cars and parking them all over London – especially in those desperate days.

Once our plans were in place, Raj and I zipped back to the

office to write the briefing notes and delivered them to the surveillance team and SO19, who then did their own recce. They needed to check for their own sight-lines, to calculate distances, vehicle locations, possible speeds, cover points and so on. Everything would be done to avoid any chance of a shoot-out or the nightmare scenarios of car and foot chases.

We collected our guns from the armoury. Outwardly I radiated calm but my heart hammered against my ribs as I holstered my Glock. I'm sure I wasn't the first armed cop to study their reflection in the mirrored doors of the Yard's lifts. This was a huge deal. It wasn't a macho thing, just a very serious feeling. I carried an awesome responsibility, the power and authority to end a life.

By 5 p.m. the people-followers had thrown a net around the mosque where the pair of weapons dealers were at prayer. Meanwhile, S-squad left TT (Tintagel House) in convoy: two vans and a car, the control vehicle. George, Jenny and I would stay in the control vehicle, while Danny and Asad manned the vans.

We wanted to be in place a few hours before the meet, so when Scarface and The Technician rocked up, they would already be in our net. The control vehicle would protect the OP vans as well, just in case they got into any trouble.

We parked up in a discreet area of a supermarket car park, our forward operating point. As I got out of the car and walked around to the back, I felt that something was wrong with my jacket and looked down. My jacket had ridden up the side of my body and my Glock was in full view.

Fuck! A terrible mistake. My gun had only been visible for a few seconds, but that was enough.

I quickly pulled down my top and carefully looked around.

No shoppers seemed to have noticed, but what about CCTV? Could the supermarket security have seen me and called the police? I needed to make a fast decision. Do we leave, risk the police turning up and launching a search for a 'gunman'. Or do we ring the local nick and declare our hand?

Red-faced with embarrassment, I told George. 'OK, it could happen to anyone,' he said calmly. 'It was less than five seconds, right?'

I nodded.

'Asad can monitor the local police radio. If a call comes out then we ring the locals.'

I was very grateful for George's understanding. Not the best start to my first op but fortunately nothing came up on the radio. Nevertheless, this incident was a real blow to my confidence; it wouldn't exactly help me to go up in my team's estimation. I wondered what they thought of their newest member now and resolved to make this my final mistake.

Jenny and I drove the vans into the spaces with Asad and Danny already in the back. They'd be there for half the night now but with food, drink and their piss bottles (you don't want to forget these), they'd be comfortable enough.

Scarface and The Technician emerged from the mosque and drove home to Newham in East London. A net was placed around their flat and we awaited their next move. The airwaves stayed silent, except for the occasional transmission of someone checking in to report nothing had happened.

Everyone was settled, waiting patiently. A huge part of surveillance is all about sitting in cars for eight hours or so – a real test of endurance. You don't even need everyone to be 'eyes on', just those closest to the action. Danny and Asad could amuse themselves as they saw fit while they waited in the streets by the Edmonton car park. Most officers now have iPhones and portable DVD players to help pass the time – or are prolific members of their local book club.

Finally, at 2 a.m., light spilled into the street from the front door of the Newham flat.

Papers were folded, sandwiches put away and book places marked. The wake-up call gave everyone a good rush of adrenaline.

The men climbed into their car and drove towards the A406.

Just at that moment Danny called.

'I got two young crack heads breaking into the car in front.'

Typical! Danny was forced to watch helplessly as they flicked a piece of the ceramic part of a spark plug at the window, an effective way of quietly breaking the glass. We couldn't afford to intervene. Danny got it on video for posterity, but we had to let the two boys go. Having to watch two lads break into someone's car, knowing we'd 'let them run' is just one of the many problems we face in surveillance. If they'd taken the car, we could have circulated it. In this case they just wanted the stereo and Danny watched as the two disappeared into the night with their booty.

Meanwhile, Scarface had picked up a friend and was driving like Lewis Hamilton, jumping red lights and breaking the speed limit between speed cameras. Whether this was a bizarre bit of counter-surveillance or stupidity, I don't know. This caused the teams following them no problems whatsoever.

He drove straight past the meeting point, then all around the area, looking for us.

SO19 were on high alert, standing by in the back of three unmarked Range Rovers, loaded weapons on their laps.

Everyone was tense, alert.

Suddenly Danny's hushed but frantic voice came over the radio: 'George! Danny here, come in, over!'

What the hell was he up to? We should have total radio silence.

'Yes, Danny, George here.'

'The two crack heads who nicked the stereo are back and are rocking my bloody van!'

Oh for God's sake, not now!

They were probably testing for an alarm with a view to breaking in to see if anything of value was inside. If they'd succeeded, Danny would have given them the fright of their lives. Although that might have been a good bit of crime prevention work for the future, we were extremely worried that they would screw up our operation, which was about to 'go down' at any moment.

Just as George was about to deploy someone on foot to check it out, the sound of Scarface's car could be heard approaching. He had finally finished his fruitless recce. This spooked the kids and they disappeared into the night. The car turned into the car park, the engine and lights were switched off and the occupants sat in the darkness, car facing the exit, no doubt thinking of a quick getaway.

We all settled back down, just in time to see a red Astra pull into the car park. It reversed into position, right next to Scarface's car. It was also facing the exit, the boot out of public view but not out of Danny's.

Scarface's passenger climbed out. The Technician, who had put on gloves, joined him and they went around to the boot of the Astra.

Scarface stayed at the wheel.

The boot opened and Danny filmed as The Technician lifted out a plastic bag. He carefully picked up and examined several 'devices' about the size and shape of a pine cone.

Danny transmitted what was happening. The three black Range Rovers that had been laid up, motionless with their engines humming quietly, crept slowly forwards. The tension across the surveillance team was now tightrope tight. The selector levers on MP5 sub-machine guns were moved to the 'fire' position.

The Technician very skilfully stripped down one of the devices before beginning a more thorough examination. He placed it on the floor of the boot and, leaning in, he shone a torch to help with his examination. The other guy started to get twitchy. He kept scratching his nose and fidgeting.

The airwaves fell quiet. Everyone was waiting for the command from the operational commander.

Suddenly, The Technician stood bolt upright and showed a section of the device to the passenger.

'Look's like there's a problem,' Danny said quietly. 'The Technician ain't happy with the quality of the goods. He's starting to lose it with the seller.'

He started to get very agitated and unhappy. I could understand it – I'd be severely pissed off if I'd had to take a risk of doing a shady deal at 2 a.m. in an Edmonton car park and someone had tried to sell me a dodgy detonator. I'd seen this sort of disagreement before with gun deals. Many are converted from imitation or decommissioned firearms; some more professionally than others.

'Scarface is still in the driver's seat,' Danny said. 'He's looking worried though, getting restless. The Technician looks like he's about to chin the third man.'

Back in 1600 the decision-makers called it.

This wasn't ideal as it meant that only two out of the three would go down (Scarface, who had stayed in the driver's seat, would claim he didn't know what was in the boot) but it looked like things were about to get ugly.

'STRIKE, STRIKE, STRIKE!'

The three Range Rovers with blacked-out windows shot out of the darkness, roaring towards the car park.

The detonator dealers spun round only to be blinded as the Rovers switched on their dazzling headlamps to full beam. They wanted to run but couldn't see in which direction to go.

For a moment it looked as if Scarface was about to make an attempt to drive off but he thought about it for just long enough for SO19 to be out, weapons aimed, screaming, swearing, total domination. The silence of the night was well and truly shattered.

Any drawing of weapons or muzzle flashes from the group at this point and the criminals would be met with a hail of 9mm bullets. This was always the most dangerous part for SO19, when they are most at risk – those precious moments when the bad guys have to decide whether they're being hit by the police or another gang. A wrong call and the bullets will fly.

Danny calmly relayed how SO19 were getting on. As he did so, he saw bedroom lights flickering on, curtains being thrown back. It wouldn't be long before the workers at the Met police's information room who deal with all non-emergency calls would be putting down their *Take a Break* magazines and books as the phone lines of Edmonton burst into life.

By this point Scarface had been dragged unceremoniously

out of the car and slammed into the grit and tarmac. It was all over in seconds.

Once the men were totally overpowered, they were searched and cuffed. There was no struggling, no fight back, SO19 had achieved their objective, a firm, hard and, most importantly of all, safe strike.

Job done, S-squad packed up, debriefed and went home and left the tidying up and questioning of the gunmen to the senior investigating officers and their teams. Sure enough, Scarface escaped jail but The Technician and the third man went down for a very long stretch.

My first armed mission was over. I'd been thrown in right at the deep end and I'd loved every moment – apart from my stupid mistake earlier. This was just the beginning, however, and it was plain to me that I still had a lot to learn. There are so many factors that have to be taken into account on these operations, not least of which was my own inexperience as a newbie manager relying on the expertise of those around me.

I would soon be running missions of greater complexity and size. And I would step inside two secret worlds – the world of the security services as well as that of our deadly opponents.

TEN

DAYS OF THE JACKALS

I was driving an OP van with Jenny in the passenger seat. We were leaving a scene after an armed arrest when a vigilant uniformed WPC who was guarding the outer cordon flagged me down.

In the back were two very tired officers, who were desperate for sleep after hours and hours of peering into the darkness and relaying events to the operational teams.

I wound down the window and whispered, 'It's all right; I'm from 15.'

The lady cop nodded. 'Oh right, I see. Hang on a sec.' She turned around and yelled back up the road. 'Sarge! Is it all right if we let these people through? They're from number 15.'

Grinning, I quietly emphasized. 'No, *SO*-15.' I hadn't been clear enough.

'Oooh!' she said, and gave me a knowing look, becoming flustered with embarrassment. 'Right then.' She lifted the tape and we continued on our way.

'It's been a long day,' Jenny said, yawning as we drove back through East London to the flight deck. I couldn't help but yawn as well. We'd been on duty since lunchtime the day before; it was now dawn. Despite our fatigue, we started talking about the burqa on the way back to TT. One of the suspect's neighbours had been wearing one and I'd seen the cover slip from her face. I'd quickly looked away out of respect but I still caught a glimpse of her beautiful features.

We knew of at least one male terror suspect who'd managed to flee Britain wearing one and another who'd spent a few weeks walking around one northern town and went undetected for a week. How many others there might have been, we didn't know.

France was considering banning the burqa in schools and Belgium was already on the way to banning them in public. We felt that this went too far.

'It's not about the clothing as such,' Jenny said, 'it's up to anyone how they should dress. After all, Danny has a serious issue with your dress sense,' she said, looking me up and down, 'and I think he's got a point.'

'Charming!' I replied. 'But yeah, I'm all for keeping airport security tight but I don't think we need to tell a woman what she should wear when she walks down the high street. That, to me anyway, sounds a bit too much like the Taliban and everything we're fighting against.'

Everybody nodded. For once I was pretty chuffed with myself. Not a bad piece of analysis for five o'clock in the morning.

'Well,' Danny said, 'you may be right but as a DCS in the fashion police, I'm telling you for all our sakes, you've got to get rid of those bloody grandad jeans!'

When our convoy got back to the armoury one of our

officers (who shall remain nameless) approached me looking really worried. 'I've lost a clip of ammo.'

That sent my heart racing.

As you probably know from seeing armed cops in the street, police weapons and magazines are black. It's these accessories that can cause problems, like misplacing your black mobile phone somewhere in your car at night; it's not always easy to find. It's the same with a clip of ammo.

Damn. If we didn't find it all hell would break loose and we could forget about going home until we'd been back to the scene and checked every square inch. We searched the car he'd been in four times but no joy. Just as I was about to order everyone back to scene he suddenly cried out, 'Got it!'

He was smiling with relief.

'Where the hell was it?'

'Believe it or not, in the "safe pocket" of my backpack.'

Typical, nothing like keeping something in a 'safe place'.

By the time everything had been put away and we stepped into the office to complete our debriefing, we were totally shattered, that heavy kind of feeling you get after a day of up and down excitement.

Unfortunately, we couldn't just 'starburst' off home. The equipment had to be safely stored, logs had to be completed properly and all accounted for. This is a dull and arduous task at the best of times but after having been at work all night it's a hellish tedium that you never see in the movies. It's unavoidable, though. If you don't get these things right then and there, they can come back and bite you. So, finally, once we were all happy, it's off for some sleep, before returning in the late afternoon.

Arriving back after having driven against the rush hour, I pushed my tired body back into TT and into the busy office.

I didn't have a pleasant day ahead of me. The SST was already going strong just one month after it had started. Officers had joined from all parts of the Met and each had brought their own skills with them. These were quickly being identified and people were being given tasks accordingly.

It had been decided that one of my 'skills' involved keeping a tab on all the new equipment coming in. It was one of those jobs that nobody wanted to do and I could see why. People just didn't use the storeroom log. I was up to my neck in missing and misplaced TomTom navigation-units when David stuck his head around the door.

'Eyes front and centre old boy,' he said with no little urgency. 'You chaps need to get your arses to the briefing room on the eleventh floor. Something big is afoot.' Excellent! I quickly ditched the TomToms and set off.

By the time we arrived the room was full and buzzing with speculation. What's going on? Who's hit the panic button? All we could do was guess that a very urgent job had broken.

Terry entered, a file under his arm. 'Settle down. As you have all no doubt guessed, something urgent has come up.' Behind him the large projector screen flickered into life, revealing the legend: 'Operation Fingerbobs'.

'We have information that an assassin code-named "White Wolf" is due to land on a flight in three hours' time.'

The room stayed silent as Terry paused and we digested the info. The first thing I thought was that this would make a nice change from the East End. I couldn't see him rolling up at a B&B in Walthamstow.

'His mission,' Terry continued, 'is to assassinate a high-profile figure. The location of the hit is likely to be a posh London club.'

'White Wolf is not an amateur, but a trained professional and will not be travelling alone. He is with his girlfriend and her thirteen-year-old daughter, using them as cover. We expect them to take in the sights of London, which I presume will include London's top attractions. So I expect we'll be going on an extensive sightseeing tour.'

'White Wolf has one problem; his weapon of choice is the gun, so he has to find and purchase a weapon with little or no history, either blind or through a contact. He won't risk any other technique, his masters' orders.'

This added another dimension to the operation, as if it wasn't exciting enough already.

'I can also tell you that he is well educated, speaks fluent English and is known to MI6 to have performed some high-profile assassinations in Eastern Europe. He plans carefully, is methodical and disciplined and is used to staging scenarios such as car accidents to misdirect the authorities. Although we don't think he is going to do this we must expect the unexpected.

'The plan is simple: from the moment White Wolf and his "family" step off that plane, we stay with them – wherever they go.'

We were instructed not to talk to those in S-squad who were not part of the case. Friends who were yesterday working closely together were forced apart; sometimes there was a bit of envy when half the unit was sent off on a secret mission but on S-squad this was a common occurrence and fortunately everyone was grown-up enough to cope.

While the spymasters at MI6 might know the whos, whys and wherefores we, quite rightly, were not told any more than this. We had no idea if it was state-sponsored terrorism, the work of a terrorist group or if rival businessmen were behind it.

Contract killing is probably the least researched and least well-understood kind of homicide there is. An Australian study[12] published in 2005 revealed that about 50 per cent of 'professional' hits are never solved and a Scottish study[13] concluded that about 5 per cent of all homicides are contract killings. There are no available figures for England and no British professionals that have been caught so far are prepared to talk about their work. All part of the service, no doubt.

What we do know is that the contract killing industry has evolved in recent years. It used to be local hit men who specialized in three target types: informants, double-crossers and, in a strange bit of self-policing, criminals who picked on the wrong person. One rapist attacked the daughter of one of London's most feared gangsters and died a terrible death as a result.

Now there are two rising trends: one is where drug gangs employ crack addicts to shoot dead rivals – these killers are known as 'Bics' because like the pen of the same name they are cheap (a life can be bought for as little as £200), disposable, and should the case ever come to court their evidence is seen as unreliable. The other is the rise of the professional assassin. Nobody really knows how much they are paid although we think they earn between £10,000 and £20,000 per hit depending on the difficulty and the status of the target.

A few years ago, an extraordinary seminar was held at the Police Staff College based in a country house called Bramshill near Basingstoke. In attendance were experts in contract killings from the National Criminal Intelligence Service; Special Branch officers; murder detectives from London as well as the Merseyside, Lancashire, Hampshire and Kent forces; the Immigration Service and the Forensic Science Service.

In response to a recent rise in contract killings, they were meeting to establish the historical failures in solving these assassinations and to see if they could come up with some fresh strategies that might improve their chances in the future. As a result, a special squad was formed, dedicated to the task of dealing with contract killers. The Special Projects Unit (which operates from a secret location) is currently running the highest-ever number of operations against active contract killers in the capital. They aren't terribly keen to release many details but they have said publicly that they believe there are about twenty hit men operating in London.[14]

This job wasn't for the Special Projects Unit, however; this was a fast-moving moment-by-moment surveillance job of massive proportions with possible links to terrorism which needed the attention of dozens of armed officers trained in the most up-close-and-personal kind of surveillance there is.

Following an assassin was going to be a unique challenge for us. Pro hit men operate outside society with no bank accounts or employment records and are seldom caught, so – especially when compared with 'normal' murders – their crimes are rarely solved. They carry out their task in a systematic, organized manner, leaving little or no physical evidence at the crime scene. Some hits are disguised as car accidents and drug overdoses – or people just go missing.

If – as in this case – the 'customer' had brought someone in from abroad, it suggested they weren't familiar with the criminal underworld in the UK. It also probably came down to trust for such an important hit. Cost might also have been a factor. In Eastern Europe, where politics are a combination of business and crime, life is the only commodity getting cheaper. For example, around 700 attempted and actual assassinations take place each year in Russia alone; the targets are often prominent businessmen and journalists, along with media moguls, politicians, ex-spies and army men.

The methods range from the professionally mundane 'three in the head you know they're dead' to the downright extraordinary (in one case a pet was dog-napped, explosives were strapped to its body and the animal was returned to its owner for an extremely short-lived reunion).

Whatever the case, our tiredness had been forgotten. A plan was put in place as we prepared to hunt the trained assassin.

'Another "fresh experience" for you, Mary,' George said as we drove through the evening rush-hour traffic, along the Chelsea Embankment on our way to Heathrow.

'Well, it's nice to have the chance to prevent a killing,' the former murder squad detective said with a smile, 'rather than pick up the pieces after the fact.'

ELEVEN

SPECIAL TWIG

Our plan was simple: pick him up at the airport, follow him wherever he went and strike at the moment he bought the gun.

Of course, this was never going to be as easy as it sounded. A trained assassin should assume that he's being followed and will do everything possible to make sure his purchase of the gun goes through as discreetly and as securely as possible.

It was possible that we would see him receive a packet in 'suspicious circumstances'. If we called the hit then and there, we might discover that he had purchased something comparatively innocent – such as a silencer. As amazing as it sounds, buying a silencer is not actually an offence and we would have blown a £1-million operation to give the smiling assassin 'words of advice'. His masters would obviously then be fully aware we were plugged into him. We had to be certain that we would strike at exactly the right time.

This is typical of the very difficult choices those working in the world of counter-terrorism face constantly. It's quite possible to make a good decision acting on the available information that turns out to be wrong, simply because we were missing a crucial piece of intel. Although the unknown can kick us very hard, the worst thing to do is make no decision at all, something that's becoming far too common in our blame culture.

'Airports fascinate me,' Danny said.

'Yup, all human life is here, heh?' Asad replied, surveying the chaotic scene.

The arrivals hall was packed with hundreds of people carrying luggage, waiting for loved ones, booking hire cars, changing money, arguing with airport staff and each other, all totally unaware of the real-life spy game going on around them. Heathrow tends to be packed with surveillance officers from all sorts of agencies and their targets; large international airports are natural focus points for cops and criminals alike.

Our target disembarked at Heathrow on time at 6 p.m. The Red surveillance team placed their net around him. He'd arrived as expected, unarmed and 'on holiday'. He was about six feet tall, had regular but unremarkable features, looked to be in his mid-forties. He looked like he knew how to handle himself and walked with the straight back of a military man.

It was slightly unnerving looking into the face of a man who – should someone pay him enough – would shoot you dead without so much as a blink. It's nothing personal of course; he works for money, idealism or hatred belong to the people who hire him.

A psychologist once wrote that killing is seen as the ultimate masculine act. It is associated with control, nerve and courage. James Bond (who famously had a licence to kill) is often cited as the 'ultimate man' who could mix sex and murder – sometimes simultaneously.

This mission was more akin to the days of the Provisional IRA who carried lists of high-profile human targets during the Troubles. Islamist extremists in the UK haven't yet successfully pursued this method, but as the battle against terrorism goes on, there is no reason to exclude the possibility.

There was nothing 'Bondish' about our man. Outside the airport, smiling and laughing, he took a photo of his 'wife and daughter'. Was he trying to get pictures of any possible surveillance team? Faces captured in the background of the photograph would be studied and memorized. A wasted effort as no one from the team was in view.

They climbed into a cab; the assassin still had his camera around his neck. We followed him among the red tail-lights along the busy A40 until he reached a hotel in Lancaster Gate. Naturally, S-squad had already been there for some time and watched as the 'family' checked in and reserved a table in the exclusive restaurant.

This was followed by a frantic scramble for volunteers and two lucky surveillance officers, one male, one female, got to join them in the upmarket restaurant at the Met's expense. Naturally they'd have to stay off the sauce but it was a pleasant treat nonetheless.

White Wolf decided on an early night and, as the surveillance teams changed shifts, we placed a net around the hotel. All exits were covered, including staff entrances and fire exits. If he decided to take a walk, grab a cab, bus, Tube or hire car, then S-squad would be right behind him.

After three days of sightseeing, in which S-squad was treated to informative tours around the London Dungeon and the Tower of London, White Wolf finally left the hotel on his own at 8 a.m. – just as we were changing surveillance teams that day, the most awkward time for us. Although it was, as David said, 'Jolly rude of him,' it was easily dealt with.

The Red team followed his cab through the morning rush hour with little problem, all the time passing any new information back to the officers at 1600. A black Range Rover full of SO19 (armed) officers joined them and followed at an even more discreet distance.

Soon, we passed Bethnal Green and entered the badlands of Hackney. This was more like it. Having worked these streets as a beat policeman and detective, I knew this was the best place in London to find a gun. There was so much gun crime here that officers in ARVs (Armed Response Vehicles) would park in Hackney knowing that they wouldn't be sitting around for long.

He ditched the cab and stepped into a cafe in Mare Street, a wide and very busy thoroughfare, making it nice and easy for us to keep tabs on him. Once again, as he ordered breakfast there was a scramble of volunteers from S-squad – a chance of a free breakfast and the possibility that they'd be the ones to grab his collar if the 'buy' was going to go down right here.

White Wolf had positioned himself with a clear view to the door and away from the other diners. After placing a cuppa on the table alongside an unread copy of the *Sun*, he walked to the toilet and checked for escape routes out the back.

'He certainly knows his stuff,' Jenny said.

I was impressed. 'It's a good habit to have.'

Back at his table, White Wolf read the paper while slowly eating a huge fry-up; letting himself become absorbed into the environment. He just wanted to look like a piece of the furniture and he did it very well indeed.

Various people came and went during the next twenty minutes, workmen, a handful of trendy young locals before, finally, a man in his early forties with black jacket and jeans walked in. He ordered breakfast at the counter and sat right in front of our man.

'Here we go, heads up one and all.'

As they leaned forward and began a hushed conversation, we called it in and a second team was scrambled out to Hackney to follow Black Jacket after the meet.

SO19's Range Rover moved closer, awaiting the call to go 'green'.

They chatted quietly for a little while longer and then sat back, looking relaxed. The business part of their conversation was over.

This was an intense part of the meeting. A gun is a small item that can be surreptitiously handed over out of view.

About fifteen minutes later, once the waitress removed their plates, Black Jacket slipped a piece of paper across the table. White Wolf took it, looked at it, folded it, placed it in his inside jacket pocket and nodded. He got up and left, walking down Mare Street to a minicab office.

As no gun exchange had happened, SO19 moved away.

Meanwhile, Black Jacket left under the watchful eyes of the second surveillance team. He wasted his time by jumping on a couple of different buses and constantly looking over his shoulder in a rubbish bit of counter-surveillance.

Then, in between bus hopping, he did something very strange. He simply stopped walking and turned round. Before him, in full view among the public, were several undercover officers on foot and in cars. For a moment we held our breath as he studied the scenery. Then, seemingly satisfied, he turned back and carried on. We housed him at a Kilburn flat, the address of which was passed on to 1600 and the Intel Team started searching various databases.

'The Kilburn address is for you, Harry,' Terry told me, 'we need a camera on it, asap.'

'No problem, boss.'

White Wolf, meanwhile, was followed back to central London where he carried on with his Happy Families charade.

By the next morning the camera was up and running, sending high-quality footage of a suburban Kilburn street back to our vantage point.

The surveillance team on the ground was able to relax a little; I'd now give them notice when our man was on his way. Despite address checks, we still didn't know his real name. So, Black Jacket became 'Tired Face', his official code name, which seemed to me very appropriate.

We were in our ops room and Raj was watching the incoming surveillance when he suddenly called me over and pointed at the screen. Something was obscuring the view.

'What's that?' I asked.

We both squinted at the screen. 'It looks like a . . . is it a twig?' Raj said finally.

It bloody well was.

'Must have fallen off the bloody tree.'

Shit.

'Well, you can still see,' Raj said hesitantly. 'Well . . . sort of.'

'Not that well though,' I said. 'In fact if our man turns to the right it's possible that we won't see him at all.'

That meant some unlucky soul from the support team would have to travel all the way to Kilburn to move it surreptitiously.

As usual, Asad was the first to volunteer but the problem was we were in the midst of an overtime cull. These culls were usually thrown at us in dramatic fashion with little or no warning: 'Right, that's it. No more overtime.' I suspect that these orders came whenever someone senior had taken a peek at our heart-attack-inducing overtime costs. I could quite understand it. Counter-terrorism is a twenty-four-hour job involving multiple teams of specialist officers and the costs quickly pile up.

Terry had a great view on these culls. 'We can do almost anything you want,' he'd say, 'just tell me what you can afford.' These culls would always eventually pass (one lasted just two hours thanks to a fast-breaking operation). On this occasion all it took was a short discussion and Asad was on his way to remove the twig currently inconveniencing our £1-million operation.

With one swipe, the offending twig was removed and we were up and running once more.

Just as well, as the next time Tired Face left home he turned right and strolled to his local gym. While he pumped iron we popped his locker and got a checkable name. Some fast research – with the help of our partner agencies – revealed he was a Romanian gunrunner of ill-repute.

At 3 a.m. the following morning all was quiet in 1600, in our ops room and on the ground where two teams were getting DVT as usual, sitting on their butts for hours and hours, waiting for something, anything, to happen.

Suddenly the radio crackled into life on the Lancaster Gate plot as White Wolf took off. .

'Here we go again.'

This time the surveillance was much trickier. Although London is one of those cities that never sleeps, the traffic was a lot lighter and our man spent all his time looking out of the cab's back window. Luckily he stayed on the main road up through Park Lane, round the Marble Arch traffic system, up Edgware Road aka 'Little Morocco', into the wide tree-lined avenue of Maida Vale before entering the far less salubrious Kilburn High Road.

The Surveillance Support Team watched as White Wolf was buzzed in by Tired Face. Three minutes later they both stepped into the street. The hazards flashed on an Audi S8.

'Very nice wheels. Fast and expensive,' Danny whispered, 'who says crime doesn't pay?'

The Intelligence Team at 1600 started searching DVLA records.

The Audi double-backed a few times in another futile exercise in counter-surveillance before they drove to the B&Q car park in Stamford Hill, where they waited in the darkness. And waited. And waited.

Suddenly, the lights went on and the Audi took off before dropping White Wolf at a minicab office. He was back at Lancaster Gate as dawn started to break. Presumably Tired Face had been supposed to hook White Wolf up with a third party who failed to show.

After a day spent shopping in Oxford Street, White Wolf again left the hotel at 3 a.m., alone. The same routine, the same pointless counter-surveillance and back to the B&Q car park. This time, after three minutes, a Vauxhall Vectra joined them and parked nose-to-nose.

Two men got out. White Wolf and Tired Face emerged from the Audi. In no time at all they started to argue.

White Wolf, ever the professional, realized he was dealing with idiots, understood the danger of arguing and immediately walked back to the Audi without a word. To end up bleeding to death from a gunshot wound in a B&Q car park in a foreign land was just plain amateurish. Squabbles over respect were for the local idiots who were prepared to shoot each other dead over name-calling.

Tired Face had other ideas; he was angry and his hand flew out, striking one of the third parties a solid blow in the chest, which caused him to take a step back. The third party flipped and his hand went to his coat.

White Wolf had already started marching back. He grabbed Tired Face firmly in an irresistible grip and practically carried him away, leaving the hot-headed third party cursing and spitting. They were lucky. Bullets in that part of town have flown around over far less.

White Wolf was back at the hotel within the hour.

After two more days of sightseeing, White Wolf and 'family' headed back to Heathrow. Something had obviously gone wrong, we had no idea what – perhaps this failed purchase had been enough to put him off – but now it was decision time.

The team leader was pressed for an answer by the guys on the ground. They badly wanted to know if White Wolf was to be arrested before he checked in. Nobody wanted an assassin to head off scot-free but what evidence did we have?

After queuing for ten minutes, S-squad watched as two men in suits approached White Wolf.

'Excuse me, sir, have you got a moment?' one said, in Special Branch's finest Queen's English.

There is only one answer to that question. You've got all the time they need.

TWELVE

CLASSIFIED LOSSES

PESHAWAR, PAKISTAN, NOVEMBER 2008

When the Pakistani Inter-Services Intelligence department picked up the intelligence they'd been waiting for, they didn't hang about.

The American, who'd just walked in to the Peshawar Internet Cafe was one of the world's most wanted men.[15] The Americans were after the one-time Boy Scout for firing a rocket launcher at their troops in an Afghan military base near the Pakistan border in September 2008. They also wanted to talk to him about the suicide bombing of the Marriott Hotel in Islamabad in September 2008. A truck carrying 600 kilograms of high-grade explosives left more than fifty people dead in what is now infamous for being the largest explosion ever known in Islamabad – and that's really saying something.

Known as Bashir al-Amriki (Bashir the American), the young man from Long Island had attended training camps in Pakistan as well as the infamous tribal-controlled Matta Cheena village in

South Waziristan. He'd discussed plans to plant bombs on the New York subway system with senior members of al-Qaeda – men who were under the direct command of al-Qaeda's number two, Ayman al-Zawahiri, as well as the most senior al-Qaeda operative from the UK, 26-year-old Rashid Rauf.

Pakistan's listening centre, the equivalent of Cheltenham's GCHQ, traced the IP address and called upstairs where an elite undercover squad was immediately scrambled to capture him – alive – at all costs.

The embattled Pakistani President Pervez Musharraf was under considerable pressure from the United States and Britain. He needed to show that he was doing something to combat the terrorists who were using the lawless and remote mountainous border regions of Pakistan as a training ground.

Although outwardly supportive, American military officials had long been questioning just how intensely Pakistan was battling the Taliban and al-Qaeda fighters who crossed their borders with ease. As a result and with a little technological and training help from the United States and Britain, Pakistan's counter-terrorism command had undergone a transformation in recent years, with many new skilled operatives, both in the IT rooms and out on the ground, being young, loyal and highly trained.[16]

As the team scrambled, a call went out to Britain's Secret Intelligence Service and to the CIA (who had installed the sophisticated surveillance equipment in ISI's offices to monitor radio and Internet communications between al-Qaeda and its sympathizers) alerting them to the fact that a major target had been located and efforts were being made to capture him.

Although Peshawar is an ancient city, still mainly fuelled by its many bazaars, there's no shortage of air-conditioned

Internet cafes with private booths. Bashir al-Amriki had selected a place not far from the bustling Smuggler's Bazaar packed full of traders from almost every ethnic background to be found in Pakistan (this bazaar was ostensibly a plain market filled with wares smuggled tax-free from Afghanistan but ask the right questions and you'll be hooked up with more guns and drugs than you could have wished for). Among the shops and food stalls are money changers, often the final stage in the laundering of dirty cash from the West.

The six-man team dressed in local attire hurried through the crowds. Their guns were concealed beneath their clothes; the local police had been scrambled and, it was hoped, would arrive sirens blaring a few minutes after they had taken their man. The local cops would need to keep the peace. Picking a terrorist off the streets of Peshawar is always a risky business, but particularly when the snatch team looks like a bunch of thieves and cutthroats – the crowds could react badly and someone would have a gun on them.

With two men covering the front door, and while two others raced to the back, the team leader and his number two picked out the American and marched up to him as he typed his email unawares.

Taken cleanly, he was whisked off for questioning and, even without a formal extradition treaty, he soon found himself being asked searching questions in a secret location in New York – and that was where he decided to talk.

Bashir al-Amriki was in fact Bryant Neal Vinas, the son of divorced parents from Long Island and a Catholic who had converted to Islam around four years before.[17] He was one of the few Americans known to have made the trek to al-Qaeda's secret Pakistani compounds[18] and as far as the Americans were concerned, the information he provided – about ongoing terror operations around the world – was gold dust.

The corridors of Thames House didn't look all that special but there was a certain atmosphere about the place. After all, M15 was a national institution; thousands of spies had come and gone through its doors since they first opened a century ago in 1909; some of whom had given their lives to protect British state secrets and to uncover those of our enemies.

I never dreamed when I joined the Met almost twenty years ago that I'd end up walking along these corridors. I was on my way to collect a secret document. The job was very urgent, hence the personal visit. I cleared Security and made my way silently through the hushed, blue-carpeted corridors until, after passing yet more checks, I finally reached the office I was after. An intercom brought a young suited man to the door and, after identifying myself in the proper manner, he handed me an unmarked A4 manila envelope detailing a huge counter-terrorist operation that was being run in the north of England.

'Try not to lose them, won't you?' he said.

'Well, I can't promise anything,' I replied with a grin and then, seeing his worried expression, quickly added: 'they'll be going straight into the safe.'

'Yes, well all right then,' he answered. 'Sign here please.'

The documents were placed within two addressed envelopes. This was a simple security measure to prevent top-secret papers from accidentally slipping out in a moment of carelessness, so they wouldn't end up scattered across a cafe, a street or train station, swept away by the wind and deposited at the feet of a curious member of the public.

As I left Box, and just before starting to walk over Lambeth Bridge towards the imposing fortress-like MI6 building, on my way to our offices in Tintagel House on the other side of the Thames, I did a little counter-surveillance, having a good look around while waiting for traffic lights to change and so on – just in case. Sometimes, when I emerged from Thames House on one of these trips, I'd notice some members of the public were looking at me curiously, obviously wondering whether I was a spy.

I'd worked up quite a sweat by the time I was halfway home. I couldn't wait to get the signatures I needed and put this damn envelope into one of our unbreakable safes.

It seemed strange that secret documents were still sometimes handled in this way – even in urgent cases. After all, both The Firm (MI6) and The Burrow (GCHQ) were able to share top-secret info with The Cousins (CIA) in Langley in just a few seconds thanks to the latest encryption software. Documents are sometimes emailed to people who sign them electronically, using encrypted code and a couple of gizmos that are a little like the hand-held pin machines some banks provide to their customers for Internet banking.

Handling secret documents is a high-pressure nightmare, and while hand-to-trusted-hand might be considered by some to be the safest way to move them about, there's plenty of human error to say otherwise.

One summer I was completing an audit of all our operations, every pink (secret) file was spread out across the desks. I was busy cross-referencing them with an Excel spreadsheet when the power went down. Sod it. I sat there twiddling my thumbs, waiting for it to come back. Suddenly, the fire alarm went off. Everyone knew the two were linked and that a power cut usually set it off, so I covered my ears and waited. When the tannoy burst into action a minute later, I was expecting the usual 'would the owner of car registration number . . .'

It was therefore a bit of a surprise to hear the metallic-sounding voice say: 'There is a fire on the eleventh floor [where I was]. Everyone get out of the building now, it is actually on fire.'

Terry, who'd assumed the same as me and had stayed put, came storming out of his office and we cleared the floor.

It was only when we were certain that the floor had been cleared and everyone had started down the first flight of stairs that I told Terry about the pink files.

'Damn! We'll have to put them away, fire or no fire,' he said. We frantically shoved them back in the fireproof safe, hoping we weren't going to be caught in a Towering Inferno and end up being rescued by fireman's ladder in front of the media.

As it turned out, there was no fire but that example is typical of the stress and hassle that handling secret documents involves. That feeling never changed for me but some people who handle top-secret documents every day of their working lives can become acclimatized – and that's when terrible lapses happen.

Although I'm all for sending secrets electronically, this has created a security nightmare in the form of the laptop. Perhaps nowhere in the country handles as much secret information than the staff at The Burrow. A 2010 report revealed that GCHQ had 'mislaid' thirty-five laptops in just one year.[19] A spokesperson said, in hope more than anything else, that there was no evidence that any of the material on the laptops had 'got into wrong hands'. This was followed by the caveat: 'there is no way of confirming that'. The 'evidence' may yet come to haunt us in the future – although I suspect they are so well encrypted that if anyone is trying to hack into them, by the time they crack the code we'll be in line for another Olympics.

A 2008 report revealed that the Ministry of Defence lost 89 laptops and 100 memory sticks in four years. In January 2008 a MoD laptop containing the details of 600,000 people interested in joining the armed forces was stolen from a car. The theft caused concern in light of a terrorist plot in which Muslim extremists planned to kill a British serviceman. The MoD then wisely banned staff from taking home laptops with unencrypted data. A senior intelligence officer in the Cabinet Office left documents, containing a damning assessment of Iraqi forces and a Home Office report on 'al-Qaeda vulnerabilities', on a train. Luckily, for the public, they were handed in to the BBC.[20]

As well as being left on trains, planes, automobiles, taxis, bars and restaurants (one senior MI6 agent lost his laptop after he reportedly drank too much in a bar), many laptops have of course been stolen. The MoD lost 650 this way in four years, including a computer that contained secrets about British nuclear weapons. One man had his stolen when he put it down next to him to buy a ticket for a Tube journey while an army captain had his swiped from under a table while he ate a McDonald's.[21]

I recently saw these thieves in action. I was sat in a coffee shop near King's Cross station. A couple entered who, to me, looked like heroin addicts. They sat near me, just in front of a woman chatting to her friend. They ordered nothing and looked around. I continued to tap away on my personal laptop doing some open-source research. The woman fidgeted for a bit and they left.

'Excuse me,' I said, tapping the woman on the shoulder. 'Have you lost anything?' I collected my laptop, readying myself for a chase.

'My purse!'

Go! I was out of the door in a flash, dived into the street and – they were gone, vanished into the rush-hour melee.

The security guard had been on his break, and they knew it. He even knew who they were. I was sat just two metres away and hadn't seen how they'd stolen her purse.

If I'd ditched my laptop I might have caught one – but another thief might have had my laptop. Besides that, catching the one without the purse would have been a waste of time. Luckily, the woman, who turned out to be a GP, had only lost £5. Even in King's Cross, you wouldn't get a bag of heroin for that. But the expertise with which she was dipped was second to none.

Of course, the scary thing about the cases described is that these are only the ones we know about – which members of the public had handed to the media, understandably keen to highlight the dreadful lapse in security. There must be many more incidents where bags containing laptops have been left in bars and cafes and their owners have suffered that horrific realization before dashing back to collect them in the nick of time.

SO15 can't claim innocence in this respect either. I was once at a briefing with an SO15 superintendent at a private venue. When I got back to the office, the superintendent had group-emailed everyone who'd attended. It started normally enough: 'Thank you for coming today, etc., etc.' But then:

'One last thing. Somebody left a laptop behind. I'd just like to say to whoever it was, you can collect it personally from me.'

The superintendent would no doubt be warming up his vocal cords for a right bollocking for whoever this unlucky, yet deserving, soul was. Ouch. There was no escape of course. It's a fairly simple job of tracking the owner of a laptop.

And it's not just laptops. In August 2009, a Scotland Yard officer who once served as a bodyguard to ex–Prime Minister Tony Blair left her Glock 17 behind in the toilets of a central London Starbucks. She'd taken off the belt holding the firearm when she used the toilet before buying a coffee.[22] Once it was recovered, all the police had to do was match its serial number to those logged at the armoury and call her up.

The problem is that when you carry something all day, every day, you get used to it. When it's in your holster, it's not so bad as you'll never take it out, but in a handbag, it's different. Because I took my gun out quite rarely, I was always alert.

Yes, forgetfulness and accidental carelessness was one massive but unexpected challenge of being security- and weapons-cleared, so it was with great relief that I delivered the secret documents safely. Phew. Now they were somebody else's problem.

After all, it's so easy to do; we've all forgotten something in a public place. In the world in which we operate, however, such negligence jeopardizes people's lives.

Early in 2009 MI5 received information that a team of suspected AQ operatives were based in the north of England and surveillance officers were dispatched to track the suspects 24/7. They soon built up a strong intelligence picture as they followed the suspects – who went to, and photographed,

Manchester's busiest shopping areas, including the Trafford Centre, the Arndale Centre and St Anne's Square in the city centre. The suspects were overheard discussing dates in mid-April, including the Easter weekend.

Carefully, over several months, the team worked steadily to build up a wealth of intelligence, gradually working towards the day they'd be able to strike against the suspected terrorists.

Until, that is, one of the UK's most senior police officers threw a spanner in the works.

Assistant Commissioner Bob Quick may have been Quick by name but he was regarded at the Yard as a cautious and considered man – a safe pair of hands, you might say. He had a distinguished service record with the police and had investigated murders as a detective before working his way up to become the head of the Met's anti-corruption command.

In 2002, Commander Quick took charge of a famous operation in Hackney, East London, to deal with a gunman who had taken a hostage in a flat. I was working for the borough's child protection unit at the time and it lasted so long (at fifteen days, it was London's longest armed siege) it had almost become a part of the scenery by the time the gunman, Eli Hall, tried to burn the flat down before shooting himself. No one else was hurt and Bob Quick was praised for his patience.

The following year, Bob Quick was promoted to Deputy Chief Constable of Surrey Police, before getting the top job as Chief Constable in 2004. Four years later he joined the Met as Assistant Commissioner where, in his £168,000 per year role, he took charge of our counter-terrorism and security department, Specialist Operations at New Scotland Yard. Since then, he'd successfully orchestrated a number of critical counter-terror operations.

In April 2009 he was photographed entering Downing Street where he was about to meet the Prime Minister and the Home Secretary carrying a secret briefing note on which details of an undercover operation – code-named Pathway – could be clearly seen on the photographs. It revealed details of the locations and manner of the intended arrests by 'dynamic entry – firearms'. It also showed where the suspects would have been held and the names of the six senior officers in charge of the operation.[23]

Obviously no one would be more surprised than the suspected terrorists that they were the subject of the investigation. The document, headed SECRET, revealed that one man was British-born, while the rest were Pakistanis staying on student visas. They ranged in age from a teenager to a 41-year-old man.

To say a major storm erupted after Bob Quick's error would be putting it mildly. This desperately important operation was now in serious danger. While the D-Notice Committee* made frantic calls to newspapers and broadcasters in an attempt to prevent the picture being published, teams were scrambled to arrest the suspects asap.[24]

It didn't help that in an effort to shut the barn door after the horse had bolted, the D-Notice Committee was able to tell editors only that they 'might be in possession' of a photograph

*The Defence Press and Broadcasting Advisory Committee oversee a voluntary code that provides guidance to the British media on the publication or broadcasting of national security information. Their main objective is to prevent the accidental publication of information that would compromise UK military and intelligence operations and methods, or put at risk the safety of those involved in such operations, or lead to attacks that would damage the critical national infrastructure and/or endanger lives.

that compromised national security, without saying what it was.

Every second counted. If the men planning an attack had heard about Bob Quick's slip-up and had either seen the published photo or suspected that they were the subjects of the operation, then they may have decided to strike immediately.

It was a sign of how closely the men were being followed that the operation to arrest them was launched within an hour of the papers being photographed. Officers shot one suspect with a stun gun. At Liverpool John Moores University, students were ordered to stay in the lecture theatres and classrooms and to keep away from the windows as a man was arrested by armed police outside the campus library. Most ignored the warning and dozens of students filmed the event on their mobile phones.

Eight addresses were searched and many other suspects were arrested on the streets, in vehicles and Internet cafes – the staff at a Homebase store had a memorable day as a hundred armed officers swooped on the shop to arrest two male shoppers. Thanks in part to the great work of the surveillance teams, everyone who was on the list was arrested.

Once the dust had settled after the arrests, Bob Quick tendered his resignation to Boris Johnson, London Mayor and Chairman of the Metropolitan Police Authority. He admitted that he 'could have compromised a major counter-terrorism operation'.[25] The price is too high in this line of work to allow for mistakes like that, however innocently they're made. Within two weeks of their arrest, detectives had to throw in the towel and release all the arrested men without charge.

Chris Grayling, the shadow Home Secretary, made an inter-esting point when he told *Sky News*: 'I cannot understand why a document of this kind was not in a locked briefcase as a matter of course.' Indeed, the double-envelope method was supposed to make this sort of thing much less likely but as I soon discov-ered, security slip-ups like this can happen to anyone.

With all the upheavals in the police, and the amalgamation and dissolution of various departments, I was asked to help set up an office for a superintendent.

I soon had everything in place – except for a printer. I scoured various empty offices that were full of redundant equipment until finally I found a fairly modern printer. That'll do nicely, I thought, and set off in search of the nearest control room.

'Is it all right if I take this printer?' I asked.

A man glanced up from his computer screen for a moment. 'Of course, no problem,' he said, and got back to whatever he was doing.

'Great, thank you.' I heaved it out to the super's desk and, just to be safe, I emailed the resources department, telling them what I'd done.

I then called someone from IT to install the printer. When he saw the machine, he took one look and drew in a deep breath, much like my local mechanic does whenever I bring in my old banger for repair. 'Can't do it. That's an old cable and it needs a new one.'

'Can you sort it?'

'Easier to get a new one really but yeah, I suppose, we have got some cables somewhere and with an upgrade—'

'Great, go ahead and fix it will you?'

I forgot all about it for two weeks until a group email

pinged on my screen late one Friday afternoon. As I read its contents they leapt out at me and slapped me round the face.

'We are missing a printer from the twentieth floor,' it said. 'It belongs to a certain partner agency. We need it back urgently. The DPS (Department of Professional Standards, which amongst other things, investigates police misconduct) have been informed and are already investigating.'

Damn, damn, damn!

Where inter-departmental politics are involved, getting a complaint can be dangerous as the blame culture soon kicks into action. Terry had a great expression for it: 'The Blamethrower'. This was to be avoided at all costs as it had been fatal to many a career.

The security problem in this case related to the printer's memory. Some printers have reasonably large hard drives on which they automatically store electronic versions of documents that have passed through its cogs for easy access, should they need to be retrieved or more copies made. Goodness knows what secrets, if any, might still have been on this printer's memory. They must have been pretty important considering this panicked reaction.

I rang the bloke who'd written the email and explained that I'd taken a printer from that floor, with permission, and had told the resources department. A quick check of the serial number revealed that the superintendent's printer was the missing one. He was reassured when I informed him that it had never left a secure environment. I was extremely pleased that I'd kept that email; that would save me from a grilling by the DPS. In the Met it's wise to keep every email, even a mundane one about moving a printer – it could save your career.

As I had recently achieved top-secret clearance, I volunteered to call the agency and hand it back. I was told to go ahead.

I called them up. 'No rush,' a posh voice said on the other end of the line when I called, 'just return it to us in due course. It's too late to return it now until after the weekend, anyway.'

Well, they couldn't have sounded less stressed about it if they'd tried. I sighed and took the printer round, grateful that I'd escaped the Spanish Inquisition. As ever, I didn't have much time to reflect. Duty called; it was time for S-squad to go to university.

THIRTEEN

UNIVERSITY OF TERROR

When Malik Ranjha* recently joined a famous London University as a nervous but bright nineteen-year-old under-graduate in computer science he was – like most students – excited but also a little nervous at the prospect. A quiet but friendly student from the north of England, there was nothing to suggest that Malik had a radical bone in his body.

His parents, who had emigrated to the UK from Pakistan in the 1970s, ran a successful business in the Midlands. His father had warned him about falling in with the wrong crowd but he was more worried about sex, drugs and rock 'n' roll than Islamic extremism.

Malik was quickly befriended by a group of fellow Muslim students during freshers' week. They encouraged him to join the university's Islamic Society.

'I don't know,' he'd said, 'my parents want me to focus on my studies. These things take up a lot of time, don't they?'

---

*Not his real name

'You should come along to our meetings and decide for yourself,' one of them said. 'We're all grade-A students and we can help you with your studies.'

At the meeting they asked him lots of questions. They seemed genuinely interested in his studies and his future. They explained that they were a proud group of Muslims who wanted to bring Islamism to other countries such as Pakistan, Bangladesh, India and Sri Lanka, as well as protect and help those Muslims who were persecuted by other faiths.

Malik was quickly welcomed into this buzzing and trendy group of twenty young men as if he were their brother. Their friendship was unconditional from day one. They were all extremely well connected, appeared to be totally in control of their destiny and were unshakeably confident in their unity. Their lives clearly had meaning and direction. It felt great to be with them, a real privilege in fact, and Malik respected their commitment to Islam.

As he attended more of their meetings in halls of residence, they began persuading him to isolate himself from other students, even from other Muslims if they didn't share the same agenda as the society.

'Why are you hanging out with that *kuffar*?' one of them said as he stood talking to a young white man from his study group.

'He's in my class, we study together.'

'You shouldn't talk to him.'

A few weeks later he visited a *madafa*, a sort of informal but private club in a nearby mosque with some of the society members. The young men were not exactly disrespectful to the local imam but they described him as being 'like all the others, a placid fool dependant on congregational collections'.

They, on the other hand, wanted to *do* something. They told Malik that Islam was a complete code of life, rather than being purely spiritual.

'Islam is more than a religion,' they told him. 'We want to see an Islamic government, we want to see Islam taken out of mosques and homes, and into all areas of life. We want to create God's government on God's earth and you don't need a ballot box to do that!'

Suddenly Malik felt grown up; these people had decided to make him part of something important. Until then he'd always been his parents' little boy. These people wanted him. No, even more than that, they *needed* him.

The leaders of the all-male group were respected by the university lecturers and, as he soon discovered, feared by others. Some of that fear and respect was soon directed at him. Malik enjoyed the feeling of power it gave him. Alone he was nothing – but now he was part of a brotherhood that stood shoulder-to-shoulder. If anyone had a problem with him, then they had it with the brotherhood – and they didn't take prisoners.

He was treated like a rising star and played a key role in the running of a very successful campus-based Islamist front organization, an organization that exhorted people to join the Islamist movement. He helped to organize events at which radical speakers drew crowds of over two hundred students. Time and again, they preached that: 'British and American politics are man-made. Our politics are made by *God*.'

He was alarmed to learn that some of the 'friends' of the organization were in prison while others openly defied the police. Malik had never broken the law. But when his friends explained why these men were in jail – for spreading the word of Islam, for carrying out the holy doctrine, his feelings changed.

'Why should we help the police to put brothers in prison,' the chairman argued, 'when their job is to deal with rapists and murderers? The persecution is everywhere, all around us, even here, Malik.'

They showed Malik horrific videos – footage of the extermination of Muslims in Bosnia; the nightmare images were burned into his mind. The tight-knit group debated the latest news from the wars in Middle East, always in a confrontational tone.

'Malik, always remember. Allah is our objective, the Quran is our Constitution, the Prophet is our leader, Jihad is our way, and death for the sake of Allah is the highest of our aspirations.'

They told him about Sayyid Qutb, the Egyptian scholar and martyr whose work had influenced millions of Muslims, including Osama bin Laden. Qutb's revolutionary book *Milestones*, in which the scholar declared that a total jihad was the only way to eliminate imperialism, became compulsory reading. The Egyptian government had hanged Sayyid Qutb back in 1966 for precisely this reason – they turned him into a martyr, the greatest outcome for any jihadist.

Malik wanted more than anything to help, to show his gratitude for their faith in him.

'Why can't we do something about this?' he'd said. 'You keep telling me that Islam is a revolutionary doctrine that overthrows governments and seeks to overturn the whole universal social order but our people are being jailed and murdered while we sit here and talk!'

The leader of the group smiled and nodded. 'I can see you are a man of action, Malik. There is indeed something more you can do.'

The inhospitable mountainous Taliban stronghold of Waziristan, in the North West region of Pakistan, close to the Afghan border. Many of our targets trained here.

SO15's weapon of choice: the ever-reliable and lightweight Glock 17. Stepping out onto the streets of London with this under my coat for the first time was an experience I'll never forget.

Bob Quick, once the UK's most senior counter terrorism officer, paid a high price and stepped down after this security error blew a covert operation wide open.

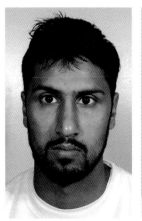

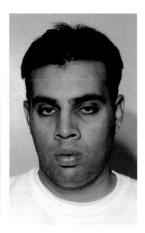

Smile, you're going to jail. Abdulla Ahmed Ali, 28, Tanvir Hussain, 28, and Assad Sarwar, 29. The convicted liquid bomb plotters took S-squad all over London as they planned their devastating attack, which could have claimed more than 5,000 lives. Below is a still from Ali's suicide video in which he warned us to 'expect floods of martyr operations'.

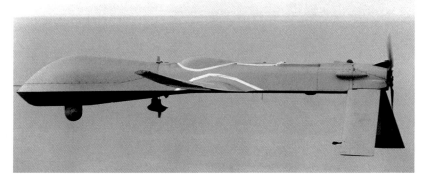

The CIA's weapon of choice: A MQ-1L Predator UAV drone capable of firing two AGM-114 Hellfire missiles. Their targets: leading terrorist targets in Pakistan and Afghanistan. Deadly accurate, they have led to the death of many terrorist leaders. Some targets on the drones' hit list made it to London.

One such target was the elusive senior AQ member Rashid Rauf, who held dual British-Pakistani citizenship. Rauf, who was raised in Birmingham and escaped from his prison guards in Pakistan, was alleged to be behind the liquid bomb plot.

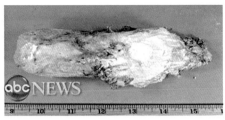

Universities of Terror: Umar Farouk Abdulmutallab tried to blow up a flight from London to Detroit with his explosive underwear. The brave actions of fellow passengers and crew made sure he failed. Abdulmutallab, a former president of University College London's Islamic Society, was one of several radical university students who attracted our interest.

Baitullah Mehsud, leader of the Tehrik-e-Taliban Pakistan (TTP). *Time* described him as an 'icon of global jihad'. Mehsud was one of the world's most wanted men and provided a ready supply of would-be suicide bombers bound for the UK – until a midnight tryst forced him out of hiding and within range of a CIA drone.

Mohammed Hamid aka 'Osama bin London', ran terror training camps in the UK that were attended by 21/7 bombers Ramzi Mohammed and Yassin Omar. We caught up with him in a Chinese restaurant in London.

Hamid's accomplice and terror ringleader Atilla Ahmet (right) was once the right hand man to the infamous one-eyed hook-handed preacher Abu Hamza (left). Ahmet sang a warped version of the Banana Boat Song to children: 'Come, Mr Taliban, come bomb England, before the daylight come, you wanna see Downing Street done.'

Yemen: Al Qaeda's new base. This hit on the US embassy cost 16 lives, providing a terrible wake-up call. Intelligence from several agencies, including ours, helped prevent the bombing of the UK embassy.

Ali Beheshti who dressed his baby in an 'I love Al-Qaeda' hat and wielded a burning cross outside the US embassy in London took exception to the British right to freedom of speech. We caught him as he tried to raze a publisher's house to the ground.

We can't do it without you: As the Intel came in after the Haymarket bombs were discovered in London we raced north, chasing after Bilal Abdullah and Kafeel Ahmed but we weren't quite quick enough. Thanks to the bravery of airport staff, policeman and members of the public however, two major disasters were averted.

The fight never ends: Hakimullah Mehsud, the new chief of the TTP sitting with Humam Khalil Abu-Mulal al-Balawi. Al-Balawi walked right into the heart of CIA's HQ in Afghanistan before detonating a devastating suicide bomb. The reason: vengeance for the CIA's assassination of Baitullah Mehsud. The TTP in Waziristan still remains a major terrorist training centre from where attacks are launched across the globe.

FOURTEEN

DEBATES WITH A DIFFERENCE

Asad and I were sat in a covert vehicle in a Tesco car park surrounded by crisp packets.

'That's the problem with jobs near a supermarket,' Asad said, rubbing his stomach.

'Yup, eating is a great way to stave off the boredom all right. And we have great loos close to hand.'

'Talking of which . . .' Asad began, reaching for the door. Just then, the radio crackled into life.

'Sit tight, "Early Dawn" has arrived.'

'How inconvenient.'

'There he is.'

'He's a young one all right.'

Dressed in Western clothes, we followed Early Dawn (Malik Ranjha) to his London university where we waited again, for another three hours, crisp packets and empty drinks cartons slowly piling up around us.

The surveillance teams changed over, but we stayed put. At 4.35 p.m. Early Dawn was back on the radar. We followed him to a house about a mile away. No anti-surveillance, just a jaunty walk.

It seemed very hard to believe that Early Dawn was of significant interest to the Security Services. But he had popped up on their radar after visiting the tribal regions of Pakistan. He then cropped up at some radical group meetings at university and his Internet activity had become a growing concern.

Still, at least he was a UK citizen, much easier to arrest than so many of those young men who are over here on a 'student' visa and whose home country has to be notified or if they make it back to their home country and have to be extradited.

'Well, we'll make damn sure he won't be getting his seventy-two virgins,' I said confidently.

'What do you mean?' Asad asked me flatly.

'Oh bugger, what have I said?' I wondered. Asad was a devout Muslim and his commitment was much respected and admired by the team. Raj, on the other hand, seemed to have no interest in religion, although he said he always ticked the box marked 'Muslim' when filling out official forms.

'Erm.'

'Exactly. You don't have a clue what you're talking about, Harry.'

I had to admit defeat. 'I thought suicide bombers were looking forward to seventy-two virgins in the afterlife.'

'No, Harry. Look, it's not your fault, really, but you need to do the SB thing and study your subject before you make reference to something you know nothing about. It's a mistranslation of the Quran. Ever since Muhammad Abu Wardeh said it . . . You don't know who he is, do you?'

I shook my head.

'He was a terrorist recruiter for Hamas and in August 2001, on national US television he said: "If you become a martyr, God will give you seventy virgins, seventy wives and everlasting happiness." This was nonsense. Ask any scholar and he'll tell you that the correct translation is "angels". Paradise is described extensively in the Quran but there are no mentions of virgins – or how many.'

I nodded. 'I see.'

'The meaning of "jihad" has become warped as well. You can be a jihadist if you're trying to become a better Muslim to overcome various temptations or whatever it is that's stopping you from being the best you can.

'Of course it can also mean true holy war, armed struggle against Islam's enemies. This is the definition the terrorists like to use but they don't seem to look at the rules involved. The Quran forbids those waging a jihad from harming those who have lived peacefully, have not attacked Islam or done anything to hurt them. It forbids the killing of women and children, torture, the taking of hostages. Al-Qaeda have done all that and more.

'Besides, a jihad has to be authorized by a significant Quranic authority, someone with a widely respected reputation, perhaps known to millions of Muslims. There's no way they would authorize al-Qaeda's "struggle" as they've broken so many rules. They've even killed Muslims.

'Suicide bombers have been fooled. The jihadi must not die by his own hand, even if the mission is indeed "suicidal" and he shouldn't even know the time and date of his death. So, although they are expecting their virgins and paradise, the suicide bombers, according to the Quran, should wake up on the other side in hell.'

'Along with those who took them there.'

'Exactly.' Asad smiled at me. 'Now you're getting it, Harry!'

I wasn't so sure, it was clear to me that I was in a world which I still knew very little about and had plenty to learn.

Once Early Dawn was back home, we waited until at 7 p.m. he finally re-emerged, dressed in religious clothing and was off again on foot.

He took us to a street where we'd been before, on another mission. He entered a house we knew all too well and Asad and I exchanged knowing looks. It was no ordinary house; it was in fact a 'secret' mosque, a place for extremists, a safe haven for jihadists. We watched as Early Dawn left the West behind and entered the world of extremism.

Having young people at university who are interested in extremism is not uncommon, but I still couldn't believe that young lad who was only a few years older than my eldest son had entered the twisted world of terror.

'No one loves the *kuffar* [infidels]! We hate the *kuffar*. We love the people of Islam and we hate the people of the *kuffar*. We hate the *kuffar*. If anyone changes his religion from al-Islam, then he would be killed in an Islamic state.'

Charming. I could only presume that these quotes wouldn't be appearing any time soon in the prospectus of this prestigious London university.

I'd decided to educate myself on university extremism and was amazed at the wealth of material available. I paused the video, which documented a meeting at another well-known London university. Someone had posted it online. The faces were too pixelated, not much to be made out there. I could, however, see that the students in the packed room seemed to me to be 100 per cent supportive of what was being said.

'And what about those who practise homosexuality?' the speaker continued. 'Let us throw them off the mountain!' This was met with much applause.

Whenever we learned that a radical speaker was coming to talk at a university we knew there was a good chance that they'd end up being arrested for preaching and inciting racial hatred. There was enough of that on this video – but as far as our present case was concerned, we weren't after the speaker, our focus was on someone in the crowd: Early Dawn.

He'd been spending far too much time on the Internet researching martyrdom and weapons training. The final straw had come when he was sent a blueprint file on how to construct the Qassam artillery rocket, which, in Terry's words, was 'a *Blue-Peter*-style, do-it-yourself steel rocket favoured by Middle Eastern terrorists on a budget'.

I carried on watching the video and the speaker continued with his hateful rhetoric. 'Allah made women to be less than man. It takes two female witnesses to match one male witness.'

Following a suspect from a university was quite a risky proposition but as was often the case with young lads like Early Dawn we weren't quite sure of where he lived yet, a common problem where people move around often, staying with friends and family. His university was the best place to start.

Contrary to what many in the media say, most young radicals don't get their ideas from mosques at all. They gather in youth clubs, gyms, bookstores – but most of all they gather in universities. I'd been surprised to see how full of Islamic militants London's universities had turned out to be – as time went on I found myself being called back to

universities more and more on investigations into possible terrorist activity.

Before 9/11 nearly all universities denied there was a
problem. But take it from me: we were in and out of universities following dangerous radicals every month of the year –
and the police had been doing so long before I arrived in S-
squad.

The would-be liquid bombers were from middle-class,
university-educated families. The reaction of their friends
and neighbours was overwhelmingly one of disbelief. They
were described as 'good as gold, a normal lad'; a 'nice guy' who
liked to play football; 'a very caring boy' who, on learning
that her dog had died, said, 'If you need me, I'm there for
you.'

It was a surprise to many to learn that the terrorists that
struck in the UK were born and raised here and not 'foreign
monsters' or Taliban fresh from Afghanistan or Pakistan.

'It's all too easy to see terrorists as inhuman monsters,' Terry
had told me over coffee. 'I think you've already seen that this
isn't true at all. Psychos make rubbish criminal gang members
and even worse terrorists. They are self-obsessed and rarely
take orders – not unless they think carrying out those orders
will benefit them directly. There's no way they'd be willing to
throw their lives away for some zealot. The best terrorists are
"ordinary". They don't commit crimes, they're great team
players, caring even.'

'So what tips them over the edge?'

'The ones who brainwash them into believing their people
have suffered, and as a consequence are being demonized, wiped
out – like the ethnic cleansing of Muslims during the Bosnian
conflict.'

'And now we have the war in the Middle East.'

'Exactly. It's easy for extremists to argue that the rest of the world is waging war on Islam and that striking back gives meaning to their lives.

'Very often these early seeds are sown in the UK's universities. Impressionable young men, many of whom have suffered prejudice, are swept up by extremist groups and suddenly find that their lives are full of excitement and meaning.'

As the information built up about the pasts of Ali and Rauf I noticed that they'd been part of radical movements while at university.

Abdulla Ahmed Ali had been born in East London, into a religious family of eight brothers and sisters, with close connections to Pakistan. Even before graduating in engineering at City University in London, he was surrounded by the extremists of al-Muhajiroun, led by the preacher Omar Bakri Mohammed.

Rashid Rauf's road to radicalization also started while he was at university and Sarwar had been radicalized long before he visited Pakistan. As George said: 'You don't just show up at a madrasa, spend a few weeks there and become a jihadi. It doesn't work that way. You need contacts, people who can recommend you as a committed young man, someone to be trusted.'

British extremist groups will often send a promising 'recruit' to Pakistan, on the pretext of visiting relatives, to link up with contacts there. They're then awestruck by the presence of famous jihadists, preachers and religious leaders. The purpose of such visits is ideological reinforcement – maybe even a blessing from an extremist leader – rather than military training. Some never return, linking up with terrorist cells and extremists there.

After all, there's no point in battlefield training when all you have to do is take yourself to the target zone and press a button – and learning how to make a bomb is a lot easier under the tutelage of an expert in the remote areas of Pakistan than from a manual printed out from the Internet in the suburbs of London.

We've asked universities for help in tackling extremism and monitoring students who are causing concern. But this was strongly rejected by lecturers from the University and College Union as an unacceptable request to spy on their students.

They argue that moderate Islamic societies are most effective at this. But they aren't. As far as the extremists are concerned, moderates are the worst kind of *kuffars* of all and remain ineffective at preventing impressionable young students from being radicalized.

While universities can act to stop illegal speeches and meetings on their campuses – such as those designed to incite racial and religious hatred – they sometimes argue that it's too difficult to decide whether some offensive arguments actually break the law.[26]

I realize that universities are there partly to debate controversial issues but, all too often, this is a weak argument. For a start they're academics so they should find it easier than most to identify whether the speaker is mainstream or not. All they need to do is study the law and research the preachers, find out what they've said at other talks. Much can be checked on the Internet; or they could even ask students. It's all straightforward stuff. For example, I think that most people are able to tell that advocating the wholesale murder of homosexuals is against the law.

A famous recent example of a student extremist is that of failed Detroit bomber Umar Farouk Abdulmutallab. The 23-year-old, who was described by one teacher as 'a dream student', was president of University College London's Islamic Society in the academic year 2006 to 2007, and organized a controversial 'War on terror week', which featured a debate 'Jihad v Terrorism'.

On 25 December 2009, Abdulmutallab tried to blow up a transatlantic flight bound for Detroit using high explosives sewn into his underwear. Fortunately, a courageous crew and passengers overpowered him as he tried to inject chemicals into the explosives.[27]

Abdulmutallab's actions have, unfortunately for UCL, helped turn parts of their current prospectus into an extremely ironic document. The UCL faculty of engineering sciences in which Abdulmutallab studied is today a major global centre for research and training in counter-terrorism. It runs a masters degree in that subject and has pioneered new technologies for airport safety and tracking.

In February 2010, radical preacher Anwar al-Awlaki admitted in an interview, published in Arabic by Aljazeera, that he taught and corresponded with Umar Farouk Abdulmutallab. Anwar Al-Awlaki gave a series of lectures in December 2002 and January 2003 at the London Masjid at-Tawhid mosque, describing the rewards martyrs receive in paradise, and developing a following among ultra-conservative young Muslims. He was also a 'distinguished guest' speaker at the UK's Federation of Student Islamic Societies' annual dinner in 2003.

The *Sunday Times* established that Abdulmutallab first met al-Awlaki in 2005 in Yemen, while he was studying Arabic. Abdulmutallab also saw al-Awlaki at the Finsbury Park

Mosque. Evidence collected during searches of flats connected to Abdulmutallab in London indicated that he was a 'big fan' of al-Awlaki, as web traffic showed he followed the preacher's blog and website. With a blog and a Facebook page al-Awlaki is often described as the 'bin Laden of the Internet'.

We've come across students from UCL who have literature entitled: 'Preparing the fighter who is going for jihad'; 'Virtues of martyrdom in the path of Allah'; 'Taking care of the family left behind by the fighter' and 'How to run a training camp'.

I don't think any of that material was on their reading list.

Among the many controversial figures that have been invited to give talks at UCL include supporters of the terrorist group Hamas, members of Hizb ut-Tahrir (their racist and fascist views had already led to them being banned from UK universities by the National Union of Students in 2004), those who have spoken in support of the Taliban, warned Muslims not to integrate into Western societies, argued in favour of domestic violence and advocated the destruction of Israel.

Sheikh Abu Yusuf Riyadh ul-Haq was invited by UCL's Islamic Society to speak on 9 November 2005. Ul-Haq had previously supported the Taliban, stating in 2000 that they were 'The only group of people upon the earth who are establishing the Sharia and the law of Allah.'

Speaking on the topic of Israel, ul-Haq previously called on Muslims to 'be willing to sacrifice anything that may be required of us'. He claimed that the al-Aqsa Mosque in Jerusalem must be liberated and 'we are willing to die in the process' and that when called upon 'we will consider it an honour and a privilege to shed our blood'. Ul-Haq has also made anti-Semitic statements, warned against Muslim integration and labelled the 'culture' of non-Muslims as 'evil'.

Murtaza Khan (aka Abu Hasnayn Murtaza Khan) regularly speaks to university Islamic Societies and was invited to speak at UCL on 21 January 2009 and at its annual conference on 6 September 2009. Khan advocates extreme intolerance towards non-Muslims. In a 2007 Channel 4 documentary Khan asked a Muslim audience: 'For how long do we have to see our mothers, sisters and daughters having to uncover themselves before these filthy non-Muslim doctors? We should have a sense of shame.'

Khan also taught Islamic Studies at Al Noor primary school in London and is described as a 'visiting khateeb' (person who delivers the Friday sermons) at the University of East London.

Abdul Raheem Green was invited to UCL to address students on 23 November 2005, 4 October 2006 and 22 January 2009. He had previously spoken in favour of domestic violence, saying that a husband may use 'physical force . . . a very light beating' against his wife and has argued that 'Islam is not compatible with democracy'.

On 25 January 2008, at a UCLU Islamic Society event entitled 'Know Your Rights', an unknown speaker argued that Muslims should retaliate by refusing to cooperate with police on tackling neighbourhood crime:

> The police always say 'Well, we are doing what's best for the country.' This is why the police lobby, the security services lobby, have to be watched very carefully . . . We'll put the word out around the whole streets, everywhere in the country, that Muslims should not cooperate with the police. And what that in fact means is, most of the police's job isn't terrorism, it's ordinary crime.
>
> And they know as well that ordinary crime, for which they need the cooperation of the communities, not just

Muslim, but Afro-Caribbean, white communities, any of the communities. We say, we'll put the word out and campaign that police have become anti-Muslim, they are political, no one will cooperate with you, all your statistics will go down the drain, you want to get drug dealers, you want to get burglars, then we'll see what we can do.

The UCLU Islamic Society are quite right when they point out that they 'unequivocally and in very clear terms denounce all acts of terrorism and violence regardless of the perpetrator'. They are there to foster debate, discussion and education, and so it's easy for radicals with unpopular opinions to speak out at such events.

I've focused on UCL because, thanks to a report published by the Centre for Social Cohesion, all this material is now in the public domain, but I can assure you this is by no means the only innocent university that has been unwittingly infected by small but powerful extremist groups.[28]

Take Waseem Mughal, for example, who was convicted of running a website for al-Qaeda in Iraq, was a former bio-chemistry student at Leicester University. Mughal was a member of the university's Islamic Society.

Would-be fertilizer bomber Jawad Akbar attended Islamic Society meetings at Brunel University, while Yassin Nassari, convicted of smuggling plans for making explosive devices into the UK, was president of the University of Westminster's Islamic Society at its Harrow campus in north-west London. His hard drive contained documents about martyrdom and weapons training, as well as instructions on how to construct improvised explosive devices. Several graphic videos of terrorist attacks and beheadings were found at his home.[29]

Although these students are of course in a tiny minority, we've known for too long that they are significant and we're paying the price for that now. As far back as 2005, Professor Anthony Glees, the director of the Brunel Centre for Intelligence and Security Services, wrote a report warning that extremists were operating on campuses. He said then that the problem must not be ignored.

'A significant number of people, either convicted of terrorist offences or who have admitted a guilt or who've been murdered or killed in the carrying out of their terrorist offences, have been students at British universities and colleges.'[30] I realize that a lot of people will disagree with this but speaking as a counter-terrorist officer on the ground, I spend far too much of my time in UK universities. Extremist groups remain firmly rooted in some of the UK's finest universities and more and more students – who would otherwise never have even dreamed of terrorism before they went to university – are in danger of being drawn into them.

When SO15 arrested Malik and confronted him with the evidence, his look of terror said it all. He told his interviewers in a shaking voice that he knew he'd made a terrible mistake in embracing extremism. There was nothing he could do about it now; it was far too late. He'd crossed a line and he was going to have to pay the price – a good few years at Her Majesty's Pleasure.

Malik's parents later said that when they went to see their son at university they were shocked by what some of the societies were up to:

We picked this university because of its world-class reputation and because of its all-round, liberal approach to education. We had no idea that our son was in danger of extremism. Some leaflets we saw were a real shock to us and we weren't alone. We're not trying to stop intellectual freedom, but what we are talking about has nothing to do with intellectual freedom. One event in 2007 was nothing but a hatred week run by extreme Islamic activist students in the university.

We were on the verge of forcing our son out when he was arrested. Now both our lives and his have been ruined. We're not alone as we've since made contact with many other Muslim parents who have been left to deal with the radicalization of their own children on their own – without help from the university, Islamic groups or the police.

After what we've been through I'd like to see outside specialists brought into universities to work on prevention so that other families don't have to go through the nightmare we've been forced to endure.

When our son arrived at university he was just a quiet but friendly nineteen-year-old boy. We trusted that a university education would give him the best possible shot at life – and just over a year later he's starting a long sentence for storing and distributing terrorist material. I don't know if we're ever going to see the young son we once knew ever again, if that radicalization will ever leave him, especially now he's in jail, with other 'heroes' from his group.

Persuading young, seemingly innocent and well-behaved students to join the terrorist cause remains a popular pastime for extremists and it seemed there was no age limit – as I was about to discover, there were some extremists who were even younger than Early Dawn.

FIFTEEN

TEENIE TERRORISTS

'You love them boards, don't you, Harry?' Danny said with a grin as I stood frowning in front of the Boards of Chaos, green marker in one hand, red in the other.

'Well, they're a work of art,' I said, not moving my gaze. The Boards of Chaos were at the centre of S-squad's operations and were the most sophisticated tool of all. They took up a whole wall on one side of our office and were constantly being scribbled on throughout the day as new intel on our targets came in and we had to find the resources to respond. It also spelled out which team was where, what their objective was, what they'd achieved so far and so on.

One of the boards dealt with all the shifts of S-squad officers. This detailed who was on what operation, any training courses they were due to attend and if they were about to take leave or were off sick. It provided a useful focal point where team members got together for an informal briefing about what the latest situation was and who was doing what. Even so, the comedians on the team couldn't help but poke fun at my obsession with keeping the board up to date.

I eventually earned the nickname 'Captain Chaos' after a number of urgent operations fell on my watch; I wasn't the only one to get a nickname but, for some reason, people thought mine was particularly appropriate.

I was staring intently at the boards, trying to figure out what I needed all these people to be doing tomorrow morning.

'I think I've got it all,' I eventually muttered to myself, and set about ringing everyone and sending out coded text messages. This was a time-consuming process. It was 4 p.m., and would take me an hour and a half before it was all done.

Needless to say, if someone wanted to change a shift, for whatever reason, it caused havoc. I couldn't get annoyed though. Our boys and girls had to live with the most incredible demands, giving them sporadic start and finish times and sudden shift changes. It was my job to ensure that we did everything we could for them in return. Sometimes it felt like I was trying to work out the seating arrangements for a massive wedding reception with an ever-changing guest list.

Of course the officers weren't always best pleased when they discovered that we'd condemned them to yet another long shift sitting in the back of the OP van the following morning, or that we'd sent them to the other end of the country, wreaking havoc with their personal lives, but *C'est la vie*, needs must and all that.

Just as I was finishing, Terry stuck his head round the door. 'Got a moment, Harry? We need to have a chat.' Terry told me he was worried that a significant number of new Asian officers were failing the courses that officers needed to pass to get into the SST. We needed young Muslim officers more than ever now and we were trying to get detective constables from the SST and in surveillance teams within eighteen months. To do this they had to be qualified as advanced car drivers and be surveillance-trained. Firearms training wasn't such a big deal, as not many ops were armed and not all of us needed to be armed when it was required, but we still had a worryingly high failure rate in driving and surveillance.

Terry was understandably concerned. As a surveillance unit, we were being sent into ethnically diverse areas, places where a pair of white men walking up and down a street or sitting in a car would be noticed, no matter how good their cover was.

'Perhaps we're rushing them,' I said, 'or their lack of experience is letting them down. It's not as if it's their fault.'

'Agreed. So what do we do about it?' Terry asked.

'I think it comes down to more intensive training, boss. As far as the driving goes, we've got an advanced instructor in S-squad, so we could work out some time for extra lessons.'

The surveillance training was trickier to deal with. The Met police surveillance course is intense and with an extremely high failure rate it's very hard to pass. It also didn't cost our department anything. If, however, we sent someone on the differently structured police national course, which was slightly easier to pass, we had to fork out £5,000 for the pleasure. We could train them to help them pass the course but all too often, when we were busy, we simply didn't have any spare officers to do this.

The Met course has an assessment that I could never pass – you have to be under a certain height (they argue that tall officers stand out). So off I went on the £5,000 national course. I thought I'd failed when on the last day I followed the 'stooge' to a bakery. He left scoffing a pie and then travelled to a

Burger King in another town for the 'meet'. As keen as I was to eat more food in the name of surveillance, it would not be wise, I thought, for me to follow him inside. My instructor, who was in the car with me, disagreed. He kicked me out and told me to 'Get in there.' Arguing with surveillance instructors meant failure, so I obeyed.

Worried that the stooge would recognize me I went to the car boot and pulled out the instructor's coat and put it on. Problem was I was double the height of the instructor and the bottom of his jacket came up to my belly button.

As I walked into Burger King I saw the car rocking as the instructor blew his top and my team-mates doubled over with laughter. During the debrief (with the potentially wasted £5,000 at the forefront of my mind) I apologized profusely for picking up 'the wrong' jacket and incredibly (and to the amazement of the team back at TT) I passed the course.

The phone rang. 'Just a minute, Harry,' Terry said, picking up the receiver. He hung up moments later. 'Right, we've been rudely interrupted. Forget all this and get yourself ready for a trip up to Leeds for first thing tomorrow morning. The SST is needed to do a recce on a private address. You'll be supporting the local Special Branch.'

Damn. I'd just sorted out my Boards of Chaos and this meant that all my texting and ringing around had been a waste of time. Thanks to the fact that not everyone was trained to do everything, we had specialist drivers, techies, trainers and so on, so it was never simple. My worst day ever was ringing an increasingly exasperated officer no less than *six times* to change his duties.

I went back to my beloved white board and picked Danny, along with two other specialist officers. After we'd sorted our equipment and checked who was best placed to pick up whom for the morning drive, we headed home.

We didn't know it then – as usual – but the Leeds Special Branch was in the middle of a major operation.

When 23-year-old Aabid Khan was called over by Customs at Heathrow in June 2006, it was just a routine stop. He was returning to his Bradford home after visiting the Balakot Mountains in Pakistan on the borders of Indian-controlled Kashmir, a pleasant land fed by the Kunhar River, home to farmers who produce apricots, walnuts and corn, grown on terraces on the green mountainsides.

It turned out to be a good call. The Balakot Mountains were also home to a Jaishe-Mohammed ('Army of Mohammed') terrorist training camp. This terror group's first aim was to wrest Kashmir from the control of India and also shared close ties with al-Qaeda.

As the officers delved into Khan's bag, they found themselves elbow-deep in the largest collection of terrorist literature they'd ever come across. There was a guide to killing non-Muslims, material about setting up a secret Islamic state in a remote area of Scotland, American and Canadian military training manuals, a terrorist's handbook, a mujahideen explosives handbook, and a mujahideen poisons handbook containing a recipe for ricin and encouragement for 'brothers' to 'experiment' on *kuffars*.

One document urged recruits to Khan's cause to join in 'assassinating named personnel and foreign tourists, and freeing captured brothers from the enemy' as well as 'blasting and destroying places of amusement, immorality and sin, embassies, vital economic centres and bridges'. He had information about London's Tube system and Tower Bridge, maps of American subways, and videos of the Washington Memorial and World Bank. There were also personal details about the Queen, the Duke of Edinburgh, the Prince of Wales, the Duke of York, the Princess Royal, and the Earl and Countess of Wessex. There were also guides to 'beating and killing hostages', forging identity documents, training, weapons purchasing, undercover operations, planning assassinations, and coaching 'brothers' in how to answer questions when travelling to and from Pakistan. He had documents providing detailed information on surveillance and counter-surveillance.

When queried about his sketches of combat suits in his Filofax (I suppose even terrorists have to be organized), Khan displayed considerable front by dismissing them as 'ghetto clothing but with an Islamic theme'.[31]

Nice try, Aabid. I think it would have taken a little more than that to fool the Customs officers. It seemed as though Bradford-born Khan had the gift of the gab. He was known as 'Del Boy' to his contacts and ran At-Tibiyan Publications, an online extremist support network.

He was pursing a jihad to be fought by small resistance units scattered around the globe, all of which would be totally separate from one another. Each unit was to be as autonomous as possible, with an individual 'emir', but of course they would share a common aim – that it was their duty (and the duty of all Muslims) to attack non-believers and that the greatest honour was to die a martyr in an act of violence. Khan wanted to be the 'fixer', the man who would establish and educate all of the autonomous cells.

To do this he primarily used the Internet. Officers soon uncovered a wealth of incriminating messages including one in which Khan spoke of finding a 'big target and taking it out . . .

like a military base in the UK'. In an email he'd written: 'What I want to do is cause trouble for the *kuffar* with hit-and-runs everywhere, cause fear and panic in their countries, make them nervous so they make mistakes.'

When the Leeds SB officers examined the huge number of files from hard drives and DVDs in Khan's suitcase, they identified two fellow jihadists. Post Office night-sorter Sultan Muhammad, twenty-three, was Khan's cousin and right-hand man. They regularly discussed killing non-believers and buying acetone, a chemical used in explosives. He fled after Khan's arrest but was captured in London two weeks later.[32]

The other jihadist was arrested as he walked home from school.

That's right. Hammaad Munshi was just fifteen years old and was still studying for his GCSEs. Khan had been 'grooming' Munshi for a year and had turned an innocent teenager into a would-be terrorist, desperate to wage war on the *kuffar*.[33]

When I heard about this, I realized it was very similar to a particular type of criminal with which I'd had a great deal of experience: paedophiles.

One of the hardest things I'd ever had to do was interview paedophiles. I've lost count of the number of crack addicts, drug dealers and prostitutes I've spoken to. Surprising as it may seem, interviewing addicts can be slightly light-hearted – both criminals and I understand that we're playing a game and – most of the time – there are no real consequences. We take their drugs, they're bailed, maybe we'll see them again, maybe not, maybe they'll clean up, maybe they won't.

But a whole different mentality is involved when dealing with the safety of kids. People who are normally quite libertarian, who are against the death penalty, find themselves struggling to justify keeping such people alive. Police officers naturally have a 'castrate and hang 'em high' disposition towards child abusers because we see, all too often, every aspect of the damage done. Most people believe that the sentences dished out to paedophiles rarely appear to reflect the seriousness of the crime, which is not surprising really.

I found it very, very difficult to get into their mindset, but you have to do this if you want them to confess. Sometimes this was the only evidence we'd end up with, as very often cases came down to the victim's word against the abuser. Very often, the paedophile had groomed their victim so well that they couldn't bring themselves to testify against their abuser, so it was crucial that we got them to admit their crimes in an interview.

Witnessing the effects of al-Qaeda and other terrorist recruiters on young boys gave me similar feelings of disgust that I had with paedophiles who 'groomed' children. A large part of paedophilia – apart from the thrill of physically abusing young children – is about control, about dominating that child, having them wholly in their power. And it was the same with the terrorist recruiters.

On the morning of our Leeds mission, Danny was outside my door at 5 a.m., bright-eyed and bushy-tailed. As we drove up, we talked about the job in general, like all officers do. Danny was keen to stay in S-squad and hoped to climb the ranks in the coming years. He'd recently hit a hurdle, though. Danny was the sort of guy who enjoyed pushing the politically correct envelope and once or twice he managed to do so accidentally.

The first I knew about it was when Terry called Danny and me into his office and asked us to 'shut the door'. This meant one of two things: he was about to tell us something very secret or we were in trouble. We quickly found out that it was the latter.

Many members of the public help us in our work; their assistance is precious and to be treasured. We'd recently managed to secure a Jewish-owned family business in East London from which to operate. Danny and another officer were sent there for a sixteen-hour shift. One of our rules about using someone else's property is that whether it's an empty run-down council flat or a luxurious penthouse, we never, ever leave any trace of our stay. If the toilet seat is down when we arrive, then it has to be down when we leave.

Danny took a packed breakfast, lunch and dinner with him so he didn't have to worry about getting food once he was settled, which was a very sensible bit of preparation. At lunchtime he was chomping on one of his sandwiches, chin-wagging with one of the staff as Danny is wont to do, making a good impression.

Unfortunately, he had been gobbling a ham sandwich on what was supposed to be kosher premises.

Although the person he'd been talking to had said nothing, the other officer told everyone. This is part of Special Branch culture; it's not 'grassing' as some would say, this is about embarrassing SB and ensuring such things never happen again. Danny had no idea where he was going to be working that day, so he wasn't to know until he arrived but still . . . The premises were quite clearly Jewish.

Terry went into orbit; the SST had been accused of blasphemy and he took it as an affront to SB's intelligence. I felt sorry for Danny, who was a truly outstanding, loyal and unquestioningly obedient officer, but I think we deserved it on

this occasion. SB officers were proud of their cultural aware-
ness and this story had whizzed round S-squad in no time.

After our rollicking was over, I took Danny for a coffee.
'I'm as much to blame as you,' I told him. 'I should have
flagged it up before we went in.'

'But I should have clocked it was a kosher place,' Danny said
glumly.

'It can happen to anyone – and we'll never make the same
mistake again.' Then, in an attempt to cheer him up, I added:
'Did I ever tell you about the time I was a probationer living
in a section house one summer and we sunbathed on the
roof?'

'What's that got to do with anything?'

'We were working nights and on one hot day we decided to
go up on the roof and get a tan. We dozed off for a bit and
when we woke up the students in the catering college opposite us had hung a sign on the window. It said "On Today's
Menu—"'

'Let me guess,' Danny chipped in with a smile. We said it
together: 'Roast Pork!'

Eventually, after we'd pulled into a service station just outside
of Leeds for fuel – for us as well as the car – we reached our
target area just before rush hour.

What hit me first was the poverty. This tight-knit Asian
community clearly had a million stories to tell as Danny and I
did a casual 'walk past' the area of interest. People here struggled to survive, and they are loyal to each other, because they
depend on each other. It was like this in many cities and I
think it was this closeness that led some parts of the media to
wrongly associate areas of Leeds and Bradford (the 7/7

bombers came from the nearby communities of Beeston and Dewsbury) with a rise in Islamic extremism. Yet it was no better or worse here than in any other large city in the UK.

I'd seen this kind of closeness in the Green Lanes area of Finsbury Park in London. As a Turkish illegal immigrant not speaking English, it's possible to live in a whole sub-society, invisible, but where your every need can be taken care of. In these communities distrust of the authorities is most prevalent – for understandable reasons, not least of which is communication. Whenever we needed the local community's help with an investigation, we always had to find a way of breaking through this layer of distrust.

That's why there's also a very high threshold for us to achieve before we can have surveillance authorized on an individual. Apart from the fact it costs a fortune we are – above all else – under a duty to be proportionate and can only target those who are a genuine threat. We can't afford to add any fuel to the fire that the police are 'spying' on Muslims. More than anything, we're desperate to gain the trust and confidence of the Muslim community.

As Danny and I passed the address, the person of interest walked out of his front door, right in front of us, black bin bag in hand. As he stuffed the bag into the already overflowing wheelie bin he nodded and gave us an 'All right?'

We replied in kind, trying not to sound like we were from London. Although this encounter had complicated things (it wouldn't be wise for Danny and I to walk back down the same street again) it was actually helpful as we now knew which bin our man used – even though it was packed with a lot of other people's rubbish. It would depend on the nature of the job as to whether those in charge thought it was worth going through a shredder load of RIPA (Regulation of Investigatory Powers Act 2000) permission forms for the pleasure of rummaging through rubbish sacks. In the good old days of 1970s SO12, permission wasn't needed and officers would help themselves – do so now and you can be charged with theft.

Danny and I kept walking, absorbing every piece of information we could until I was happy.

Back in the car we analysed what we'd seen that morning. The best option we had was to place a camera – and that meant getting permission. However, there were risks in tight-knit communities; we could easily end up asking a relative or close friend of our target.

The first thing to do was to return to the target area to check out the view from an adjoining street. As soon as we'd parked up my phone went. It was Terry. He was interrupted almost immediately. 'Hang on, Harry, I'll call you back.' Almost as soon as I hung up the phone, there was a tap on the window right by my head.

'What ya doing?'

Two young Asian lads were peering through the window at us.

Shit. Keep cool and act natural. Danny wound down the window.

'Come to buy a car, mate, but we're early, from London like.'

Nice try, but the lads weren't happy. I could feel their eyes scanning the inside of the car. I couldn't risk turning round. Was there anything on the back seat that would show us up as the law? No, just map books, which fitted with Danny's story; I was pretty sure we were home free on that front.

Yet we were still two white London blokes in their area and

they didn't like it. We could be debt collectors, drug dealers, wheel-clampers, Inland Revenue, benefit fraud investigators, MI5 or police.

'Right then, later, bruv, yeah?'

They walked off, giving us an over-the-shoulder look.

We'd survived, but our cover story wouldn't allow us to be out in the open again. It would be up to someone else. We needed more Asian officers for jobs like these. We were picked on because we were two white geezers sitting in a car that had stopped in the wrong part of town. This is one important reason why officers in any police force should reflect the community they serve.

My phone went. It was Terry. 'Forget it, Harry, the local Special Branch are going to take it now. Some officers have been freed up. Get yourselves back to London.'

'Typical!' I said once I'd hung up. Although I was glad to know that the Leeds team were back up to full strength, I couldn't help thinking that I'd have to now revisit the Boards of Chaos yet again.

When Leeds SB arrested Hammaad Munshi, officers found two bags of ball-bearings – the shrapnel of choice for suicide bombers – in his pockets.

Munshi lived just ten miles from Khan. They'd spent a year corresponding with each other over the Internet and had swapped documents about the manufacture and use of explosives. Khan told Munshi that he wanted to help him go abroad to fight jihad.

Munshi was an IT whizz-kid; his online Arabic profile 'fidadee' means a 'person ready to sacrifice themselves for a particular cause'. He ran a website selling hunting knives and

Islamic flags and several al-Qaeda propaganda videos and recordings were found on his PC's hard drive.

He had led a double life for almost a year. He came from a much-respected local family and was the grandson of Sheikh Yakub Munshi, president of the Islamic Research Institute of Great Britain at the Markazi Mosque in Dewsbury. On the surface he was a good student but he spent every spare moment he had searching for jihadist sites, to send out terrorist material to others as part of a conspiracy to wipe out non-Muslims.

Notes were found under his bed. One read: 'One who is not taking part in the battle nor has the sheer intention to die is in the branch of hypocrisy . . . I don't want to be a person like it has been mentioned about, I don't want to be deprived of the huge amounts of lessons Allah has prepared for the believers in the hereafter.'

Just because Munshi was Britain's youngest terrorist didn't mean he'd escape prison. He was sixteen by the time he was arrested and so in 2008 he found himself in the unenviable position of standing in the Old Bailey being sentenced for making a record of material likely to be useful for terrorism.

Telling Munshi that he had 'brought very great shame upon yourself, your family and your religion', Judge Timothy Pontius continued: 'There is no doubt that you knew what you were doing . . . However, in the light of the evidence, I have no doubt at all that you, amongst others of similar immaturity and vulnerability, fell under the spell of fanatical extremists, and your co-defendant Aabid Khan in particular . . . They took advantage of your youthful naivety in order to indoctrinate you with pernicious and warped ideas masquerading as altruistic religious zeal. Were it not for Aabid Khan's malign influence, I doubt this offence would ever have been committed.'[34]

With this in mind, the judge sentenced him to a lenient two years. Khan was jailed for twelve years on three counts of possessing articles for terrorism while Sultan Muhammad, Khan's cousin, was given ten years for three similar charges and one of compiling information for terror.[35]

After sentencing, Munshi's grandfather put his concerns to the media: 'As a family we have always tried to abide by and uphold the laws of the United Kingdom of which we are proud to be citizens. We respect, therefore, today's judgement. But like any other family in this country, we are deeply upset by the situation in which Hammaad finds himself . . . All of us feel there are lessons to be learned, not only for us, but also for the whole Muslim community in this country. This case demonstrates how a young impressionable teenager can be groomed so easily through the Internet to associate with those whose views run contrary to true Muslim beliefs and values.'

Khan's arrest came after his third four-month trip to Pakistan since 2003. By this time he'd been preying on vulnerable young people for years, recruiting them to his cause, using Internet chat rooms to lure them in before inciting them to fight. He arranged their passage to Pakistan for terrorism training, and talked about a 'worldwide battle'. We don't know how many other young boys Khan and others may have influenced in this way.

It remains a lesson worth heeding and parents need to be aware that such dangers exist. Just as we are now more aware that paedophiles use the Internet to snare victims, we should keep in mind that terrorists operate in the same way.

SIXTEEN

THE COMMISSIONER AND I

I was at home, clearing out the car in preparation for our family holiday in France. It was full of all sorts of rubbish. Being so busy over the past few months with house moves, job changes, working long hours – not to mention our three lively kids, aged two, six and fifteen – meant that we lived in barely organized chaos. Although I still had plenty of time before I needed to leave, I seemed to have a never-ending list of jobs to complete and as a result I was rushing.

Buried in the back of the boot was a tin of magnolia paint. I was pulling it out, wondering how on earth it had got there, when the phone rang.

It was Jenny. 'Harry, we've got an urgent job, we need you down at TT, asap.'

'I'm on leave from early tomorrow.' But of course, that was the point. My name was still on the board, tomorrow is another day and twenty-four hours is a long time in Special Branch.

'Not till tomorrow, officially speaking, according to DI Caudle,' Jenny said. 'Sorry, flower, a big one's come up.'

Holidays had been in short supply over the last few months and my family really needed one. I really didn't want to have to tell them that the job had interrupted our lives once more. They'd put up with so much from me. They understood that what I did was important and that my job was a huge part of who I was but I'd been missing more and more family occasions, from sports days and school plays to birthdays and anniversaries. I couldn't complain; I'd known the score when I applied for SO12. As Terry had told me once: 'You can sit on the merry-go-round or ride the rollercoaster, it's up to you. I chose the latter and never looked back.'

In frustration I grabbed the tin of paint and yanked it out of the boot. As I lifted it out, it slipped from my hand, the lid popped open and a couple of litres of emulsion poured down my front.

'Oh for f—!'

'Dad? What's going on?' my eldest son, who'd suddenly appeared at the garage door, asked. Wiping myself down, I explained that I had to pop to work and that I'd be back as soon as I could. I didn't want to mention that I had no idea what awaited me there or how long I would be. I got the worst of the paint off, changed and drove straight down to TT while calculating the cost and logistics of having to rebook the ferry. I tried not to think of the disappointment on my family's faces if I had to tell them our holiday was postponed – or that they would have to go without me. We had to squeeze in a break while the kids were on holiday and my wife couldn't just swap her leave around in her job. I'm sure these dilemmas are shared by every emergency worker in the land.

My phone started to ring again. This time it was Danny – he told me I had to stop via the Yard and collect some paperwork.

An hour later I was in the lift at the Yard, on my way to the office where the paperwork was waiting for me. On the way up, it stopped before it got to my floor.

The doors opened. Oh no. Could this day get any worse?

Before me, immaculate in full-dress uniform, was Commissioner Sir Ian Blair. I was unshaven, with wild uncombed hair, in jeans and an old shirt and my shoes splattered in paint. The only clean thing was my ID card which showed my name nice and clearly for Britain's most senior policeman.

He raised his eyebrows and looked me up and down. This couldn't pass without comment.

'Been painting, have we?' Sir Ian enquired.

'No, Sir Ian, it was an accident.'

'Hmmm. I see.'

Damn, Damn, Damn. The doors opened. Even if it hadn't been my floor, nothing would have stopped me from leaping out of the lift at that point.

'Hello, mate,' Danny said when I finally made it to TT. 'Turned out it's all cushty, false alarm, so off you go, enjoy your 'oliday tomorrow after all.'

This was one of the toughest parts of the job, which was both a relief and a curse. Off we'd go scrambling to a breaking operation only to be told to stand down by the time we arrived. Sometimes we'd be told that the mother of all jobs was on, but that was it. Nothing further until decisions were made, and we'd sit twiddling our thumbs for hours. We had a phrase for it: 'Hurry up and wait.'

'Er,' Danny added, seeing the paint on my shoes, 'what happened to you then?' He never missed an opportunity to expose my poor dress sense, let alone a paint explosion.

I could have strangled him. I'd been dragged all the way

down to work urgently just to embarrass myself in front of the
Commissioner of the Metropolis.

'Merde!'

I then told the office my story and, as the laughter came,
Danny offered me a coffee to commiserate over before I
started the drive home.

Once I had my macchiato, George, Theresa and I ended up
chatting about Ramadan. While all surveillance 'terror cops'
are generally knowledgeable about the religious behaviour of
the people they hunt, the idea was always to understand and to
empathise fully. Very often this was for reasons of investigation.
If our subjects were using the Islamic calendar, for example,
it was very useful for us to know when they were talking
about without having to go to Google. This sort of knowledge
can be crucial in planning an operation.

Our reason for discussing Ramadan was different. We had a
number of Muslim officers on the team and wanted to ensure
that their needs were met. Theresa asked each Muslim officer
what he or she wanted to do, as there are often subtle differences.
We knew where each prayer room or mosque was in relation to
where the officers were posted and wanted to make sure that we
could cope with demand. In terms of planning and executing
covert operations – as far as I am aware – we didn't turn down
one religious request, and we were very proud of that.

We also discussed the long, arduous and sometimes dangerous hours that officers would be expected to work while they
were fasting (driving at high speed and carrying guns while
faint with hunger is not recommended). We also suggested
that officers spoke to their imams about their needs so that
they were fully supported. We wanted to make things work
and they did.

I'm sorry if this sounds a bit like recruitment drive material but it really was true and we weren't doing it to tick some performance box when we had our appraisal. We felt it was a matter of respect for the individual and part of the old Special Branch culture of 'paternal management'.

Having said that, Eid ul-fitr, the holiday that marks the end of Ramadan, was a bit of a pain for us. Some officers could only give us limited notice of when the three days of celebration would be. We all knew roughly when but the exact date often came down to individual imans as the Muslim year is based on the lunar calendar and Ramadan moves forward by ten to eleven days each year. But we coped; any rearrangements were usually handled quickly with few problems.

Two weeks later, I returned to work much refreshed and, upon arrival, I attended our regular Tuesday morning tasking meeting, chaired by the head of S-squad. At this meeting, MI5 would tell us their surveillance priorities for the coming seven days and then alongside officers from SO13 (investigations) they'd bid for surveillance teams, officers from the SST, covert photographers and Technical Support.

What they were actually bidding for is what we call 'coverage', i.e. they want a subject followed, photographed and recorded. Every movement would be fed back to 1600 and passed on to intelligence teams who do a lot of things I can't tell you about.

But it isn't just S-squad that causes al-Qaeda wannabes problems; it's also the public. Their vigilance and attention to detail has provided us with huge help on several operations.

The previous week had been especially busy and Theresa had come along as she was handing various jobs over to me.

The MI5 representative this morning was a lady who called herself Yvette. I had no idea if they go by real names or not but I do know it would have been rude of me to ask.

Yvette fitted a particular stereotype. She was one of around 3,800 people who work for MI5. In terms of gender the organization has an almost perfect balance but, like the Metropolitan Police Service, it still needs to achieve more to reflect the diverse communities we serve. She was similar to Marion, attractive and an Oxbridge first. One question I've always wanted to ask MI5 operatives is whether or not they told their partners who they work for. This was forbidden in the past, but MI5 has changed in recent years, developing a more publicly accessible role, and so perhaps spouses can now be told.

As we waited for Yvette to arrive, Terry suddenly entered the room. His face looked like thunder. He was carrying a red plastic box under his arm.

'Uh-oh,' Theresa whispered, 'I don't much like the look of this.'

I nodded in agreement and then watched, amazed, as Terry walked to the front of the room, took the red box and emptied its contents on the floor.

Now the room was full of terrified S-squad detectives. We all knew that someone had really screwed up and everyone, me included, was praying it wasn't them – or their team. I leaned forward in my seat and eyed the contents strewn across the floor. There were some evidence bags, plastic boxes and an unused incident management log.

Terry stood there in silence and stared at us.

Theresa and I exchanged glances in bewilderment.

'I found this lot in a bin,' Terry said, barely controlling his anger. 'And it wasn't a Scotland Yard bin. It was on public property, somewhere we were supposed to never have been.'

Oh crikey. While I was relieved it wasn't me, I sat through the bollocking that drummed home the fact that we cannot afford any careless moments in this line of work.

Once he'd finished, Terry collected the bits and left, slamming the door behind him. We all sat in an uncomfortable silence for a few moments, hanging our heads in shame.

'Blimey,' I said, turning towards Teresa, 'I was hoping to get his signature this morning.'

'I'd give it a little while,' she replied, and I readily agreed to wait until after lunch.

MI5 walked in a few moments later and failed to notice our shell-shocked silence as they listed their requirements for the following week. As usual, most of the requests were for 'yesterday' and I jotted down each job and what it meant for my team. Unfortunately for Box, setting up surveillance operations takes time. You can cut corners of course, which increases the risk of compromise, so we don't – ever. The first job on the list came under my remit. They needed a camera installed with a good view on a suspect property in, surprise, surprise, East London.

After the meeting, I took my list of tasks and went through the office. Once I'd planned what needed to be done, I had to cost it, tally up the price of the surveillance job before trotting back to Terry's office to ask him what we could afford to do.

'Afford' isn't exactly the right word, it was more to do with what we could actually justify spending. I could achieve a great deal with the SST, but everything came at a cost. I had to put options forward with the relevant costing. Different managers have different attitudes to budgets and once you become aware of every detective inspector's foibles, you start to get a feel for what they'll agree to or not.

There are many different ways we can install cameras; they can go almost anywhere but of course we have to ensure they remain undiscoverable. So this means we first need to do an 'environmental survey', aka a recce. This was usually a really good way of training a newbie and I'd send them with an experienced person so they could be tested and taken through the problems of certain locations, certain things that are definite no-nos, and so on.

In this case, we needed to get into an East London council estate. These were extremely problematic but I had a great deal of experience of these areas during my crack house days, so I decided to go on this one with Raj. We prepped ourselves by dressing down as much as possible. Gangs are divided by the postcodes in which they live. Many of London's housing estates are guarded and are divided into territories – unmarked, but they are there and if you don't fit in or if you haven't been seen before, you will get attention – something we most certainly didn't want.

This was a notorious estate where cars were blown up with fireworks, tyres were slashed in front of the neighbours, where windows were broken and where locals were threatened and robbed. The alleyways that connected the blocks and which led to the surrounding roads were a real rabbit warren, perfect for muggers to lurk, strike and disappear with ease. I didn't need a police incident report to tell me that there was a huge amount of gun and violent crime in this area.

This estate was a typical 1960s low-rise block, drab and covered in menacing but incomprehensible graffiti. The temperature seemed to drop the deeper I got. A wave of paranoia hit me; was I being watched? We kept our shoulders hunched and eyes down, hands in pockets. Looking confident here would only increase the chances of a confrontation.

I felt pretty certain about our appearance; we weren't wearing the usual undercover crime-squad uniform of clean Timberland boots, nicely pressed jeans, designer top, short, neat haircut and expensive aftershave. This is usually topped off by the biggest giveaway of all – the wedding ring. Even if you are in the most convincing undercover gear, that little flash of gold is a dead giveaway. Luckily, I was thin and pasty, was wearing loose clothes and my hair was in a right state, as usual. Raj had also dressed appropriately for the neighbourhood.

We checked the address out, which was on the far side of the estate, a short line of newer, friendlier-looking rows of houses and businesses. I decided that the best way to get a camera on the target was to try approaching a member of the public to see if they would agree to help.

It's no secret that we put cameras in various locations and this is something we take very seriously. We sign a document whenever we install a camera on private property and this allows the court to sanction the non-disclosure of evidence that would identify certain locations from which we'd got our observations. An officer in charge of surveillance of at least the rank of sergeant (in this case, that's me) would have to give evidence about visiting the premises, the attitude of the occupiers to their identities being revealed and the difficulties of finding suitable sites in the locality.

Before any trial, an officer of at least the rank of chief inspector has to be able to give evidence that, immediately before the trial, they ascertained whether the occupiers of the premises were the same as when the surveillance took place and whether they were happy to be identified or preferred to remain anonymous.

Of course, as in this case, we researched them thoroughly before knocking on the door. We have a strict policy in that we never lie to them but we also tell them very little. All we can do is express our extreme gratitude to them for trusting us. We never take risks.

Members of the public react in different ways. In this case, Raj and I returned to the estate on a hot summer afternoon. The neighbours were from Pakistan and as Raj spoke Punjabi I decided that the approach was probably better coming from him, so I waited in a covert car down the road.

Raj knocked on the door and an elderly lady opened it. She was tiny, about five feet tall and spoke no English. No problem, Raj was fluent in Punjabi. As Raj started to talk to her he quickly established that, as is all too often the case, she didn't actually live there. The other, more important problem was that she was terrified. I could see that Raj was doing his best to placate her but she quickly became more and more hysterical. She was disturbing the environment, her friend's house, and our plot.

'Time to go, Raj,' I said to myself from my vantage point in the car.

Sure enough, just at that moment Raj started to walk away. Once he made it back to the car he climbed in, closed his eyes and sighed.

'What is it?' I said.

'I don't think she believes that the Met has Asian cops who speak Punjabi. She panicked and I couldn't calm her down.'

I sighed; our surveillance options had been much reduced but no problem. Five minutes later my thoughts were interrupted by the sudden increase in volume of what had been a distant siren. An IRV (instant response vehicle) turned into the street.

Fuck. Time to go. Raj won't be going back to that street for a long time.

To date, hand on heart, we go about this type of thing in such a desperately cautious way that I can safely say we have never had a problem. The officers involved are highly trained and we don't take risks; we always cut and run if there is any doubt with regards to our being exposed or, even more importantly, to public safety.

Of course, we still managed to set up surveillance without the help of any local people. In this case it turned out that there was a perfectly innocent explanation and the person of interest had no links to terrorism. We departed from their lives as quietly as we had entered and they never knew they had been under intensive scrutiny.

The details of these aborted operations never reach the public, but the Muslim community should be reassured that we are not hell-bent on proving everyone is a terrorist. The last thing we want is to waste our resources on the innocent. We can't disclose information about these cases for obvious reasons.

As ever, almost as soon as we'd packed up, we were drawn into yet another extremely fast-breaking operation to pick up a would-be bomber, whose shoes were still covered with dust from the mountains of Waziristan.

SEVENTEEN

WAITING FOR A BOMBER

A sudden commotion from across the office made me look up from my desk. Everyone stopped what they were doing and looked on in amazement as two detectives stood nose-to-nose, rowing furiously at full volume about a current fast-moving operation. I'd often seen PCs and the odd detective lose their rag in a high-pressure operation but this was most definitely not the norm in the offices of Special Branch.

I quickly strode across the room, fearing things were really going to get out of hand or – as SO13 liked to put it – we were about to end up with a 'blood on the carpet situation'.

Although people often work best under the constant pressure, it can get rather volcanic sometimes, leading to the odd unexpected eruption when a big job is breaking. We all care passionately about our work and disagreements are inevitable when lives are at stake.

Some of the biggest explosions took place between SO12 and SO13 officers. These were two very established opposing cultures and had very different ways of getting someone to do something. In SO12, a manager would say: 'Would you mind awfully', which in SO13 talk was translated into 'JFDI' ('Just fucking do it). SO12 referred to this as the 'shouting' culture and found it most unbecoming while SO13 sometimes felt as if there was a lack of intensity of purpose from SO12, as they were all too busy holding doors open and saying, 'After you.'

In this case the warring detectives' teams were short of officers. We were at a minimum level of staffing because a number of people needed time off and many were on annual leave or on courses but of course the operation was super-urgent and wouldn't wait. It was no one's fault. Sod's law often meant we'd end up getting 'hit' when we were at these low levels; it was extremely frustrating.

Having separated the two warriors I told them that I might be able to sort everything out and would check the Boards of Chaos. My plan was scuppered just a few minutes later when I was hit with another new urgent operation and so was forced to withdraw my offer. It didn't go down very well.

The two disagreeing detectives quickly calmed down however, regrouped and reached a compromise. These flare-ups, although rare, sometimes occur when we try to meet impossible targets. It's understandable. We're fighting terrorism, we can't afford to mess up – any cock-up or delay can lead to mass murder. The long hours, night duties and endless changing orders and mission-swapping can take their toll, but nearly all of the time we rise to the challenge.

Differences resolved we shot off on our separate operations. My team and I were soon blasting towards Heathrow on an urgent job, being briefed as we went.

KARACHI, PAKISTAN, SEPTEMBER 2008

Even in autumn, the temperature in Karachi sometimes soars to the unpleasantly humid high 30s. On that sweltering autumn afternoon, those of its 15.5 million residents who were fortunate enough not to have to make their living on the teeming streets hid away from the sun in the city's many coffee shops or made for one of the city's beaches to catch some cooler air.

Karachi Money Exchange was right at the heart of this anarchic mega city, Pakistan's financial centre. The streets here are many and ancient; built haphazardly, they zigzag drunkenly through the Old City and join several other busy thoroughfares, many of which are often no more than ten feet wide. It's all too easy to get lost.

The young men sitting at tables behind the pillars lining al-Rashid Street smoked and exchanged the idle banter of those with little to do. They were outside an unfashionable cafe where the elderly patrons chewed the fat about nothing in particular. Lounging in a colonnaded area they were shielded from the afternoon sun, their loaded guns concealed in cloth bags, grenades in their coat pockets – just in case things got 'complicated'.

At 2 p.m., the doors of the large Money Exchange were pulled open; a security guard – their inside man – emerged and looked up and down the street knowingly. Seeing his contact step out from behind the pillar he nodded and started to walk away.

As clerks came and went through the large doors, the men walked quietly up to the entrance, knowing that if their man had done as he should have the safe would be open.

The cameras showed the security guards inside straightening instinctively as they saw the group of smartly dressed men enter. But before they could make any move the men withdrew their guns and fired into the ceiling. Once everyone was on the ground, two of the men walked up to the vault, removed $1.8 million in cash in several bags and exited again, but not before shooting one guard dead for not lying still enough. They stepped out into the streets, climbed onto two motorbikes and vanished into the warren of chaotic streets.

The following morning the guard who had walked away was found lying sprawled on the edge of a sewer in one of the poorest parts of the city. He'd been shot three times in the head. The Tehrik-e-Taliban Pakistan (TTP) don't much like accomplices from outside the organization. Just the fact that they have a price is enough to warrant their doom – not to mention their nasty habit of talking after being kicked around a prison cell for a few hours.

Karachi has long served as a hideout for several al-Qaeda fugitives, including Khalid Sheikh Mohammed, the alleged mastermind of the 9/11 attacks. In a city with more than 2,000 mosques, surrounded by millions of their fellow Pashtun tribesmen, there are plenty of places to hide. In this safe haven, free from the American drones that patrolled the skies over Taliban strongholds in the border regions, al-Qaeda raised funds and recruited eager youths from the madrasas for jihad.

This time though, Pakistan's ISI were on to them. There had been a sudden rise in large armed robberies in 2008. This was a good way of raising cash for jihad, especially as the drugs trade along the border with Afghanistan had been hit hard in recent months. The ISI managed to trace the delivery of $1.8

million in cash to al-Qaeda leader and head of the TTP, Baitullah Mehsud, in Waziristan, the terrorist stronghold in the mountainous region of north-west Pakistan that borders Afghanistan.[36]

The Taliban are criminals. They operate more like the Mafia than a standing army. They're a global criminal network raising money from operations across the world to keep their warlords equipped for the fight in Iraq and Afghanistan.

Apart from drugs, millions arrive in 'shadowy donations' which flow into Pakistan through illegal banking channels. After the devastating 2005 earthquake which claimed the lives of 50,000 people, strong sentiment to help victims provided a rare opportunity for terrorists to exploit a huge influx of cash.[37] Rashid Rauf's father had helped set up Crescent Relief, a charity based at Ilford, in Essex, which raised and sent more than £100,000 to Pakistan following the earthquake. A significant portion of that was said to have been diverted to Islamic militants. There is, however, nothing to suggest that Mr Rauf senior, who stepped down as a director of the charity in 2003, knew about terrorists benefitting from donations, and Crescent Relief's aims were entirely humanitarian.

It was fair to say that Baitullah Mehsud, a major tribal leader who commanded a highly organized army of up to 5,000 men, was Pakistan's most wanted man. Even though he had never finished school he had masterminded a suicide-bombing campaign that hit schools, police stations, bazaars and garrisons across the country, killing hundreds.

He was also suspected to be behind the assassination of Benazir Bhutto. Despite this, Mehsud remained practically invisible to the authorities who didn't have so much as a photograph of him. American drones had been circling the mountains of Waziristan for months with no sign of life. *Time* magazine placed him in their top 100 list of the world's most influential people in 2008, calling him 'an icon of global jihad'.[38] Since 2001, Mehsud had also earned the wrath of the United States by creating a unit tasked to kill people who were pro-government and pro-American or who supported the American occupation of Afghanistan.

In a January 2007 interview with the BBC Urdu Service, Mehsud extolled the virtues of jihad against foreigners and advocated taking the fight to the United States and to Britain. Islam forbade suicide attacks, he said, so other ways of making a sustained campaign must be found.

Mehsud was extremely close to Mullah Abdul Ghani Baradar, the second most powerful figure in the Afghanistan Taliban. This is the military commander who developed the Taliban tactic of planting 'flowers' – improvised explosive devices (IEDs) – along the roadsides of Iraq and Afghanistan. He's been described by terrorism experts as even more cunning and dangerous than Taliban supreme leader (and his old friend) Mullah Omar. Mullah Baradar was a most elusive target.[39]

Mullah Baradar has been credited for rebuilding the Taliban into an effective fighting force and has been running the group's daily affairs for many years, since Mullah Omar was forced to take a less active role in the organization due to his failing health. Besides heading up Taliban military operations and running its budgets, Mullah Baradar also ran the group's leadership council, known as the Quetta Shura, named because its leaders have been thought to be hiding near Quetta, the capital of Pakistan's western province of Baluchistan. A photograph of him has yet to surface.

Born in 1968 in Weetmak, a village in Afghanistan's

Oruzgan Province, the young Mullah Baradar joined the
Afghan mujahideen war against Soviet forces at an early age. It
was during this war that he came to know Mullah Omar; the pair
fought alongside each other against the Soviets and some reports
suggest the two even married a pair of sisters.

After the withdrawal of the Russians and collapse of the
Communist regime in Kabul in 1992, Mullah Baradar and
Mullah Omar both settled down in the southern Afghanistan
district of Maiwand where they ran their own madrasa. When
Mullah Omar started a revolt against the local warlords in 1994
with a force of some thirty men, Mullah Baradar was among
its first recruits. This was the beginning of the Taliban movement which swept Kabul in 1996, establishing the hard-line
regime.

Mullah Baradar became Mullah Omar's most trusted military commander. He was at Omar's side when American
bombs pounded Kandahar in November 2001. It was Mullah
Baradar who hopped on a motorcycle and drove his old friend
through the ring of American and Afghan army lines to safety
in the mountains, in a legendary escape worthy of Steve
McQueen.

Mullah Baradar's men were responsible for inflicting heavy
casualties on Western forces. He ran the Taliban's day-to-day
operations, both military and financial, allocating Taliban
funds, appointing military commanders and designing military
tactics. He was the first to change to guerrilla tactics, instead of
trying to meet American troops head-on, and begin using
roadside IEDs.

He often travelled to Karachi to consult with fellow strate-
gists, raise finances and hunt for new technology. Yes, he hated
all things modern and Western, but like all terrorists he found

mobile phones extremely convenient and if they could be used against the enemy, then why not? His flexible approach had served him well over the past thirty years or so.

In contrast, the rigid approach of both the United States and Pakistan had helped Mullah Baradar. Pakistan's military helped establish Mullah Omar and his Taliban fighters in Afghanistan in the mid-1990s after the Russians pulled out. Their aim was to create a powerbase from which they would control Afghanistan, something that never really came to fruition.

At first, the commitment from Pakistan to join the Americans in the fight against the Taliban wasn't there. But now, since Rashid Rauf, American and Pakistani forces along the border began to share intelligence in real time, as it happened. The American military passed on GPS coordinates of the bases used by the Pakistani Taliban, for example. These tribesmen see Islamabad as their first enemy, not the NATO troops across the border in Afghanistan. Thanks to the Americans, the Pakistani military were able to hammer them with artillery or aircraft strikes.

The United States had also helped the ISI hunt for terrorists in the forested valleys of South Waziristan, which was crawling with Pakistani and Afghan Taliban and al-Qaeda fighters. The relationship between the United States and Pakistan is hardly rock solid; there are many complications as Pakistan still needs to show its anti-American side since many of its citizens despise the drone attacks and see the Americans as interfering, so what's publicly admitted is a fine art.

Now the ISI wanted the heads of Mullah Baradar and Baitullah Mehsud on a plate and came to Washington for help – and the Americans were only too happy to oblige.[40]

Tracking the gang of Tehrik-e-Taliban bank robbers wasn't easy but over the following few months the CIA and the ISI managed it. After pinpointing their general area, they were scooped up by the ISI in a slum town teeming with Pashtuns from Afghanistan just outside of Karachi. The money was long gone but no one except the owners of the Money Exchange was really concerned about that. As far as the CIA and ISI were concerned, they had achieved their first crucial goal – getting close to Mehsud's lair in Waziristan.

Getting a foothold in Waziristan was desperately important as other unrelated terrorist cells were being trained in this area before flying to the West on a variety of missions. And that was why S-squad was waiting outside Heathrow on a winter's evening – waiting for a would-be bomber from Waziristan to land.

EIGHTEEN

DRAWING THE NET

Thanks to a tip-off from a member of the public who'd been on a walking and camping trip in the Lake District, a surveillance team had already been put onto a group of Asian men who seemed to be going through military manoeuvres.

Sure enough, the team had watched incredulously and with some amusement as the amateur soldiers attempted forward rolls with branches cut to look like guns and nearly broke their necks in the process. But of course, as they realized, these amateurs were no laughing matter. The 'warfare' they were practising may have seemed pathetic, but the physical aspect wasn't the important part, it was all about the bonding that would help brainwash them to the point where they were prepared to murder hundreds of innocent people.

It was quite different from the days of the IRA, when the terrorists were trained to a relatively high military standard in everything from withstanding interrogation techniques – including torture – as well as the handling and use of weapons and explosives.

Also, there was another difference: language. Deciphering Arabic in seized documents was a fine art but we had no shortage of Arab speakers since 9/11 when it was decided that we were going to need to understand every word, turn of phrase, slang and dialect – after all, British criminals often spoke in hard-to-decipher slang, so why wouldn't terrorists?

Of course, Arabic is more than one language. It is spoken by 530 million people in over fifty different dialects and accents – it's perfectly possible for one Arab speaker to meet another and not understand a word of what the other is saying. It helped to have a speaker from exactly the right area, someone who could catch every nuance, phraseology, inference – people who were able to see past all the similes and metaphors, one of which was repeated reference to 'planting flowers', improvised explosive devices.

Thanks to the ISI and some relatives who feared their cousin had been indoctrinated, we knew that one of the men had recently been to Waziristan and was on his way back, possibly with the knowledge and desire to make a series of car bombs, using everything from washing-machine timers to various household chemicals. The feeling was that instead of suicides, these men were planning a sustained bombing campaign, much like the IRA.

Their targets and exact methods remained unknown but one thing was certain, these men were in the early stages of planning an attack using IEDs and we needed to be 'eyes on' at all times. We were in a race against time to pick our target from the airport and throw a net around him before drawing it tight at precisely the right moment.

A few days later, after following the bomber from Waziristan from the airport and across London, we once again found ourselves in the east of the city. I was armed and doing a walk-by of the target address at 2 a.m., on my own as usual. To walk by the property twice without looking suspicious I decided to head back past the address with a kebab, as if I'd just popped out for a late-night feast.

The halal kebab shop, coloured red and white, at least looked clean. It was doing a roaring trade as well, so I took this to be a good sign. The Asian man behind the counter seemed cheerful enough as I ordered two large shish kebabs with chilli sauce (one was for Asad who was waiting for me in our covert car). I took a seat and waited along with a bunch of other customers as he cooked them. Even though it was 2 a.m., business was booming.

I stared at the portable TV jammed high on a shelf while I awaited my supper. Four drunk young men came in, and immediately started shouting and ordering all at once. The smile quickly vanished from the Asian man's face as he tried to interpret their confused ramblings and they started to verbally abuse him.

'Wassamatter? You no understan' English?'

This insult caused them much laughter.

'Shall I spell it out fer ya?' the biggest of the four said. His face had tiny features that wrinkled in concentration as he picked up a squeezy bottle of tomato sauce and started to 'write' his order in tomato ketchup on the counter.

I stared at them in fury.

'What you lookin' at?' one of them demanded.

'Nothing.' Damn. I was armed; they were up for a fight. It was time to go. Any other time I would have taken immense pleasure from politely arresting them but not now. I got up, stretched myself up to my full six feet five, hoping it would put them off, and started to make my way past.

'What's your problem, then?' the man with the sauce bottle said. The others had started throwing chips at one another and I fought to get past them without banging my gun into them.

'Hey!' the kebab shop owner said, 'what about your shish?'

'Don't worry about it. Give it to one of them, on me.'

A moment later I was out and on the street, severely pissed off at having to leave the man to his fate. I hated running and tried to console myself with the fact that the shop owner could always call the police if he felt things were getting too much and chances were, at that time of the night, that they'd get there quickly.

Surveillance cops always end up seeing things at inconvenient times, including crimes. In such cases, whether to act or not is very often down to that officer. We all find it hard to hold back; if we see someone committing a crime, no matter where, when or what, we like to get involved.

As I skulked guiltily back to my operation, I wanted to believe that the shop owner could handle it, that this was part and parcel of running a kebab shop in this part of East London and he was able to deal with it. Cops are used to abuse; it's a regular part of the job and although we don't like it, we don't let it bother us. But I was of course kidding myself. No member of the public should have to go through that kind of abuse, night after night.

'And?' Asad said when I returned kebab-less.

I explained what had happened and we sat in silence – well apart from our grumbling stomachs – until I finally got round to asking Asad a question I'd been wanting to ask for a while.

Asad had been brought up in the UK, but had many friends

and family in Pakistan, and he was a frequent visitor. I wanted to ask him some stupid questions and late at night sat in that car I knew I could get away with it. There's no better place to get to know someone than at 3 a.m. on stakeout.

I wanted to know what it was like being a Muslim cop in SO12 and what he felt about what we were doing. I asked him if it seemed we were spying on his 'own community'.

'How do you feel about the far right in the UK?' he replied. 'Would you have a problem or feel awkward about jobs in that area?'

'Of course not.'

'And if they were Christian?'

'No.'

'Well, there you go then. Are you religious?'

'Not really.'

'Well, I'm not like you. I'm very concerned about religious practice, I go to the mosque a lot and I proudly tick the box that says "Muslim" when filling out application forms.'

We'd both just read an article in the *Daily Mail*, which said that there were four al-Qaeda moles working in police stations around London.[41] MI5 chiefs reportedly believed that the suspected moles were planted as sleepers – agents under deep cover – to keep al-Qaeda informed of any anti-terror raids we planned. The IRA had used similar methods in the 1970s, when they infiltrated the police and army in Northern Ireland.

I found the story worrying in the sense that it was going to alert the men concerned while also increasing paranoia. We wanted to attract officers from ethnic minorities and this was hardly going to help.

We'd already heard how the exiled cleric Omar Bakri

claimed Islamic extremists were working at the heart of the NHS and other vital services in the UK. An asylum seeker had recently been jailed for nine years when he was found to have manuals on how to build and detonate car bombs. Before his conviction he'd applied for a job as a cleaner for the police force (he didn't get it).

Asad was clear about what some people in the Muslim community think. 'Scare stories like this are typical, true or not. At the end of it all, the Asian is the bad guy. For years, certainly since the first Gulf War, Muslims have seen the media as being completely biased and prejudiced, presenting distorted images of the Islamic world, lies and propaganda, concocted for an English audience. That's why we have to work harder to win over the Muslim community.

'The truth is a lot harder to believe when a large part of the audience already feels like it's been misled. One of the key things is for us to understand how the community feels – whether we agree with them or not. Then progress can be made.

'There is a view that some newspapers have helped create two camps: extremist Muslims and corrupt white people. Columnists feed the fire with their haphazard and thoughtless labelling, which dehumanizes. You notice how they didn't speak to any Asian police representatives for that article?

'When I was a kid, and an Asian person was going to be on telly, the whole family would stop what they were doing to watch as it was such a rare event. Now, Asians are on all the time – but there's a perception that it's only when something negative has happened. Muslims are dragged up to condemn and apologize for those who claim to kill in the name of their religion. They think an Asian person can't appear on TV without reference to religion and conflict. We've got to challenge this view; no wonder some kids look elsewhere for their role models.'

I asked him about whether UK foreign policy in Iraq, Afghanistan and elsewhere was fuelling the fires of extremism.

'This doesn't mean they're extremists; thousands of people from all backgrounds joined the "Stop the War" protest. No weapons of mass destruction were ever found and many thousands of civilians had died. That didn't mean that UK Muslims wanted to support Saddam, just that many people feel the way the West had gone about getting rid of him was deceitful and wrong. How are the people of any background able to trust our political leaders when they are perceived as deceitful?'

'So how can we repair the damage?'

'You know what the way forward is? We need to *talk* with Muslims. We've been so slow at this. After 9/11, *everyone* in the Muslim community was talking about it but those running the mosques were too slow to join the debate. The imams didn't do enough and this allowed extremist groups to get a foot in the door. Many of us just thought they were nutters, just like we do of the far-right white extremist groups. They talked about it incessantly but in a one-sided manner, you know? All this: "You have to defend Islam from America!" and "This is the excuse America has been waiting for!" Total nonsense.

'This is why we end up spending so much time in universities. They're full of young people eager for new ideas; universities are an exciting environment, far removed from the conservative mosques. Most people running the mosques weren't born in the UK, they're elderly, reserved and the extremists have little trouble convincing some young undergraduates that they have no idea about the problems young

Muslims in this country face. The "preachers" turn potential recruits against the true Islamic scholars and imams. They peddle the dangerous view that kids should hate the mosques and the mullahs, because they're corrupt. Many of these young people are easily convinced, it wasn't as if all of them were flocking to the mosque to listen to the men of authority before 9/11.

'Those that remain good Muslims and go to the mosques are preyed upon by the men who educated our bomber friend here. They hang like jackals around the exits and ambush the young men that emerge feeling relaxed, happy and full of love for their fellow man. They "attack" them with leaflets, telling them about all the people dying in Afghanistan and Iraq and how it was all for oil. Suddenly these young men are feeling angry and understandably so, that good feeling is gone and they go home in turmoil. It's a tough battle for them, a dilemma that too many young men in Britain today are trying to deal with, and why a twisted interpretation of a jihad is, occasionally, too attractive to resist.

'The best way for us is to get involved and help them resolve their dilemmas. Hell, join the police, I did and I feel like I'm making a difference. If we repeatedly engage with the communities, then bonds will be strengthened, we'll win trust and support and remove many misconceptions about the police that have stopped people from coming forward.'

'What do you think about taking Muslim community representatives on big raids?'

'Yeah, it's complicated but not without merit.' He considered for another moment. 'Why not? We could manage it safely and we shouldn't restrict it to just anti-terrorist raids, either, they could come on other operations. I'd love for them to attend a briefing, just to see how serious we are about protecting the public and avoiding harm and insult in general. But we are at least starting to talk to the community more and more. But it's been a long time coming and it's not enough. In the meantime, many in the Muslim community feel like we're spying on them.'

I grinned. 'Well, we don't.'

Asad gave me a look that said 'Don't be so stupid' and then grinned as well.

'Well, tonight's target has certainly earned it. You really have to have done something special to get our attention.'

'Yeah, well, it's not as if we have the resources to spy on every Muslim in the country who we suspect of having the slightest terrorist sentiment – contrary to what many people think.'

'But those are exactly the sort of people we should be talking to – those with a feeling that the terrorists may have a point, not in their intended act, but in their grievances. Every time a drone mistakenly hits an innocent target in Pakistan, the coffers of the terrorist front organizations swell with donations.'

I didn't know it then but a Channel 4 poll carried out in 2006 had surveyed a large group of Muslims, and found that no less than 22 per cent of them agreed with the proposition that the 7/7 bombings were justified because of 'British support for the war on terror'. Those under twenty-four were twice as likely to excuse the attacks as those over forty-five.[42]

'That's not easy though,' I said. 'I'd be pretty outraged about that. Imagine that happening here. A foreign power with the permission of our government to fire Hellfire missiles at people they think are terrorists. I can't imagine how I'd feel and react if my kids' school was hit by a missile and it was considered by our powerful ally to be "an acceptable loss".'

I clicked my seat back a bit further and stretched out. My muscles ached. So much of this job involved sitting in cars night and day. I rattled my brain for other topics.

'What's it like in Pakistan at the moment?'

'It's funny; whenever I go there I get a very clear picture that I'm not the same kind of Pakistani as people living in Pakistan. To them, in Pakistan, I'm British. Some British Pakistanis get a shock when they go for the first time, thinking it's their heritage and when they arrive they're treated differently because they're British. You could end up feeling a bit isolated if it wasn't for the support of your family, as if you don't "belong" to either world. I never had that problem but I can see how some kids would. As far as the situation goes, in some places it's pretty awful. Karachi's always been a mess. There's loads of Brits over there though. Who knows how many head out there for terror training?'

We had no figures but there's no shortage of radical groups and global Islamic networks based in the UK – and most of these are based in London thanks to its financial, logistical and intellectual wealth.

'Do you even know what the aims of some of the groups actually are?' he said.

It was odd. When I thought about it I wasn't so sure – apart from to attack the West. 'The terrorism we're facing now feels more like revenge than anything else,' I replied uncertainly.

'Well, there's a bit more to it than that. Some extremist groups want to revive the caliphate, a theocratic pan-Islamic state. That means one man – the caliph – heads the state but is under God's divine guidance. This way all the Muslim lands would be united under a single leader. They want to inspire revolution somewhere in the Muslim world where a caliphate would be declared, from where it would conquer the world.

'Pakistan is understandably the number one target; after all it's a nuclear power. And it's easy for revolutionary groups to operate there. Vast areas of the northern parts of the country are tribal and operate under their own laws. I don't know how many exactly, nobody does, but it could be that hundreds of young British men of Pakistani origin have journeyed to Pakistan to join this struggle over the years.'

Asad paused for a moment and I sat quietly, waiting for him to carry on. Outside the car, all was quiet.

'Do you know what amazes me about Pakistan?' Asad asked.

I shrugged. 'The prevalence of the AK47. They're common as muck. Cheap and reliable and passed on to eager recruits who end up using them against our boys out there—'

'Who are fighting the same war we are for less money, more danger and more hardship,' I said, completing the sentiment for him. There are no known figures on how many treacherous British fighters have fought or died attacking our own soldiers.

'It's possible that some of those men are back in the UK. Maybe our man, who seems to be tucked up in bed for the night, was one of them.'

'Sweet bloody dreams.'

Dawn was cracking the London skyline and it glowed orange and blue. I imagined where this man's life would take him. Would he end up in Belmarsh, in the hands of the ISI or vaporized by a drone? He was a bomb-maker, so I hoped for the latter.

★

On 18 January 2008, the *Washington Post* reported that the CIA had reached the conclusion that Baitullah Mehsud was behind the assassination of Benazir Bhutto, Pakistan's former prime minister. As a result, President George W. Bush placed Mehsud on a classified list of militant leaders the CIA and American Special Forces were authorized to capture or kill. He also put a dead-or-alive bounty of $5 million on Mehsud, which on 28 June 2009 was matched by the Pakistani government.[43]

The wily Mehsud managed to evade the *machay* ('wasps', as the drones are called by the Pashtun) no less than *sixteen times* in fourteen months. He even outlasted George Bush's presidency.

In the end it was Mehsud's desire for a son that was his undoing. His first wife bore him four daughters, so out of desperation for a warrior son, he married the daughter of an influential cleric.

On the night of 5 August 2009, Mehsud emerged from his mountain hideaway and visited his new wife at his father-in-law's house in Zanghara, a village in South Waziristan.

Officials at the CIA in Langley, Virginia, watched a live video feed relaying close-up footage of Mehsud who was reclining on the rooftop of his father-in-law's house. It was a hot summer night, and he was joined outside by his wife and his uncle, who worked as a doctor; at one point, the remarkably crisp images showed that Mehsud, who suffered from diabetes and a kidney ailment, was receiving an intravenous drip.

The image remained just as stable when the CIA remotely launched two Hellfire missiles from the Predator drone.

The figures leapt up in an instant (people running for cover from Hellfires are such a common sight that the drone pilots call them 'squirters') at the sound and sight of the approaching missiles – but it was too late.

Once the dust settled, all that remained of Mehsud was his torso. Eleven others died: his wife, his father-in-law, his mother-in-law, a lieutenant, and seven bodyguards.[44]

Mehsud was someone both the United States and Pakistan were happy to see go up in smoke. There was no controversy when, a few days after the missile strike, CNN reported that President Barack Obama had authorized it. Two weeks later, speaking in a public radio address, President Obama, who had been in office just seven months, emphatically confirmed the hit on national radio: 'We took out Mehsud.'

According to a recently completed study by the New America Foundation, during his first nine and a half months in the hot seat, President Obama authorized as many CIA aerial attacks in Pakistan as George W. Bush did in his final three years in office. Washington was letting the Taliban know that Pakistan, once a safe haven, was now off-limits. In fact, there was nowhere left for them to hide.

To emphasize this, after Mehsud's hit, a grateful Pakistan was asked to return the favour by arresting Mullah Abdul Ghani Baradar. The CIA gave them the location – the town of Baldia, just outside Karachi – and the terrorist was captured in February 2010 as he left a seminary.[45]

As it happened, we never found out what happened to the bomber we were following. As ever, the changing interna-tional picture, especially major hits such as the obliteration of Mehsud, influenced terrorist cells. Our job ended up becom-ing another piece of coverage that went into the huge pot of intelligence for MI5 and our target flew away without having bought so much as an AA battery. Another agency followed him to his next rendezvous, as part of the never-ending quest for intelligence.

We would have absolutely loved to have the full picture, but there was no time or reason – the world of counter terrorism moved too fast. It was frustrating for S-squad, but that's real-life policing for you. As usual, the following day, we were desperately needed elsewhere as part of another fast-breaking operation, this time to conduct research on a terrorist house that was about to be raided.

NINETEEN

'WELL DONE' DETECTIVES

As usual, the intelligence told us this was potentially very serious. S-squad's remit was to confirm whether a property was in fact a bomb factory but, like so much intel, it needed reinforcement. We often only had one chance to 'strike'. If we missed any crucial evidence we could only claim 'disruption', which, although important, is always second best and not the victory so many people had worked so hard for.

Even though it was before dawn, I was already sweating as I rocked up at work. It was summer and we were in the midst of one of those very British heat waves that turn London bone dry and fill the air with dust, producing some spectacularly red sunsets that we watched through the dirty windows of TT while longing for a cold beer and a sunlounger. Our air conditioning struggled to cope and pushed the air around the office with little conviction.

I was still at my desk when I noticed that one of our younger DCs, who shall remain nameless, was wearing flip-flops. I chuckled, this was hardly appropriate police footwear but I supposed you could just about get away with it in this heat.

He'd been working long and hard on a counter-terrorism report about developing terrorist strategies for the Cabinet Office and he'd finally sent it off with Terry's approval after several long days of careful writing and rewriting.

'I'm so glad that's finally done and I can relax at last,' he told me and sat back in his seat. Fatal words. Just then, Terry stuck his head round the corner.

'The Cabinet Office were very impressed by that report,' he said.

'Thank you, Terry.'

'Don't thank me yet, I want you to come with me to Downing Street asap.'

'What?'

'Yes, it's cracking up-to-the-minute stuff, and they want us to brief the people who'll brief the PM in person.'

'What?'

'Are you deaf?' Terry said, his face reddening.

'No, boss.'

'Good, come on then.'

A few minutes later, Terry and the DC were walking along the marble floors of the Cabinet Office. Terry hadn't yet spotted the footwear and the enterprising DC did his best to disguise their distinctive *slap-flap* by making sure his footsteps matched Terry's as he marched just behind him.

It was only when Terry stopped to shake the hand of a senior Cabinet Office spin doctor that the flip-flops of the DC, who was two steps behind, suddenly slapped and flapped with loud echoes.

Terry turned and looked down at his DC who was dressed in a suit plus the flip-flops. For once, he was speechless.

The spin doctor peered over his glasses at the mortified young DC's shoes. In his finest Oxbridge accent, he said: 'Ah, I see you're from the Branch.'

Once Terry returned, he took great delight in briefing me on the flip-flop incident and then asked for an update. I didn't have too much to report at this stage. We were watching a flat on a large South London council estate (it made a pleasant change from the East). Although we had nothing as yet, MI5 had told us to 'stay with it 24/7', so they must have had something of significant interest in one of their files.

The following morning, once I'd finished briefing Terry, I checked in with the monitors and those watching the cameras. All seemed to be fine. Then as usual, as I started to ring round the incoming day shift, a problem cropped up, someone's replacement was running late and I was out of staff. So I decided to sit in until the late arrival made it past the accident on the A13 they were stuck behind. Lateness is an annoyance and an extra expense for the department – and then there's the person who'd been looking forward to going home after a very long night staring at foxes, rats and the occasional drug dealer. It can create resentment, even when the excuse is a good one, hence my decision to step in and let the night-shift officer go home.

I stared at the images on the monitors. The flat was typical of thousands of council flats on hundreds of council estates that sprawl across London. At its centre was a collection of tower blocks; around these sat squat low-rise blocks of flats, which overlooked a largish green field – in which was the rusted frame of a burned-out Nissan. Time and time again I'd been called out to these estates, with the drugs squad, the child protection team and now in our new battle of the twenty-first century. I felt as if I'd made a significant difference in my previous two roles but it was harder to see how much of an effect I was having in defeating terrorism. We never had the full picture, and I had no idea how many operations were being run up and down the country. I didn't even know how many operations had been termed as successful by MI5, as very often I'd never get to know the outcome. At some stage we'd be pulled off this job and sent straight on to the next.

I quickly forgot my early morning mulling when the screen flickered. This always made my heart miss a beat. We needed to be eyes on 24/7; I never wanted to have to stand up in front of a room full of counter-terrorism officers and say that the crucial bit of intel, which would have wrapped up this operation, was missed because my department had installed a faulty camera.

I focused on the screen and sure enough it flickered again. Oh damn, I thought, I've seen that sort of flicker before. I was already on the phone as it started to die, cutting in and out with a burst of white noise.

To make matters worse, dawn had come and gone and the chance of replacing the camera under cover of darkness had passed.

'Danny here, boss.'

'Great. I need you and one other in the OP van, eyes on the address. Our camera's down.'

'Got it, on my way to you now.'

'Head straight for the flight deck, Raj will meet you there.'

It wasn't long before they'd plotted themselves up nicely on the address. All was still quiet. I set about trying to get the camera fixed but we were low on technical staff and its location made any alterations tricky.

It was already incredibly hot; despite this Danny and Raj took the news that they were going to spend the next fourteen hours in the back of a van together on the hottest day of the year very well indeed.

'And we're parked in the sun,' Danny said cheerfully, as if this was a bonus.

I heard Raj chip in with: 'Our very own personal sauna.'

'I'm sorry, guys . . .'

By lunchtime they were roasting, unable even to crack a window open. Their working day had become a major test of endurance.

I called them whenever I could just to check they were still able to stick it out. I had no one to replace them and we were desperate.

'No worries,' Danny answered when I called him after lunch, 'we're down to our Adam Ants, and it's a bit more bear-able now.'

'Just as long as you're sure. Don't be a hero now.' But of course, that was exactly what I was asking from them and they did both me and the Force proud. Although this perhaps seems a little trivial, to me this is just one example of the everyday sacrifices our dedicated officers were prepared to make in the line of duty. We would often preface a difficult request with the words 'I know this is a big ask but . . .' Terry was shrewd enough to select officers who would always answer that question with 'No problem, I'll do it.' I've witnessed many other scenes like this which I can't talk about, but the public should remain reassured that I think they have a fine body of men and women looking out for them. Whatever it took – if we had to spend fourteen hours in an unventilated tin can in 100-degree heat – then that's exactly what we would do.

Finally, just as the sun started to sink behind the tower blocks, I managed to get the camera fixed. I called them with the good news. 'Job done, lads, you'll be pleased to know we've got crystal-clear images once more.'

'Oh, thank God for that,' Danny said. 'Raj and I were at the end of our rope.'

'I'm afraid we're going to have to hang on a little longer, old boy,' Raj said. 'You've left something on. The van battery's died.'

'Bollocks!'

After some careful background research, we asked members of the local community for their help, and they were just fabulous. This also provided me with a rare chance to interact with the public, something I missed from days on the drugs squads and in child protection.

'Would those boys like some tea?'

I looked down at the tiny old lady beside me.

'Which boys?' I asked.

'Those nice young men in the van,' she said, peering through the net curtain. Poor Danny and Raj had drawn the short straw once again and were sitting in the van on another sweltering day. The old lady melted my heart with such a polite and innocently made request. She'd also made my heart jump with her perceptiveness in relation to our OP van, but I suppose she'd seen us coming and going and knew what to look for. I knew I could trust her.

'Oh, don't worry about them,' I told her reassuringly, 'they've got everything they need in there.'

This wonderful enthusiasm to help us was really lovely to encounter and a real reminder (not that we needed it) of the values for which we were striving. Often we got to talk to the public when we revealed who we were, something I always enjoyed. Their stoical attitude and trust in what we were doing, despite various cock-ups that had been relayed over and over in the media, was fantastic.

We had a lot more to learn about the subject of terrorism as the elderly husband of the little old lady explained: 'Things are in such a mess now. There is a huge difference between the young and old in Islam, and both sides have a different picture of what we should be trying to achieve as Muslims. It could be so simple, it really could.

'Until all Muslims are able to show that they're concerned for the welfare of all of our fellow human beings and I mean all, then we're not being faithful, that is why we have to stand proudly on the front line against extremism.'

He shook his head sadly. 'There's too much talk about "defending the honour" of the Prophet.'

Then leaning forward he smiled and said, 'Now what would you think of Muslims if we all pulled together and did everything in our power to end hunger in the world? Now that would be something!'

'Are you troubling this man?' his wife interjected, entering the room with yet more tea. 'Can't you see he's busy?'

'It's all right,' I said.

'See?' the old man said testily, turning to look back at his wife. 'He's interested – aren't you?'

I nodded, but cautiously, I did have plenty to be getting on with.

'If we ended hunger instead of worrying what other people thought about the Prophet then we'd be heroes!' He beamed. 'Everyone would want to become a Muslim. Suppose then we decided to end war? To make sure that good medicine was made available to every nation on earth?'

'Can't argue with that, can we?' Jenny said. I couldn't and it was time to end the conversation anyway. This operation was taking us close to the edge. It was a 24/7 job and after several days of very intensive work we were seriously under pressure. The longer an operation runs, the more chance there is that someone – who is expecting to attract attention – will rumble that they're being watched.

Once it was decided we had enough intel to justify it, the decision was made to smash the suspect's door in at 4 a.m. the following morning. Of course, S-squad had a front-row seat, as usual.

Looking out of the window onto a quiet East End street at the dead of night, I felt as if I could have heard a pin drop. Then I heard the familiar (to me anyway) rumble of black-clad SO19 officers' boots on the pavement. Seconds later the front door imploded. Shouting, screaming, neighbours' lights going on, dogs of all sizes barking, cats starbursting across the street. The SO19 shouted so loud that the neighbours came out with their hands on their heads thinking it was their home being raided. It was over in seconds and our target was soon snugly contained in a top-security cell.

TWENTY

STOLEN SECRETS

A great deal of government business gets done in the cafes around St James's. Scotland Yard is a stone's throw from the royal park of the same name where, for generations, spies, civil servants from the nearby Home and Foreign Offices as well as junior spin doctors from Downing Street have plotted countless deals and coups in sight of Buckingham Palace. The police are no exception and have nicknames for some cafes; one favourite is known as the Goldfish Bowl. It's usually full of cops in smart suits having clipped and hushed conversations.

In May 2007, in one such cafe, a journalist from the *Sunday Times* was waiting to meet a source, a 59-year-old man who worked for Special Branch.

The contact was just about to leave his top-secret department, on a floor that required special passes to access. He picked up a brown folder. On its cover was the legend: 'Joint Terrorism Analysis'. Every page of the report was marked as 'Secret'. Inside it stated that Iraq-based leaders of al-Qaeda were planning terror attacks in the UK.

He took the file, left the Yard, crossed a couple of streets and entered the busy cafe where the journalist was waiting to meet him.

A few days later, George and I were sat in the Goldfish Bowl, mulling over Danny's 'ham sandwich' incident and licking our wounds after the team's bollocking from Terry.

My phone rang. I looked down and saw Terry's name flash up.

'Oh God, what now?' I wondered out loud to George.

'Maybe the owners of the business have complained,' he replied. Unhelpfully, I thought. That's the last thing I needed.

As it turned out, we were wrong: it was time for another urgent briefing. Leaving our coffee we marched to the Yard where we met someone from the dedicated briefing team. These guys are specialized in getting massive amounts of info across to us as concisely, accurately and memorably as possible.

A short while later I was running down the steps two at a time on my way to the flight deck. An Iraqi man, codenamed 'Broken Strap', was flying in to Gatwick from Karachi, Pakistan. He was in the UK to meet an unidentified male (UI) and to pass on 'instructions' before flying on to Germany for reasons we did not know. It was likely that this was an MI6 job as he was only here on a brief stopover. SST had been asked to help cover the meet and to 'home' the unidentified male (follow him to wherever he sleeps or calls home). A team had already been sent to Gatwick but things were happening that demanded my presence and authorization. I was pleased to see that my favourite car was on the flight deck (every cop has one) and ready for take-off.

As soon as I was half a mile from the office I plonked the magnetic blue light on the roof, turned on the siren and started to hack my way south through the London traffic. Cars, vans and lorries parted without question and I drove fast; I was well over the speed limit in the outside lane of the M3 when my blue light suddenly flew off the roof.

'Shit!'

A long cord connected the light to a socket in the car, from where it drew its power. Glancing in the rear-view I saw the light – which was still flashing – bouncing merrily along at 100 mph behind me.

The cord was unravelling at a frightening rate and I caught the end as it was yanked out of the socket and just before it flew out of the window. I was now barrelling along at 100 mph holding the steering wheel with one hand and a hundred yards of cable with a flashing blue light bouncing along behind me.

That's got to be a first, I thought as I slowed down, and started to yank in the cable. By the time I got to the end there wasn't much left of the blue light. Still, it had been a lucky escape; it could have been much worse – it could have smashed into somebody's windscreen.*

I managed to find my way to Gatwick without any further mishaps and met the team in the bar where Broken Strap and the UI were expected to meet. After signing the paperwork and surveying the venue – everything from the toilets to the kitchen – I drove off to the airport to meet the local SB and the Red surveillance team who would lock on to Broken Strap as soon as he disembarked.

---

*The problem, as it turned out, was a lack of magnetism in the roof.

We had no information about the man that Broken Strap was going to meet; we had to second-guess each move, try to work out the logic of what they were planning. While the rest of the team merged into the background in the bar, I had a look around the train station and checked the bus routes, just in case either of them decided to use public transport.

As usual we were forced to wait, and wait and wait. And wait. Broken Strap's flight had been delayed. Finally, once he emerged, the team was right behind him.

He stopped at the Avis desk. That's odd, I thought. We were told he was on a stopover, so why hire a car?

Once he'd got the vehicle, he drove it out of the airport then parked near the bar and began walking towards it for his meet. Meanwhile, we'd got the info on the hire car. He'd used his cousin's ID. Naughty, naughty. Technically, he'd taken the car without consent and wouldn't be insured, but as expected the senior investigating officer let him run. We're not going to blow a massive multi-agency international operation for a £500 fine.

Broken Strap was beardless and wearing trendy designer labels. Of course, al-Qaeda come in all shapes, sizes and styles and the more Western they look and sound then the easier it is for them to move around without arousing suspicion.

We spent a long time with him in the bar as he waited for his connection to show up. He didn't, so Broken Strap completed his stopover and continued with his journey. This was one of many frustrating missions where nothing happened. Although it never felt like a waste of time, it was an extremely unsatisfying part of the job.

The next day we found ourselves pottering about the office. I had a mountain of paperwork to get through from about five or six different completed operations. I couldn't put it off any longer and set to it with a resigned sigh, arranging my Leaning Tower of Pisa in-box into order of urgency. Fighting terrorism also means fighting off a never-ending tide of forms with a trusty biro: expenses, duty rotas, cars, logistics, technical equipment – each demanded a form to be filled.

Just as I put biro to paper, George stuck his head round the door. 'Everyone to the conference room, something big is up.'

Hurrah! Needing no encouragement, I threw down my pen and trotted along with the rest of the office, already discussing what we could be up to next.

Sometimes, however, these large meetings have nothing to do with an operation. For instance, Sir Ian Blair came over before the Health and Safety trial began to talk about Stockwell. He was genuinely worried about it and gave a very engaging and interesting talk.

Once we were all sat in the conference room, looking out across London's magnificent skyline, one of our big bosses walked in and shut the door behind him. Met bosses come in different shapes and sizes, with very different personalities. This guy was very well respected, extremely smart and very imposing, a real force of nature. Although I hadn't served under him directly I suspected that many officers would have had no problems laying down their lives on his command, such was his stature.

He wasn't afraid to muck in with the lower ranks. During a particularly demanding operation, a risk-assessment issue had been raised over an arrest. The arrest strategy was considered too dangerous. When our boss learned of this from home he said 'I'll do it then' and climbed into his high-performance sports car, went round to the address, nicked the suspect, chucked him into a police cell at Paddington Green and zipped off again. This was a brilliant bit of leadership that turned him into a legend at SO15.

Like Terry, he never lost his temper unless something really bad had happened. As soon as he'd entered, the atmosphere in the conference room changed instantly – it went from excitement to worry in a couple of seconds. What had we done? Who had screwed up?

He had to walk the length of the room to get to the front and, without breaking his stride, he grabbed an empty chair and carried it with him. Once he was at the front, he slammed it with a tremendous thump on the floor.

I think we all stopped breathing at that point. I'd never seen anything like this before, certainly not from a senior officer. Somehow he managed to eyeball us all at the same time. We held our collective breaths. After what seemed an age, he picked up the chair, sat down on it (it didn't break, thank goodness) and began to speak, calmly and clearly.

'I am going to tell you a little story.'

A longstanding SB officer had been arrested, he told us, for the worst betrayal.

The relief that we felt knowing that it wasn't 'us' was quickly culled by the shock of what he'd just said.

This was an out-and-out betrayal of the worst kind, he told us. The officer had been charged with 'Misconduct in a Public Office', which is about as serious an offence as you can commit. It carries a maximum sentence of life imprisonment.

He'd disclosed a secret Joint Terrorism Analysis Centre report to a journalist and the *Sunday Times* had published an article as a result. The report detailed an Iraqi-based al-Qaeda cell's plans to carry out Hiroshima-scale attacks on British soil.

What shocked us all was that Thomas Lund-Lack was a retired detective inspector who'd spent most of his unblemished 33-year career in the Metropolitan Police. He'd retired in 2003 but had been hired by Special Branch as a civilian (this is fairly common, retired officers can be trusted and understand how the police operate – it also makes for a nice earner on top of a police pension). As a result, Tom had been cleared to see the top-secret material on Britain's security threat levels.

I couldn't understand it. Why would a career-SB chap do such a thing? Apart from risking the lives of the men and women working on this international multi-agency operation, he must have known he would lose his pension and end up in jail. We didn't really get an answer in the meeting as it was still so soon after his arrest.

I wondered whether it had any connection to Broken Strap and his contact's no-show. I had no way of knowing of course, but once this article had been published, it could quite conceivably influence the behaviour of the terrorists we hunted and disrupt the work of agencies across the world.

When he had his day in court, Tom said he'd done it because he was 'annoyed' and wanted to 'bring out the problems that he believed he had seen'. It was all about the break-up of Special Branch and its merger with SO13, which had been a difficult experience for some officers – but for some reason none more so than Tom.[46]

It was no excuse – as far as I could see the gradual ending of Special Branch had not led to any security lapses or compromises in any operations whatsoever. If we're going to defeat the terrorists then we're going to have to accept change, and there's simply no room for hurt feelings. As Tom said later, he was a 'silly old man' who'd become 'angry' about what he perceived as the effectiveness of the Counter Terrorism Command. I wondered whether there was any way his actions could have been anticipated or intercepted. It seemed unlikely but I thought that a security review would be required.

The judge, Mr Justice Gross, put it very well when he said: 'Mr Lund-Lack will understand the need, as anyone in court will understand, that to protect your free society it is essential that some intelligence must be kept secret. Secrets must be kept and they cannot be kept if an insider breaks his bond of secrecy.'[47]

The judge gave him eight months to think about what he'd done. I can't imagine how terrible it must have felt for Tom, entering prison as a retired Special Branch detective inspector, to be inside with people he'd spent his entire career putting away.

TWENTY-ONE

THE LAST SUPPER

It was 11 a.m. on Thursday 31 August and George was in good spirits as he greeted me in the office. 'Good morning, *Capitan* Chaos,' he said cheerfully. 'It's a lovely summer's day and all's right with the world.'

I stared back glumly. 'I'm doomed,' I told him.

'Why's that, old boy? What on earth's been going on in my absence?'

The weekend had been truly awful. I'd been the duty sergeant the previous Friday night when I discovered that two of our radios – mine and Mary's – were missing. They were supposed to be locked in the office safe. I'd spent most of the afternoon searching for them, growing more and more panicky by the minute. I rang our radio chap, but he didn't have them. Once word got out, our unit would be humiliated, and as the radios were my responsibility, Terry would tear me to pieces.

On Saturday I'd called in favours and got a little team into work for 9 a.m. After thanking them profusely (the prospect of telling Terry on Monday morning was giving me nausea), I got them to search and search and search . . . and search again.

My team were the only ones in the office on a sunny Saturday; it was pretty depressing. My strategy was to perform a POLSA-style search of the office. POLSA (Police Search Advisors) are the guys in navy outfits who take the term 'rigorous search' to the next level and beyond. Their work is crucial in catching terrorists, murderers and rapists. I have the utmost respect for these guys, mainly because I believe they have the most boring, and therefore most difficult, job in the entire police service.

I'd made it sound like an investigation and as far as I was concerned, it was. We set about performing an extremely methodical search of the office and everyone's pod. As with all such searches, unusual things started to crop up. When I was asked to help search the locker room at Tottenham Police Station as a young sergeant, we ended up with over fifty 'exhibits'! These included a whip, a baseball bat and an imitation firearm (it was for training probationers), prisoners' property and interview master tapes. Fortunately, everything had an explanation, and for the most part had simply been stored incorrectly.

After two hours we had finished. I looked at the team's discoveries that lay on the table before me. Bits of cameras, batteries and other odds and ends; things we'd soon return to their rightful places, but no radios. We then moved beyond our immediate space to the rest of the office, but nothing was found.

On Sunday we returned and repeated the exercise. Still no radios.

I got into work very early on Monday morning. I checked the radio store and the logs for the umpteenth time. Nothing.

As I came out of the store at about 9 a.m., I spotted Terry walking down the corridor. He saw my 'Oh no!' expression and after wishing me a good morning he added: 'You'd better just tell me.'

After I'd finished explaining he stared at me and said, 'You have until midday.'

Now, after another two hours' searching, it was 11 a.m. and I was resigned to my fate.

Suddenly I saw Mary striding across the office towards me, a big smile on her face.

'We found them!'

'What? How, who, where?'

'They're being phased out; we should've been told, but they were collected last week.'

Not believing the good news, I checked our stock sheet. They were still listed. I then checked our disposal sheet, which was our record of what equipment was being shipped out of the office because it was obsolete, due for service or needed repair. They weren't listed but when I called to check I was told that they had arrived safely at disposal. Whoever had collected them had forgotten to clear them off our stock sheet, or to tell anybody.

Suddenly I could relax. It wasn't my fault. I wanted my weekend back!

I was exhausted; the stress of this had been unbelievable. I had spent three days crapping myself over two radios. It all seemed so petty but equipment loss was, quite rightly, regarded as a serious problem.

At the end of the day I started my journey home by walking past Vauxhall Cross and the MI6 building in the evening sun, looking forward to a quiet evening in front of the TV.

I'd reached the zebra crossing by the bridge and was just yards from disappearing down to the Tube when my phone went.

It was Terry.

'Get back to the office, we have a job on.'

I loved that understatement. As my pulse raced, and the adrenaline coursed through my veins, I forgot my tiredness and raced back to TT.

I was back in less than five minutes. Operation Overamp was going executive. Terry calmly went through what was about to happen. 'Tonight, ten subjects are dining at a Chinese restaurant called "The Bridge to Chinatown" in Borough Road, Southwark, South London.'

This restaurant was popular with students from the nearby South Bank University and was on one of London's busiest roads; it was just a short distance from the barely organized chaos of St George's Circus. The group had used the restaurant four weeks in a row.

'This will be the group's last supper together,' Terry said. 'It's the perfect way to sweep them all up in one go rather than increase the risk to the public by raiding multiple addresses. There will be members of the public, not forgetting the staff inside, so the first concern is their safety. Having said that, the targets are dining in a private room, which should help minimize risk.'

Terry said that the TSG (Territorial Support Group) would make the arrest and because there wasn't much time, we had to get them all the info they needed to effect this safely, which meant doing recces while our targets were still enjoying their last supper.

The TSG roam the capital six to a van ready to provide a

rapid response to any emerging situation where brute force might be needed to restore the peace. I'd called upon their services dozens of times when raiding crack houses, so knew what they were capable of and how incredibly brave they were – very often they'd charge through the door of a crack house not knowing what awaited them.

Of course, this would be a very different kind of raid. For ten terrorist subjects to be arrested simultaneously in such circumstances was a huge undertaking. We needed to ensure that none escaped or had a chance to resist or cause harm to any member of the public.

I had about ninety minutes to get the TSG all the information they needed, which would be no mean feat. I needed to cover the details of the surrounding area as well as the restaurant itself. They'd also need a set of contingency plans in case the situation changed.

I began ringing around and getting people back, some of whom had set off for home. Those on the Tube wouldn't get the message until they surfaced. Those in hire cars would have to amble back at 30 mph. Those in high-performance cars would be here in minutes and I planned accordingly – at break-neck speed. Always at the forefront of my mind was that there was no margin for error.

Steadily the team came in and I gave them their roles. George, then Raj, Danny and Asad, Jenny and Mary, all got to work and flew round to the restaurant, checking exits, surrounding streets, alleyways and a nearby estate which would make a good bolt-hole for a fleeing terrorist. Although this was the fastest job we'd ever done, there was no panic, just quiet professional haste. There was no banter either, not a word was wasted. Precisely ninety minutes after we'd been given the job the briefing pack was ready to be read out to the TSG.

The briefing room was packed. People had spilled out into the hall. Asad fought his way through the crowd to the front and passed the pack to Terry.

Terry fixed me with a firm stare that said all I needed to know in terms of his gratitude of what we'd managed to achieve.

I nodded and we began. We spoke to the team supervisors, explaining strategies, outlining the route, showing floor plans and possible contingencies. They then went and discussed tactics with their respective units.

I was buzzing with excitement – I'd hardly had any sleep for the past few days but didn't feel tired in the slightest as the TSG climbed into their vehicles. Everything had to be perfect, even the order in which we pulled up at the address – we had to give them as little warning as possible. After I had everything in place, I reported on the latest activity: 'The Last Supper has begun.'

The hit was on.

TWENTY-TWO

SOLDIERS OF ALLAH

Almost three years earlier, seventeen-year-old Kader Ahmed had joined a radical group after visiting the Da'wa stall run by Mohammed Hamid on Oxford Street, in front of Debenhams' flagship store. At a Da'wa stall, Muslims 'invite' other people to talk and read Islamic literature in an effort to get them to join their group.

Ahmed was Somalian. His family had moved to London to escape the ceaseless Somali Civil War, fought between extremist Islamic groups. He'd been taken out of his secondary school at the age of fourteen and educated at home in Plaistow, East London, by his Muslim mother.

Mohammed Hamid was a controversial figure with a remarkable history. He'd been arrested following a disturbance at the stall. Police officers had been called to reports of three men blocking the pavement with a trestle table stacked with religious books. Hamid refused to move and the officers were threatened with abuse.

As Hamid was handcuffed and dragged to the police van he

yelled: 'I've got a bomb and I'm going to blow you all up!' He gave his name as 'Osama bin London' and failed to turn up at Horseferry Road Magistrates Court because he had travelled to Pakistan where it is thought he met with senior members of al-Qaeda.[48]

Some time after this, MI5 officers managed to plant a recording device inside Hamid's house in Almack Road, Hackney, East London.

Ahmed was invited to Hamid's home for the group's regular Friday evening meeting, where he was welcomed with open arms.

Hamid was engaging, charismatic and persuasive; he spoke in a northern accent but used cockney slang and Asian mannerisms as he talked of an inevitable war between Muslims and the West.

Hamid was born into an Indian Muslim family in Tanzania and arrived in the UK as a child. Initially the family lived in Heckmondwike and Batley, in Yorkshire. Then Hamid moved in with an older brother in London at the age of twelve. He first got into trouble for shoplifting fish-fingers and a tin of sweetcorn. By the age of nineteen he was in borstal; jail terms for robbery followed. Hamid separated from his first wife, Linda, in his early thirties and looked after their two children. Shortly afterwards he met a woman who introduced him to drugs and he soon became addicted to crack and sold everything he had to feed his habit, until all he owned was a blanket.

A chance trip to a mosque with his brother saved him and he decided to leave the country for India to clean up. While there he met his second wife, an observant Muslim, and she came back to England with him, moving into his council house in Clapton.

The couple had four children together. Hamid became ever more devout, adopting traditional Islamic dress and growing a beard. In 1996 he opened the Islamic bookshop al-Koran in Clapton. He started to become a popular face in the community; he was a volunteer youth worker and managed a Sunday football team.

The 9/11 attacks changed him and he became radicalized, attending rallies at Speakers' Corner in Hyde Park. He also raised money for refugees from the war in Afghanistan. At the Speakers' Corner rallies in 2003 he first met the 21/7 bombers Ramzi Mohammed, Hussain Osman and Muktar Said Ibrahim, as well as other young radicals, and they joined him in meetings at his house. He exchanged 155 calls and text messages with the four would-be bombers, including one message sent to Hussain Osman on the evening of 7 July in which he used the alias 'Al-Quran': 'Assalam bro, we fear no-one except ALLAH, we will not change our ways, we are proud to be a Muslim an we will not hide. 8pm Friday at my place, be there food and talk, AL-QURAN.'

He also became embroiled in the crisis at Finsbury Park Mosque in North London, where the hook-handed, one-eyed radical cleric Abu Hamza held open-air prayer meetings after being evicted by the mosque trustees. Hamid helped negotiate an end to the stand-off in October 2004, and that was where he met Hamza's right-hand man, Atilla Ahmet.

When Ahmed met Atilla Ahmet at Hamid's house, the 42-year-old preacher from Lewisham was quick to boast that he was the leader of the group as well as being the number one al-Qaeda operative in Europe. Ahmet had already been denounced as 'Atilla the Scum' by tabloid newspapers.

Born and raised in South London, Ahmet's family were Turkish Cypriots. He'd worked as a soccer coach in south-east London's Bexley League, managing Sydenham Boys, Athenlay and Fisher Athletic. By all accounts he'd taken it far too seriously and had to be held back from other managers during some matches. The married father-of-four abandoned football in favour of radical Islam in 1998 and he was accused of being an al-Qaeda official after he gave a controversial interview to American news channel CNN in February 2006.

During a second interview with CNN in August, he said 9/11 was 'a deserved punch on the nose' for the United States and described former Prime Minister Tony Blair as 'fair game' for a terrorist attack. His hatred of *kuffars* was matched only by his contempt for *munafiqs*, the Arabic word for hypocrite, which he used to describe any moderate Muslim who did not back his extremist agenda.

In one talk, Ahmet told the group that the Muslim Council of Britain, one of the main umbrella groups for Muslims in the UK, was the enemy. He said they needed to be 'taken out', adding that they should not be afraid of death, that Allah wants them, the jihadists, to punish the *kuffar*.

Together Hamid and Ahmet started to 'groom' Ahmed who they saw as having great 'potential' to join their twisted version of jihad. At first, Ahmed's parents were pleased when their son became more devout after meeting Hamid but, within a short space of time, Ahmed became estranged from his father.

As Hamid said, Ahmed had become 'like a son' to him. This was exactly what Hamid was attempting to do – to groom naive and impressionable young men to 'join him' in his jihad. Two young brothers had also been recruited in the same way.

They asked Ahmed if he'd like to come on trips with members of the group and were delighted when he agreed. The 'camping trips', which included trips to Cumbria and the New Forest, were the first time Ahmed had been outside London since he'd arrived in the UK.

Ahmed travelled with them all over the country on training trips where about a dozen men went paintballing in the English countryside and were taught military techniques. As the group became more and more united, Ahmed grew closer and closer to Hamid and Ahmet.

What none of them realized however, was that police photographers and the security service were already watching the training camps.

On 23 July 2006, they travelled to an Islamic school in East Sussex, which was set in fifty-four acres of woodland that the group used for camping and training for jihad.

Hamid and Ahmet discussed the 7/7 bombings.

Hamid: I turned round and said to one of the brothers, you know what happened on the tubes, right, how many altogether, four people shaheed (martyred). Allah wa Allah I have to say this is as well, but four people got shaheed, right, how many people did they take out?

Ahmet: Fifty-two.

Hamid: Fifty-two, that's not even a breakfast for me.

Ahmet: I know it's not.

Hamid: That's not even a breakfast for me, for me in this country, do you understand me?

Ahmet: Hmm.

Hamid: Now, at the same time, how I look at it, I would

take my breakfast and I still be with my children and my
wife and I'll be looking after them. Remember Jack the
Ripper.

Ahmet: Hmm.

Hamid: Remember this people that never get caught, right,
don't let your ego go forward, let your intelligence go
forward for the sake of Allah, use your *hikma* [wisdom]
and be effective, effective, see how many gets it, see how
many you can take at the same time, see how long you
can last out, then if you have to go, then you're going for
a good reason.

At another of these gatherings, Atilla Ahmet sang a song to the
children on the weekend camp. Using the calypso tune of
'The Banana Boat Song', Ahmet sang: 'Come, Mr Taliban,
come bomb England, before the daylight come, you wanna
see Downing Street done.'

Both men talked of shedding blood to implement sharia
[Islamic law] and suggested Parliament as a target, with Ahmet
saying: 'The House of Parliament, the big people, the MPs,
the police, the army, the city slickers are all halal [permitted].'

The others who came to form the ten-man 'cell' who met
in the Chinese restaurant included a builder and an ex-bus-
driver. Three were converts from Christianity and four had
been born overseas.

One of the men, Kibley da Costa, twenty-four, of West
Norwood, south-east London, had been born a Jamaican
Christian in one of Kingston's ghettos. After moving to the
UK in 1995, he became a bus driver but was left traumatized
after a drunken pedestrian fell under the wheels of his vehicle
and died of his injuries.

He converted to Islam in 2003 and began calling himself Abdul Khaliq and worked with youth groups in South London, volunteering to talk to black Muslim youngsters in an attempt to steer them away from street gangs such as the Muslim Boys.

Mohammad al-Figari (real name Roger Michael Figari), forty-four, of Tottenham, North London, was a convicted drug smuggler and convert to Islam. Born in Trinidad, he was brought up by 'very religious' grandmothers – one Catholic, one Hindu. He moved to London in 1989, studied law and economics at Kilburn Polytechnic and worked for the Inland Revenue and the Department of Social Services.

After becoming a chauffeur under contract to the BBC he drifted into crime. He supplied clients with drugs and 'female partners' and obtained a criminal record for theft and assault. By 1997, he had fallen in with a smuggling gang importing cocaine from Jamaica using drug mules who swallowed packets of the drug.

Al-Figari said he converted to Islam ten days before his arrest for smuggling, having been interested in the black American organization Nation of Islam. He was eventually convicted and sentenced to eight years. While a prisoner in Wandsworth he came across one of the extremist documents that formed one of the terror charges against him. Unbelievable as it sounds, he borrowed a pamphlet called 'How Can I Train Myself for Jihad?' from HMP Wandsworth's library.

Al-Figari had met Hamid shortly before being sent to prison and the preacher continued to send him Islamic literature. After his release on Christmas Eve 2002, al-Figari became a loyal follower. He joined Hamid on the same camping trip to Baysbrown Farm that was also attended by the 21/7 bombers. At this time al-Figari was working as supervisor of deliveries of pharmaceuticals at a London hospital – despite his drugs conviction.

At one meeting in 2009, Hamid told his followers they were 'Soldiers of Allah' who were 'fighting for sharia'. And: 'The whole aspect is for you to get shahada [martyred] for you to be shaheed [martyr].'

The powers that be had heard enough; it was time to strike.

TWENTY-THREE

THE GREAT CHINESE TAKEAWAY

And now here we were, driving in our multi-vehicle convoy, on our way to arrest Hamid and his gang. We drew curious stares as we snaked quietly through central London, along the short distance from TT to the Chinese restaurant.

The streets around the restaurant were already packed with officers and agents from various agencies in various guises.

A few hearts had leapt when da Costa was overheard suggesting that MI5 had probably bugged the restaurant but we knew they said this sort of thing all the time, so we carried on as planned. There was simply no time to bring anything forward anyway – if they left before we got there, we'd simply have to find another way to scoop them all up.

I couldn't help it but the thought did enter my mind: 'Christ, I hope they aren't armed – or worse . . .'

The vehicles rolled up and the TSG climbed out, their boots clumping on the pavement as they jogged towards the Chinese restaurant. This was going to be one hell of a takeaway.

They charged in – and a polite Special Branch voice at their head shouted clearly and above all the noise. 'Sit down! Hands on the table, please. Everything will be explained to you.'

And the men, seeing their situation was hopeless, remained sitting, the remains of their dinner cooling before them.

Finally, in the small hours, I started my journey home again and just managed to catch the last train. Apart from a handful of sleeping commuters who'd overindulged in readiness for the bank holiday weekend, I was alone.

I mulled over the operation through a fog of tiredness as my exhaustion started to settle in. This had been quite something to be a part of, even as the tiniest cog. Right at that moment, as I travelled home, Hamid was getting his very own personal tour of Paddington Green police station, the famous holding centre designed for terrorist suspects.

I didn't know it then but the first to fall apart was Atilla Ahmet. He started having claustrophobia-induced panic attacks after just a few hours. Not long after he was moved to Belmarsh he decided to plead guilty and confessed. This left him friendless on the inside and he became paranoid, accusing his fellow defendants of being MI5 spies before sacking his legal team.

The five-month trial at Woolwich Crown Court was the first to deal with a new offence introduced under the Terrorism Act 2006 of attending a place used for terrorist training.

Of course, the men argued that we'd got it all wrong; they were only going on these trips for 'fun and fitness'. Although I'd be the first to admit that their training didn't amount to much, the jury were quick to disagree.

There always exists the danger of not taking the threat seriously enough. To quote the IRA, the terrorists only have to be lucky once – as they proved on 7/7 – whereas we can't afford to slip up – ever. We should never trivialize these people, no matter how amateurish they may seem. After all, the danger lay in Hamid's grooming of young people, in creating monsters who would be prepared to kill hundreds of innocent people at the push of a button. He repeatedly talked about fighting and killing 'non-believers' and bent and twisted the teachings of Islam until they were almost unrecognizable but fitted his own sick agenda. As to *why* someone like Hamid does what he does, I liken it to a kind of perversion.

Hamid was found guilty of organizing terrorist training camps and of encouraging others to murder non-believers. He was jailed on 7 March 2008 under special Imprisonment for Public Protection powers. The judge said Hamid should serve seven and a half years – but would not be released until he has reformed.

I suspect that may take some time.

Atilla Ahmet pleaded guilty to three counts of soliciting to murder in connection with Hamid's camps and home talks and was sentenced to six years and eleven months.

Kibley da Costa was found guilty of providing terrorist training, two counts of attending terrorist training and one count of possessing a record containing information likely to be useful to a terrorist. He was sentenced to four years and eleven months.

Mohammad al-Figari was found guilty of two counts of attending terrorist training and two counts of possessing a record containing information likely to be useful to a terrorist. He was sentenced to four years and two months.

Kader Ahmed was found guilty of two counts of attending terrorist training. He was sentenced to three years and eight months.[49]

I've listed these men's sentences because, sadly, it won't be long before most of them will have done their time. Offenders are freed when they reach their release date – usually halfway through their sentence, with deductions for time served on remand. They then serve the rest of their time on parole. Many men and women convicted of terrorist offences in recent years have already been freed or are on probation.

They've been convicted of helping bombers, raising funds for terrorism and recruiting young men to fight a holy war. I suspect that in many cases the short stay inside is unlikely to have changed their beliefs.

Five convicted terrorists released into the community have already been returned to jail after breaching parole. One was recalled to prison after assaulting a police officer while another has been questioned about breaking restrictions on Internet access. Another man was suspected of attempting to buy a gun. Although this sounds worrying, it's also reassuring to know that they're being picked up as soon as they overstep the mark.

There are plenty of prisoners arrested since 2001 that are classed as 'high risk' and are due for release. Since 1999, at least 150 men have been convicted of terrorist offences, with 120 linked to al-Qaeda. Of those, 115 were given determinate sentences, which means they will be released after serving two thirds of their terms, despite being refused for parole in many cases. About 75 are due to be freed in the next three to four years.

The National Association of Probation Officers (NAPO) has said: 'It is extremely difficult to deal with any individual whose criminal behaviour is politically motivated because established assessment programmes do not work.'[50]

They are quite right, terrorists are 'special cases' as their murderous behaviour stems from moral conviction (as warped as it is) as opposed to the more traditional murder-related offences, which are usually something to do with family arguments, or money, or disputes between criminals. Placing convicted terrorists in hostels supervised by staff more used to dealing with drug dealers and thieves might yet prove to be problematic.

The police would be expected to watch those most likely to re-offend. The financial cost of monitoring them in the community is far greater than keeping them in jail. It costs the taxpayer around £40,000 a year for a prison inmate and £25,000 for a hostel place. But those who pose the greatest risk need constant police surveillance upon release, which is extremely expensive as it involves several teams of officers permanently working twelve-hour shifts. As more and more convicted terrorists are released, we could soon find ourselves stretched to the limit.

TWENTY-FOUR

EAGLE EYE

I was staring out of the office window through tired eyes and munching a late breakfast when I was perked up by the sight of one of the 'Duck tours' waterbuses that drive tourists across the Thames stuck on the mud flats just near to its entry point beside MI6. Another one had turned up to try to pull it free and was struggling.

As I strained to see the result, I was interrupted by Jenny. 'It's Danny for you,' she said, transferring him to my phone. I had just taken a big bite of my bacon roll and chewed quickly as I put the receiver to my ear.

'Danny?'

'Yeah, I was coming back over Lambeth Bridge and I saw two guys taking pictures of Thames House (MI5). I'm not happy about it.'

'Right,' I said sceptically. People are always photographing the buildings of London. Personally, I don't much see the sense; my holiday snaps of buildings always seem to end up in the bottom desk drawer or buried somewhere deep on my hard drive. Even so, every time I walked to Scotland Yard I saw tourists posing for their very own snap of our famous revolving sign. I was puzzled, therefore, that Danny had actually rung me about this. Why would he do that? Where's the evidence? Taking photos of London's buildings isn't a crime in itself.

'Do you think they should be stopped?' I asked.

Danny replied without a moment's hesitation. 'Definitely.' He was emphatic.

I considered. I could either spend a lot of time on the phone trying to work out why Danny, who was a very experienced cop, had such an odd hunch, or I could just get on with it.

There'd been much fuss made in the media about tourists having cameras taken off them and memory cards being wiped, so I knew this could go badly. I didn't want to alienate young Asian tourists against the police. I was sorely tempted to tell Danny to let them go and get back to the office. After all, he wasn't operationally deployed, there was no intel; I'd only sent him over to the Yard to fetch some paperwork for me.

When officers come straight from uniform into Special Branch they have to go through a transition programme. The keen cop is always looking for crime, it's in our blood, but in SB we had different roles and had to deal with things differently.

So I wondered whether Danny was being a bit 'keen' or was he 'on to something'? Danny was an eager cop, he really wanted to make a difference. The problem with being in the SST is that we were very often divorced from the criminal side of policing. We were the watchers who let others make the arrest; we had no face-to-face interaction with our suspects whatsoever. I know I missed that part of the job and I was sure Danny did too.

I decided to go with Danny's gut feeling. 'Stay with them, Danny, I'll get them stopped for you.'

I called the local uniforms on the non-urgent phone line but asked them to be quick; I didn't want Danny 'showing out'.

We were able to stop them under Section 44 of the Terrorism Act 2000, where police officers may randomly stop someone *without* reasonable suspicion, providing the area has been designated a likely target for an attack.

Danny called five minutes later. 'They're here; details are being taken.'

Another five minutes and I was shaking my head in disbelief. Danny had only gone and done it! They *were* of interest to us, even if they weren't exactly the brightest tools in the box. As Danny put it, 'There's Google Maps for all that stuff now.' That's very true, the Internet is the terrorist's weapon of choice and these days it's easy for someone in Karachi to take a virtual 'walk' through central London. Nevertheless, once the local police had let them go, it would be recorded and passed on. I think Danny's action had spooked them sufficiently to forget about whatever it was they were thinking of doing and we certainly never heard from them again.

What was particularly interesting to me was that – against all the odds and my best judgement – I'd trusted Danny's instinct. I was so uncertain about the need to stop people taking pictures because it made us look so draconian and we were getting so many of these stops wrong. Take MP Austin Mitchell, for example. He's a keen photographer and was amazed to be stopped by the police from taking pictures on two occasions.

If you are a normal person going about your business and you see something you want to take a picture of, then go ahead and take it. The only time it becomes a problem is if you're photographing something or someone inherently private – and then you're into paparazzi territory.

It seemed as though some inexperienced officers weren't stopping people taking pictures for the right reasons and I hated the fact that this reflected badly on the police as a whole – after all these stories had made the front pages of newspapers.[51] You could hardly blame the press when seven armed police were apparently sent to detain a renowned architectural photographer who was photographing a London church. Of course, the consequences of not responding to a police officer's concerns could conceivably end up being far more serious.

Some campaigners, understandably worried about police powers, actually went out of their way to film and photograph government buildings and then filmed their encounters with the police before posting them on the Internet – none of which is illegal.

There's a great deal of paranoia around but the police officers who patrol our streets are on alert for anything that vaguely resembles terrorism. It's difficult because the more professional a photographer, paradoxically, the more likely they are to be stopped or questioned, which is odd because you'd imagine a terrorist would try to be a little less obvious.

As far as journalists are concerned, guidelines agreed between senior police were adopted by all forces in England and Wales in 2007. They state that the police have no power to prevent the media taking photos and 'once images are recorded, [the police] have no power to delete or confiscate them without a court order, even if [the police] think they contain damaging or useful evidence.'[52]

It is so hard to get the balance between security and freedom right. The many Acts passed by parliament to combat terrorism (the Terrorism Act 2000, The Anti-terrorism, Crime and Security Act 2001, The Criminal Justice Act 2003, The Prevention of Terrorism Act 2005, The Terrorism Act 2006, The Counter-Terrorism Act 2008, The Terrorist Asset-Freezing (Temporary Provisions) Act 2010) give the police tremendous power to limit many freedoms in the interests of protecting the larger public. It's therefore essential that we execute the law in the spirit in which it's intended. As a police officer, I'm always delighted when the public stand up and tell us when we're getting it wrong – as in the case with photography.

Sometimes, the public can be wrong though, as in the case with stop and search. It was widely reported that figures published in 2004 revealed a 300 per cent increase in the number of Asians being stopped and searched under Britain's new anti-terror laws. We were unjustly accused of Islamophobia as a result. In reality, according to a 2005 report, 'Terrorism and Community Relations' by the House of Commons Home Affairs Committee, we'd stopped and searched 21,577 people, 2,989 of whom were Asian. We don't ask for people's religions when we stop them so I can't tell you how many of them were Muslim, but as about 50 per cent of Asians are Muslim we can guesstimate that we stopped about 1,500 Muslims – about 7 per cent of the total. Muslims make up 13 per cent of the population of London, where most (80 per cent) of these people were stopped and about 7 per cent across the rest of the UK.

Of course, the police do make mistakes but many of these

are understandable. Uniformed police officers, patrolling our streets with their eyes peeled, are performing an essential role. They're out there day after day, looking hard for anything that could relate to terrorism – after having attended countless briefings about terrorism. The beat officers' vigilance, as well as their power to act, is crucial – as I would soon see for myself.

TWENTY-FIVE

THE MAN FROM YEMEN

The American embassy in Sana'a, Yemen's capital, is a short distance from the country's finest architectural achievement, the al-Saleh Mosque, a gleaming palace that can hold 40,000 worshippers. The mosque cost at least $60 million to build, an unheard-of fortune in Yemen, and it sits in stark contrast to the dusty slums that surround it.

Locals say that stepping into the mosque is like stepping into paradise. Stepping out again is like stepping into hell. A lack of running water, food, electricity means that almost all of Yemen's 23 million citizens live in total poverty.

On 17 September 2008, just as the sun started to climb the sky, as the embassy guards changed shifts after completing their last meal before beginning the day's Ramadan fast, the al-Qaeda terrorists struck. They arrived in a truck and were disguised as uniformed Yemeni police. After pulling up at the outer perimeter checkpoint, they asked to be let in. Their plan was to drive up to the heavily fortified second perimeter, the front entrance to the embassy compound, and blow a hole in it.

A second vehicle loaded with al-Qaeda commandos armed with automatic weapons and grenades was waiting around the corner, ready to speed through the breach left by the truck bomb and enter the embassy. Once they'd made it inside, their plan was to shoot all the diplomatic personnel on sight.

But the suspicious Yemeni security guards refused the vehicle entry. The militants opened fire and detonated the bomb, killing several guards in the huge blast. One of the suicide bombers' arms was later found several streets away.

As a huge plume of black smoke rose over the capital and as the second vehicle full of terrorists raced past the carnage bound for the front gate, American diplomats headed for a specially designed panic room in the basement of the embassy building.

The terrorists engaged Yemeni guards in a ferocious gun and grenade battle. Twenty minutes later the al-Qaeda men were all dead. They had taken six guards and seven civilians with them.[53]

Jenny and I were in one of West London's loveliest squares, trying to get an angle on a bedsit. We'd completed two walk-pasts, and I'd allow us no more so we were considering how we could provide a 'lift' or 'trigger' for the surveillance teams (this is slang for alerting the surveillance teams that the suspect was about to leave the property).

My phone went. It was Terry.

'Get your arse out to Newham, there's a job we need to start in one hour.'

He gave me the address but told me nothing more. That was all I needed for now. Problem was, we were in West London, Newham was in the east.

'We're gonna have to hoof it, Jenny,' I said.

She smiled. 'I'll drive.'

It was lunchtime and the sun was shining; this meant that the traffic would be bad and the bright sunlight would neutralize the stick-on blue light which meant the public would hear the two tones of the siren but might not see which car it was coming from.

Jenny pushed the car hard through the traffic flowing slowly over the Westway and into central London. I gave her directions from a map book. We had TomToms but they didn't take traffic into account and sometimes got left behind when we shot through roundabouts 'too quickly' and ended up telling us to turn left ten times on the trot.

Fifteen minutes later, I freed my white knuckles from my legs. I had to hand it to Jenny, she was a fabulous driver and had pushed the tyre grip to the limit as we squealed our way around some corners. We were half a mile from the address, so we pulled the blue light back into the car and switched the siren off. After having 'cleaned' the car of any sign that might give us away as cops and lost all the traffic that had seen us with the blues and twos on, we parked up and finished the journey on foot.

We can't just watch a premises, we need to be cleared under RIPA (Regulation of Investigatory Powers Act 2000) which regulated the powers of public bodies to carry out surveillance and investigation. In other words, we needed written or, as in this case, verbal authority, as it was urgent. I called Terry and confirmed that the 'oral' clearance was in place. The job was on.

The address was a flat above a religious bookshop. Once the others from the SST arrived, we were given a description of the target, a man from Yemen. He'd landed in the UK a few days previously after having travelled from an al-Qaeda camp hidden in the country's coffee-growing fields. He was of significant interest to some of our international partner agencies and they were hoping he would lead us to senior al-Qaeda leaders in the UK, with whom he hoped to discuss the potential funding of al-Qaeda in the Arabian peninsula as well as terror attacks and training in Europe.

This was just my kind of operation – fast-moving, with lots of unknowns and the chance to bag some extremely valuable intel. As ever, though, things were not going to go quite how I hoped.

Al-Qaeda tends to set up camp in lawless areas where they're able to move freely, and Yemen was one such place. About two-thirds of the country is out of government control and in the hands of either separatist groups or local tribes, some of whom have a bad habit of kidnapping foreign tourists to use as bargaining chips in disputes with the central government. Yemen is also in the grip of an intractable, ethnically driven civil war, which started back in 2004. The usual tragedies have abounded – from blockades of medicine and bombing raids by the government to torture and terrorism by the militants.

Add to this Somali pirates menacing ships trying to reach Yemen's ports, an economy over-reliant on a dwindling oil production, and a looming water crisis, and it would be fair to say that the government has enough to worry about without having to think about tackling al-Qaeda training camps.

Under pressure in Saudi Arabia and Iraq, al-Qaeda has turned the lawless mountain areas of Yemen into a new staging area. The United States has tried to orchestrate attacks on al-Qaeda in Yemen and the government even helped the Americans track down one al-Qaeda leader in 2002, who was, as usual, taken out by a Predator drone.[54]

Yemen also has a colourful recent history of extremism; an Islamic school in Sana'a once provided teaching to John Walker Lindh, the so-called 'American Taliban' captured in Afghanistan in 2001.

Another visitor was Umar Farouk Abdulmutallab, who studied at Sana'a Institute for Arabic Language from August to September 2009. He routinely skipped his classes at the institute and attended lectures at Iman University, notorious for its suspected links to terrorism. Also present in Yemen was Anwar al-Awlaki, the self-styled 'bin Laden of the Internet'.[55]

The Bush administration had targeted al-Qaeda leaders Naser al-Wahishi and Qasim al-Raymi in Yemen in recent years with disastrous results. Naser al-Wahishi became al-Qaeda's leader in Yemen after the 2002 drone strike; he is believed to be behind a 2007 bombing that killed seven Spanish tourists and two Yemenis as well as the attack on the American embassy. Qasim al-Raymi ran the training camps and trained the men in preparation for the embassy strike. He also put Abdulmutallab through his paces.[56]

Attempted drone strikes on both men by the United States had missed their targets and killed innocent women and children, sparking a public outcry and fuelling anti-American sentiments across the country, and helping al-Qaeda garner more support.

Poverty and unemployment are prime recruitment factors for al-Qaeda, who promise to help end both. The new American administration has caught on and is now trying to pump millions of dollars into easing poverty in Yemen by increasing the country's coffee production. It's early days, however, and there remain a lot of people that still need convincing, as was evident from the increased terrorist activity from this new al-Qaeda stronghold.[57]

Although I had no idea if they stocked a Yemeni brand, Jenny and I were enjoying cappuccinos in the sunshine while watching the target's flat.

'This is more like it,' I said.

'Makes a change from sitting in a parked car, that's for sure.'

While we watched the world go by, like any 'happily married couple' would, the rest of the SST were busy doing recces and finding a selection of decent ops, among other things.

Meanwhile, our man's description had been given to a hurriedly assembled surveillance team back at TinTac (another nickname for Tintagel House).

My phone rang. 'The job's gone armed,' Terry said. 'Had to let you know as the surveillance team are coming equipped but I'm afraid there's no chance of you getting your kit now.'

'I understand,' I replied.

People came and went from the bookshop all afternoon, but there was no sign of life in the flat.

'Looks like the excitement is over,' I said a few minutes later. I planned to give us ninety minutes in the coffee shop before we changed vantage point. Ninety minutes would give the rest of the team plenty of time to get in place.

Asad arrived a short while later and joined our table.

I was half looking at the paper and noted the phrase 'Terrorist Fundamentalists' in one headline.

Asad sighed when he saw it. 'These people aren't fundamentalists,' he said.

'What do you mean?' I asked with interest.

'They say they want the world returned to how it was over a thousand years ago, what they would call "Islam's Golden Age". But that's nonsense. Terrorists aren't going back to the old ways that the concept of fundamentalism implies at all. They just try and find those parts of the Quran they can twist in a hopeless attempt to justify bombing innocent people, as if fundamentalism necessitates violence. Real fundamentalists tend to live a chaste life in poverty – they don't believe in indiscriminate mass murder to further this cause.'

'But don't the suicide bombers believe that they're helping return the world to the "Golden Age"?'

'They may buy the idea after a long period of skilful brain-washing by terrorist trainers. They are the simple believers who are devoted to their masters and believe that Allah will reward them in heaven.'

'Not the brightest tools in the box then.'

'Exactly – not smart as such but very, very keen and unswervingly loyal – not just to their religion.'

Our time was soon up and so we swapped with two others from the SST. Jenny, Asad and I found views elsewhere and were joined by a photographer. The people-followers rocked up and settled down to await the appearance of their prey.

We'd been watching on and off for ten hours but we were expected to go through the night. This man was clearly a Very Important Terrorist. As darkness fell, the photographer left us to it.

I shivered. We were on the second night's surveillance and this time I was partnered with young Marion in a covert car. To keep the windows from misting up (bit of a giveaway as well as obstructing our view) we had to keep the car cold. We couldn't leave the fan on all night otherwise we'd have a flat battery in the morning, so we cracked open the windows.

As usual, a long night allowed me to quiz away.

'I'm curious,' I said, 'to know why, when you have a degree from Oxford, you decided to join the police. You know you could be earning megabucks in the City.'

'What are you trying to do? Put me off?' Marion answered with a smile. 'I wanted to achieve something tangible, something real. Buying and selling stocks and shares by pushing buttons on a computer and making a few phone calls just doesn't appeal. I'm challenged every day in this job, and I've learned some very amazing skills.'

'But life would be a lot easier as a rich and high-flying banker. I mean, look at you now, stuck with a Jim Carrey lookalike in a freezing cold car in East London from midnight till dawn, watching people that would happily kill us as soon as look at us.'

'Jeez, you really are trying to put me off! Believe me, as strange as it seems, I love every minute of this job.'

Some time later, Marion reminded me of this conversation when Lehman Brothers went bust.

She threw the paper down on the desk: 'And you told me I should be a banker!'

'OK, point made,' I conceded.

While Marion and I were at least able to have a good chin-wag while we slowly froze through the night, poor old Asad was struggling to stay 'eyes on' on the target's front door from the OP van.

'Eyes on' means you're posted to watch someone's front door, for example, and you don't remove your eyes for more than a second at a time – for eight hours straight.

Most of East London is in bed from about midnight. As the traffic dies away you watch people's lights gradually going out. All you can do is stare in envy at the thought of them climbing into their nice warm beds. From that moment until dawn, any movement in the street would prove to be total excitement for Asad. He broadcast every now and then, just to let us know that he was OK.

Although the back streets of East London were now asleep, you always got to see the odd sight at night. I don't know why but there'll always be someone doing something odd. Not necessarily illegal, just odd. I've seen someone walking down the road with a single mattress balanced on their head at 3 a.m., someone else pushing an old-fashioned pram at 4 a.m., people jogging, the occasional drunk fast asleep on the pavement. And then there's the wildlife; I've seen countless foxes on bin raids, cats fighting, singing, hunting or being chased by shockingly huge London rats.

The closer to dawn you get the harder it becomes to concentrate; your eyes get tired from staring at the same point for so long. Any activity is a cause for rejoicing, something new on an otherwise unchanging frame.

As dawn approaches, postmen, early shift workers and mosque attendees appear; they're all cause for fascination, something fresh for your tired eyes. The worst part is when your eyes hang heavy and you think you see a flash of movement. You jerk awake and look around. What was it? An animal? A gust of wind blowing leaves or rubbish? A moving branch? Has the target successfully sneaked out?

It's on these long nights that I think that this is a hard way to earn a living. Asad could be totally relied upon. I knew I could tell him to watch paint dry all night and he'd do it without question and without falling asleep.

Sadly, I could not say the same for myself. When I was with another department, some years ago now, I was with a colleague, hiding in a bush all night, waiting for a criminal to emerge from his hideout. We stayed awake until dawn cracked the sky at 6 a.m. and then the exhaustion got to us.

We didn't wake up until 9 a.m. and the rest of the team had gone home without telling us. We kept quiet about falling asleep; if we'd confessed I'm sure we would have earned ourselves another night in the bush. In those days if you were late for work or committed another misdemeanour, you usually ended up in the OP van as it was considered one of the dullest jobs.

Asad, Marion and I were eventually relieved at 5 a.m.; the only thing of interest we'd seen all night had been a passing milk float, a rare sight in London these days.

I was back in the office by midday. Terry had called us all in: 'This job is escalating, the hours are going to be long and I need you to install more "technical surveillance assets".'

It may have been escalating in Terry's eyes but our man hadn't left the flat for three days and it felt like the op was dead in the water.

Finally, on the fourth day he appeared, but just long enough to chuck a black bin bag in the communal wheelie bin down the road. We collected it in the dead of night. After donning our Marigolds and having a good old rummage, we discovered nothing of interest – except for some khat, the ubiquitous amphetamine herb of Yemen. What the hell was he doing in there that necessitated the chewing of khat?

On Friday he took us off to the mosque, and for a bit of shopping, then twice more to the mosque. Then back inside the flat again for another three days.

I hated the waiting but I forced myself to accept it, to become more patient. I knew that this was an essential asset when hunting terrorists.

But, *two weeks* later, nothing had happened and still we were told to keep on it 24/7.

That night I was sat with an officer in a car, waiting for the target to return home after a rare trip outside. If he appeared on time and in the right place, we'd say he'd 'read the script'. It was bloody annoying if these chaps sometimes went 'off the page' but of course we were prepared for most eventualities.

It was quite possible for us to end up doing quite a bit of police 'admin' while sat in the car and as I was her line manager the officer had decided this would be a good time to 'raise an issue'. I agreed.

'Some of the girls have a problem with the attitude of one of the male Asian officers towards women,' she told me. 'It's not me personally that has the problem, I'm raising this on behalf of a friend.'

This was pretty important. Not only was it sensitive, we really needed to maintain good relationships between all members of the team because two people who didn't like each other could end up being posted to watch a suspect together in a confined space for sixteen hours. That could make work unbearable and lead to valuable team members asking for transfers as a result.

'What is the problem exactly?'

'Well, shall we say he has an old-fashioned attitude towards women.'

'That they shouldn't be carrying guns and driving fast cars?'

'Something like that, yes.'

I decided that I'd try to deal with this by talking it over with

George and Theresa. Talking to detective inspectors is fine but
it ups the ante and can add to the damage, as it becomes more
of a formal complaint. I looked forward to getting George and
Theresa's views on the matter.

I'd need to tread carefully, however. If I dealt with the problem ineptly then I could end up causing havoc on the team.
'Can you give me some examples?' I asked.

'Well yes, he—'

'Wait!' I hissed suddenly. We froze. I'd just seen our man in
the rear-view mirror. He'd walked right up behind us and
stopped. Not only had he arrived home early, but his normal
route never took him past this section of the street. He was
most definitely off the page. I watched carefully in the mirrors.
He passed by and just kept walking. We breathed a sigh of
relief; we hadn't been compromised.

I resolved the problem after talking to George and Theresa
and then by talking to the Asian officer concerned. He hadn't
realized he'd come across in such a conservative way and said
he had no problem with women officers doing everything the
men did. We fed this back and it was quickly resolved. The
issue was all about perception. It's easy to take the attitude of
'Tough, just get on with your work', but it's incredibly important to have a healthy atmosphere on the team – especially
when you spend hours working together under pressure.

Finally, there was a break in the routine. Our target took us to
a mosque where the photographer got some snaps of him
joining a huddle of older men. They chatted for twenty minutes and then our target walked to an Internet cafe.

'That was it,' George said, 'that's what we've been waiting
for.'

'I hope it was worth it,' I said doubtfully.

'It's always worth it, old boy. These chaps are planning something big. Any link we can uncover is a massive step in the right direction.'

'He's booked a ticket back to Yemen,' Danny told me much later, after being given the result of the checks into our man's computer history.

So that was it, he'd done his job after two weeks of sitting in an East London flat and one twenty-minute meeting. The next morning he left his flat at 5 a.m. with his suitcases. We followed him to Heathrow. We were desperate to know – what were we to do? Were we going to let him leave or not? 1600 was suddenly buzzing with activity and an urgent meeting was held among senior agents at Thames House as our subject strolled into the terminal.

My phone rang. 'We're letting him go, Harry,' Terry announced.

And that was it. No debriefing, no tea and medals, just on to the next job while our man flew back to his alien world in the hills of Yemen.

But we'd got his meeting on record and new lines of enquiry had been set up on some previously unknown individuals in the UK. Connections were being made that we didn't know about. This had been an awful job for us but it was an essential piece of intelligence gathering and, as George liked to put it, 'The intel was hard won but priceless, old boy.'

In December 2009, an attack on the British embassy in Yemen was foiled after an al-Qaeda cell in Arhab, twenty miles north of the capital, was dismantled.[58] The attack, using a truck bomb and a second vehicle full of armed and trained terrorists, was based on the assault on the American embassy, which had left sixteen people dead. It was prevented, the Defence Ministry said, thanks to a much-improved intelligence picture of al-Qaeda operations in Yemen.

TWENTY-SIX

FAHRENHEIT 451

It was 2 a.m. on Saturday morning in September 2008. Upper Street in Islington, North London, was still busy with week-end revellers. In a nearby leafy square, however, all was quiet. Officers from SO19 sat in covert cars, 800-rounds-a-minute MP5 sub-machine guns at the ready.

Our targets were currently across town in the golden-domed Regent's Park Mosque. I was nervous. We were planning to catch the men at the very moment they planned to strike, so timing was everything if we wanted to secure a long conviction. If we pounced too early then there was a good chance they could deny everything, and we would have a hard time persuading a jury to convict them.

Besides that, this was a highly sensitive mission that involved freedom of expression. Our chief target had been a leading protester outside the American and Danish embassies in 2006. These protests were born out of the outrage caused by the publication by a Danish newspaper of twelve cartoons that depicted images of the Prophet Mohammed.

The images had been intended to be a bold assertion of free speech and Danish cartoonist Kurt Westergaard – who found himself the primary target of death threats thanks to his drawing of the Prophet with a bomb in his turban – said he wanted to illustrate how religion was exploited to justify terror. Many Muslims were furious, stating that his cartoon portrayed the Prophet as a terrorist, while others argued that simply drawing an image of Mohammed is in itself a blasphemous act. Denmark became the focus of a worldwide protest as a result – even more so as it had a presence in Iraq and Afghanistan. The vast majority of the protests were peaceful but a few had turned sickeningly violent.

Mobs in Damascus, the capital of Syria, had torched the Danish and Norwegian embassies while rioters set fire to the Danish consulate in Beirut and protesters petrol-bombed Denmark's embassy in Tehran. A demonstration outside an American military base in Afghanistan left two people dead after local police opened fire on the crowd. In all, a hundred lives were lost in the violent protests.[59]

Two years on and the cartoons were still being used to justify violent attacks. Just three months earlier, in June 2008, for example, a Taliban suicide car bomber had struck at the Danish embassy in Islamabad, leaving six people dead.[60]

In London in February 2006, six hundred or so protesters marched from the Regent's Park Mosque to the Danish Embassy in Sloane Street where they shouted 'We love Osama bin Laden!' and waved inflammatory placards reading:

'Massacre those who insult Islam', 'Europe you will pay' and 'Europe you'll come crawling when Mujahideen come roaring'.

Our current target, whose long beard reached past his chest, had held a burning cross and also paraded his twenty-month-old daughter in an 'I-love-al-Qaeda' hat, proudly calling her 'the youngest member of al-Qaeda'. He waved banners vowing to 'Massacre those who insult Islam' and promising 'Europe, your 9/11 will come!' He called himself 'Abu Jihad', aka Holy War, as he was interviewed by ITV.

His real name was Ali Beheshti, forty years old and unemployed (although he had written 'pilot' as his occupation on his daughter's birth certificate). He lived with his family in a smart semi-detached house in Ilford, East London, and drove a Mitsubishi 4x4. His 28-year-old wife, Hannah, was the daughter of a sales consultant for an engineering firm who grew up in a smart home in a Bristol suburb.

Yes, we knew Ali pretty well. We'd been following him and two of his friends for a couple of weeks. The others were Abrar Mirza, a 23-year-old mobile phone salesman, and cab driver Abbas Taj, who was thirty, both from East London.

Their target was a small independent UK publisher, which had taken on a controversial book after American publishing giant Random House cancelled a £54,000 deal with the author, fearing a violent reaction by 'a small radical segment' of Muslims, according to, they said, 'credible and unrelated sources'.

It brought back the uproar following the publication of Salman Rushdie's novel *The Satanic Verses*, published twenty years earlier, which was interpreted by some Muslims as an attack on their faith. That also led to death threats, riots and the murder of the book's Japanese translator. Salman Rushdie himself had a lucky escape in 1989 after a bomb exploded prematurely in a London hotel, killing only the assassin.

The American writer was Sherry Jones, first-time author of

The Jewel of the Medina, described by critics as a tale of 'lust, love and intrigue in the Prophet's harem'. Its central character is A'isha, Mohammed's favourite wife. It tells of her marriage aged nine to Mohammed, who is much older, and how she copes as he takes another twelve wives and concubines.

While the basic facts were generally accepted, some critics argued that the novel 'misinterprets and falsifies sacred history' by adding imagined scenes. The most controversial of these was where the Prophet and his fourteen-year-old wife consummate their marriage.

Denise Spellberg, a professor of Islamic history at the University of Texas, who had been sent a proof copy of the book, was the first to take exception to this scene, labelling it a 'very ugly, stupid piece of work . . . you can't play with a sacred history and turn it into soft core pornography.'

Jones insisted that her book was respectful towards Islam. 'I have not dishonoured the Prophet,' she replied. 'I say: read the book, I wrote it with the intention of honouring him . . . [Spellberg] used the most inflammatory language . . . If you want to incite heated emotions from any religious group you just use the word "pornography" in the same sentence as their revered figures.'[61]

I think that Jones had a point. It was that kind of inflammatory language that got Salman Rushdie into so much trouble and meant that many did not read the *Satanic Verses* to judge for themselves – they simply accepted the interpretation of others.

Spellberg's criticisms were passed on to some students whose only action was to suggest peaceful and perfectly appropriate methods to deal with them – such as studying the book and bringing the most controversial parts to the attention of other Muslims, with the ultimate goal of getting an apology from the author.

Rushdie's book had been published even though both author and publisher had been threatened with death and even though Rushdie was forced into hiding for a decade. It was published across the world even though the book's Norwegian publisher was shot three times as he left his house one evening and after its Japanese translator was stabbed to death.

Random House America announced they were pulling out of their deal with Jones 'to postpone publication to the safety of the author, employees of Random House, booksellers and anyone else involved in distribution and sale'. This act alone, done without any threat being made, implied that Muslims were a violent people; that they would turn violent simply because they were upset by the book's content. It was this that drew the attention of extremists to the book.

Publisher Martin Rynja, who runs his company Gibson Square Books from the basement of his five-storey Georgian home, strongly disagreed with Random House's decision and had bravely taken on Jones's book. He said: 'In an open society, there has to be open access to literary works, regardless of fear.'[62]

Quite right too. Although having said that, UK law imposes a number of limitations on freedom of speech not found in other countries. Incitement to racial hatred and incitement to religious hatred are both crimes and, thanks to the Racial and Religious Hatred Act (2006) we were able to arrest and successfully prosecute some extremists.

For example, 23-year-old web designer Mizanur Rahman called for the killing of British troops outside the Danish embassy in the February 2006 protest.

'We want to see their blood running in the streets of Baghdad,' he told the protesters, before adding: 'Oh Allah, we want to see another 9/11 in Iraq, another 9/11 in Denmark, another 9/11 in Spain, in France, all over Europe.' He was filmed calling for troops to be brought back to the UK in body bags. He was also photographed holding placards that said: 'Annihilate those who insult Islam'. Found guilty of stirring up racial hatred and inciting murder, Rahman was sentenced to six years in prison (reduced to four years on appeal).[63]

'Now, I'm sure I'm not alone in spotting this,' George said after Rahman had been jailed, 'but this is quite possibly the greatest definition of irony I've ever encountered.'

'How's that?' I asked.

'Well, Rahman and others took offence at the cartoons of the Prophet Mohammed, right?'

'Yes, and?'

'Well, they wanted those cartoons banned, in other words restriction on freedom of expression, specifically to protect the culture of minority communities. We've now introduced those laws but they've been used to send *him* to jail for protesting against those cartoons!'

While Sherry Jones's book may have been seen as insulting by some Muslims, she certainly didn't intend to stir up religious hatred. She had written a fictional story based on historical fact; it was simply some imagined scenes that had caused offence among some members of the Muslim community. So far, although the threats to the publisher had been very real, they were limited to one or two extremist groups, and the book had not yet drawn much mainstream attention and criticism.

As far as I was concerned, by calling for the murder of those who insult Islam, Ali Beheshti had already broken the law.

Now, so we had been led to believe, he was planning to go even further than that. After following him for two weeks, during which time both Beheshti and Mirza carried out reconnaissance 'drive-throughs', we filmed him filling a green fuel can with diesel. He placed it inside a white plastic bag and put it in the boot of Abbas Taj's Honda Accord.

'Seems as though he's got arsonist tendencies,' Danny said, recalling the protest outside the embassy in which Beheshti had set fire to a cross, badly burning his hands in the process.

Beheshti's plan was to burn Martin Rynja's house down in the middle of the night while he slept. If it worked, it was quite possible that the smoke from the fire would suffocate the publisher in minutes.

On the night of 27 September, twenty years to the day since the publication of *The Satanic Verses*, the three men stayed a short time in the Regent's Park Mosque before leaving and driving down the Marylebone Road towards Islington, oblivious to the fact they were being closely followed.

Taj, the taxi driver, became the getaway driver for the night. He dropped Beheshti and Mirza close to the publisher's home before parking a couple of streets away, close to Highbury and Islington Underground station.

Beheshti and Mirza quickly found the publisher's house (Martin was already in police protection by this point). While Mirza kept watch, Beheshti took the can out of the plastic bag and started to pour the diesel through the letterbox before setting the liquid alight.

'STRIKE! STRIKE! STRIKE!'

Suddenly the road was full of screaming and shouting armed police. Beheshti and Mirza turned in shock and froze. At precisely the same moment, more armed officers surrounded Taj, pointing their MP5s directly at him, yelling at him to get out of the car. We had struck with overwhelming force. There was nowhere for them to run and the men quickly surrendered.

As soon as the armed officers had Beheshti and Mirza pinned up against a wall, a team of firemen, who'd been waiting around the corner, charged down the street towards the publisher's front door, which was now engulfed in flames. As thick black smoke poured into the street they smashed it down and had the fire out in a few seconds. Luckily, the damage was minimal and we made sure the door was quickly repaired.

Even though Mirza had tried to wipe his computer's hard drive a quick check told us he had been researching Gibson Square Books, including a Google Earth map search. We also found some charming photos of a smiling Beheshti posing with a gun and a large sword.

Taj's car had jihadist tape recordings in it, as well as mobile phones belonging to Mirza, which had been used to take photographs during their reconnaissance trips earlier that month.

When faced with the overwhelming evidence, Beheshti and Mirza both pleaded guilty. Taj tried to convince a jury that as he had not gone to the property in question, he didn't know what was about to happen. He failed.

They were all found guilty of intending to destroy or damage property with intent to endanger life, and 'being reckless as to whether the life of another would thereby be endangered'.[64]

Sadly, but understandably, as the very real threats continued – Borders books were told they would be firebombed if they sold The Jewel of Medina – Gibson Square Books decided not to publish the book.[65]

I hated the fact that these terrorists continued to abuse our right to freedom of speech – even after we'd caught these attackers and would have done so again and again in the name of freedom. I hoped it was for this reason at least that the threats died away after the attack.

The book wouldn't die, however, and it was eventually published in the United States by Beaufort Books (who quickly followed this with the sequel *The Sword of Medina*) and then in seven other countries – including Sweden.

As she sentenced the three men to four and a half years apiece, the judge, Mrs Justice Rafferty, told them: 'If you choose to live in this country, you live by its rules.'[66]

I couldn't have put it better myself.

TWENTY-SEVEN

GETTING THERMOBARIC

I walked into the office first thing on a Friday morning in June 2007 and prepared to resume my Captain Chaos mantle, ringing round everyone to check their status; officers in 1600, in observation posts, and to check in with my contact from the Security Service.

But as soon as my newspaper hit the desk my phone started to ring. Good grief, I haven't even taken off my coat yet, I thought.

I'd been on the Tube for twenty minutes with no phone signal; that can be a long time in our world. I picked up the receiver: 'Can I help you?' I asked wearily. As with many police departments we never automatically identify who we are.

'Harry, it's the DCI here,' a voice said, before adding his name.

Unusual I thought, but I let it roll over me.

'Hi, Boss, you OK?'

'How many people have you got available?'

I screwed up my eyes and started to decipher the Boards of Chaos, the one reliable source of information of what everyone was up to.

'Errrr . . .' I said as I put it together, just to let the DCI know I was getting there. I was thinking that I needed a shot of caffeine.

'Don't fuck around, Harry, I am sat on a live bomb here!'

OK, now I'm awake! 'Almost everybody,' I quickly replied.

'I'll ring you back.' Bang, the phone went down.

Oh God, I thought, here we go.

As I started to call everyone in, word came down that I was to cancel all of that day's surveillance. The situation was clearly developing and I had a feeling that this wouldn't be the only bomb we'd see that day.

At about 1.40 a.m. that morning, Andrew Shaw, an off-duty fireman, had been walking up the Haymarket, in London's West End. He stopped when saw a clear vapour coming from an empty green Mercedes parked outside the front entrance to the Tiger Tiger nightclub, which, being a Friday night, was packed with partying Londoners.

He tried the car door and was surprised to discover that it was open. A quilt was laid across the back seat. Shaw could smell gas and spotted a metal cylinder wedged between the two front seats. It was leaking, so he did what any self-respecting fireman would and yanked it out and turned off the valve.

It was then that he saw several kilograms of nails and other bits of shrapnel lying next to another cylinder in the footwell. He also saw two Nokia mobile phones with wires coming from them placed in front of the gear stick. He called the police.[67]

Thanks to the IRA, the simple car bomb has been a part of

British life longer than the Internet and as a result our bomb disposal squads are the best in the world and they were more than ready to deal with anything thrown at them.

The first question any bomb-disposal expert asks is: what kind of device is it? Is it timed, set off to explode at any moment? Is it a command-initiated device to be set off by radio control, or a victim-operated device – a booby trap?

The Haymarket bomb was command-initiated. The idea was that a call made to the mobile phones would lead to the detonation. In this case, the ringing circuit in each phone was wired to a light bulb, held in a syringe and surrounded by match heads.

The simple devices were intended to ignite the volatile vapours swirling inside the vehicle and explode the gas canisters followed by the 100 litres of petrol divided into four 25-litre canisters in the boot. Then there were the 2,000-odd nails that would act as shrapnel.

These bombs were rudimentary – with none of the dreaded biological, chemical or radioactive elements – not even any 'proper' explosives such as C4. Historically, terrorists have tended to favour pragmatism and economy over more sophisticated methods. The nails were a bit of a giveaway that these were first-time or amateur bomb builders. An exploding cloud would not project anything at its centre outwards at any great speed. Of course, what matters is not the technological complexity of a device but how many people it can kill – and this bomb could definitely have killed.

These were fuel–air explosive bombs – thermobaric bombs – designed to produce a huge fireball by igniting aerated liquid gasoline. Fuel–air bombs produce a blast wave of a significantly longer duration than those produced by traditional condensed explosives, increasing the number of casualties and causing more damage to structures. They're just about the most vicious weapon you can imagine – igniting the air, sucking the oxygen out of an enclosed area, and creating a massive pressure wave crushing anything unfortunate enough to have survived the initial blast. The American military used thermobaric bombs to clear acres of jungle in Vietnam and, ironically enough, the UK used thermobaric weapons in Afghanistan, in Hellfire missiles fired from Apache helicopters.

It seemed likely that there would be a second device. In 2002, bombers in Bali killed 200 night-clubbers and wounded hundreds more by detonating two separate devices, one to draw curious onlookers and a second that exploded in the midst of the assembled crowd.

A first explosion outside Tiger Tiger might well have drawn onlookers to the edge of a police cordon and into the range of the second potential car bomb. But where, if it existed, was it?

Finally, back at TT, the command came in: 'Prepare to deploy for three days.'

Right. I got the team together in the office and briefed them with what little I knew myself.

'I've no idea what's going on except all hell is about to break loose and we need to be ready. I can't say when we'll be going home. You need clothes for the next three days and food and drink for the next twenty-four hours. In the meantime, charge your phones, radios and batteries and pack everything. Fill the cars' tanks to the brim. When we get the call, there will be no time. I do *not* want to hear "Hang on, Harry, I've just go to do this, that and the other." So call home, let your family know you're going away and anyone who's not available for the next seventy-two hours should make themselves known now.'

Danny raised his hand. 'Can I go home and get me clobber?'

'No chance. Sorry, Danny. I know you're not far away but if you get stuck in traffic or the Tube then you're no use to me.' Grinning, I added, 'We'll go to Tesco round the corner. At long last you'll be able to join me and dress in the finest clothes Tesco has to offer.'

Danny pulled a face but accepted his fate.

After stocking up in Tesco, filling the cars with petrol and loading the boot we sat and waited.

Frustration soon started to set in. We were one reactive missile waiting for the intelligence to catch up with our suspects. As soon as the intelligence came up with a location, then we'd be launched after them.

The time dragged on and on and we sat in front of Sky News, watching out for any developments, but it was recycling the same headlines over and over. What were we waiting for? I wondered. Where were the bombers? On TV terrorism experts came and went. 'Car bombs are cheap and simple to make and easy to hide,' said one. 'You can buy books on Amazon that tell you how to make a car bomb.'

Danny performed a search of Amazon. 'He may be right about car bombs being cheap but I can't find anything on Amazon.'

'Car bombs,' the expert continued, 'really are the terrorist weapon of choice in terms of sheer brutality and destructive reach.'

We found the second device, thanks once again to public vigilance. A car bomb had been illegally parked in Cockspur

Street, just around the corner from the southern end of the Haymarket, on the edge of Trafalgar Square, and had been quickly clamped and towed. It was now in an underground car park in Park Lane. The clampers had heard about the first bomb on the news and called the cops when they checked the cars they'd picked up that night and spotted the metal canisters inside the Mercedes.[68]

Still we waited. At 10 p.m., I curled up in a ball on the floor at the back of the office, pulled my hood over my head and tried to sleep. The former army boys always advised me to 'Eat and sleep when you can, for you never know when you'll be able to do so again.' I suggested that the others try to do the same, but I couldn't sleep; I found myself listening to Danny's, Raj's and George's banter. I was too full of excitement, anxiousness and frustration.

Finally, at 11 p.m. we were sent home. I allocated the police cars to those I'd call out first (including myself) and we headed off, our adrenaline all but gone.

I awoke at the crack of dawn and prowled around the house like a caged lion. I suspected that the rest of the squad were doing exactly the same thing. My bag was packed and sat ready by the front door. I checked and rechecked it.

So much of this job is about waiting. Far too much, I thought. I couldn't distract myself and spent the rest of the morning walking round the kitchen table and staring at the phone, while my family tried their best to get on with their lives with me there – but not there.

It was tough on my wife and the kids but they also knew that scenes like this came with the territory. They'd seen the news and had naturally put two and two together. The job put them under a lot of pressure as well as me. So many families have been destroyed by the job; I've been to loads of police weddings and commiserated with many a bride or groom months or years later, once the job had taken its toll.

The Stockwell tragedy was still fresh in everyone's mind. This was an almost identical situation to 21/7 – bombers on the run after a failed attack, every resource at the Met's disposal activated to track them down before they struck again.

I was lost in thought about all of this when the phone finally rang. I nearly jumped out of my skin.

TWENTY-EIGHT

BLUE LIGHTS TO SCOTLAND

'Things are happening, Harry,' the DCI said. 'Muster your team at TT and stand by.'

Excellent. This meant the investigation was going somewhere at last. I rang Asad and Danny first; my two very trusted lieutenants. Like me, they were licensed to carry firearms and had their 9mm Glocks stored in New Scotland Yard's armoury. They both picked up the phone on the first ring. All I needed to tell them was 'Get your arses in and wait', and they were on their way.

I quickly rang round the others, some of whom weren't licensed to carry, and told them to start making their way in. I had complete confidence in them all. It was a fantastic team to be a part of and now we were being assembled for what could be our most important mission yet.

That done, I started to march out of the house. Oh crap. I'd forgotten something. I remembered the police officers who were caught up in the Madrid bombers' booby trap; one of them hadn't made it back home. I headed back in to my family and hugged, kissed and told them I loved them, an all-too-brief and precious moment.

And then I was gone.

The investigation was still in the frantic stage, but SO15 was closing in on the bombers. At that time, I wasn't being given updates on the intelligence. Mobiles aren't considered a secure form of communication, so we rarely share operational details this way.

Then, just as I entered North London, my mobile went. It was the DCI. I pulled over in a lay-by to take the call.

It was a brief conversation, the essence of which was: 'Take your team and blue light it to Scotland.' Still in the lay-by, I quickly called the rest of the team with the update. I then affixed a new improved version of our blue light on the roof, hit the horn button to activate the sirens and gunned the V6 turbo-charged engine towards TT.

The busy roads were greasy with drizzle, making the drive more hazardous, but I still made good time to TT. A fantastic sight greeted me as I entered the office. The lads had laid out all our equipment on the desks in a line and briefed me as to what they thought we should take. Their military training had taught them to do this and I was delighted, they really were a supervisor's dream. The whole team was packed and ready to go minutes later.

Finally, we were on the warpath. Although all I knew was that we were going to Scotland, it was clear the hunt was on. That Saturday, despite very heavy traffic, the public quickly melted before our blue-lit unmarked cars. They knew who we were and who we were after.

I so wanted to blast up the outside lane of the M1 at 140 mph, but I needed to keep the slower vehicles with me and held us at 100 mph. So, still not knowing where in Scotland we were headed, the news radio on, each of us with our own thoughts, for the moment at least, wondering what awaited us.

What to make of it all so far? We were in familiar territory: home-made bombs, near misses, extremists targeting innocent people. But the car bomb was a new development. Was that influenced by Iraq? Car bombs in that troubled country had really taken off in recent months. They might also have been influenced by the IRA – the undisputed masters of the car bomb.

On the other hand, it might be a completely closed-off cell, a self-start-up group inspired by rhetoric posted online. After all, bomb-makers no longer need to travel to Afghanistan, Pakistan or Iraq to learn their trade; they don't even have to meet a bomb-maker. It's possible to obtain bomb blueprints and network with like-minded jihadists over the Internet.

No one is safe from a car bomb. They're unstoppable and impossible to detect – needles in a writhing haystack of vehicles. They're also cheap and simple to make. While our greatest fears may be of dirty bomb and chemical weapon attacks, the car bomb and IED are the terrorist's most effective option, as our brave soldiers are learning to their cost in Iraq and Afghanistan.

I hoped this wasn't a sign of things to come. I recalled the IRA's car-bombing campaign in the early to mid-nineties. Their truck bomb attack in 1993 in Bishopsgate, which had ripped apart the heart of the financial district of the City of London, caused a billion pounds' worth of damage, killed one and injured forty. The casualties were so low because the bombers struck on a Sunday when the City was deserted. The bombing created a financial crisis for insurers, particularly Lloyds of London. There are some who believe that it was this new approach of the IRA, one intended to affect the economic health of the country, that persuaded the British government to sit round the table with the terrorists.

The Haymarket bombers had set out to kill as many as possible and although they'd failed in that respect, they'd managed to create fear and tension and had got themselves a whole heap of attention.

As we travelled north we spotted a few familiar cars from other departments and when we stopped for petrol in a service station, as we raced in and out, we met some 'friends and acquaintances' heading the same way as us. As usual in these situations, it was all calm, quiet and hurried professionalism.

We pushed the cars as hard as we dared. Not much further now.

TWENTY-NINE

GATE CRASHERS

The dark-green Jeep Cherokee bypassed Glasgow Airport's high-tech numberplate-recognition system with the greatest of ease. The system activates a barrier at the entrance to the inside lane around the airport. Only taxis and buses with registered numbers are allowed through. When the Jeep pulled up, however, it simply tailgated behind a registered car and sped through before the barrier closed.

Airport baggage handler John Smeaton was having a cigarette break when he saw the Jeep hurtling towards the airport doors, flames spewing from its chassis. It crashed into the concrete bollards and came to a halt just shy of the airport doors. As the flames grew, and as two men climbed out of the burning vehicle, Smeaton ran towards them, determined to do something.

He wasn't the only one; airport police were already running towards the vehicle, one carrying a fire extinguisher. Constable Stewart Ferguson, forty, was off duty and had been talking to father of two Sergeant Torquil Campbell when they heard the crash.

As they ran around the corner to get to the scene, horrified witnesses watched the driver climb out, pour petrol over his head and set himself alight. As the flames enveloped his body, Ferguson, who had grabbed a fire extinguisher, sprinted towards him, spraying as he went.

Campbell, meanwhile, was wrestling with the passenger, who was trying to stop them from reaching the burning car. As soon as the burning man had been extinguished, Ferguson aimed the extinguisher into the man's eyes to disorientate him.

The police officers knew this was a terrorist attack and could hear cracking and popping coming from the jeep. Was a bomb about to explode? Were the fuel tanks about to go? As airport staff arrived to help they got the man under control and quickly cleared the immediate area.

'They were just waiting for death,' Campbell said afterwards. 'The fact that they were still alive perplexed them a little bit and they didn't know what to do.'[69]

The burning man was rushed to the Royal Alexandra Hospital in Paisley where doctors discovered he was wearing a suspect device – thought to be a suicide belt of explosives. The casualty ward was quickly evacuated and not long after a brave policeman made the decision to remove the belt and sprinted from the hospital before throwing it into the middle of a nearby cricket pitch.

We were too late. We listened, horrified, as the news came in of an attack on Glasgow Airport. While we were delighted to hear that the suspects had been caught and that the only serious injury was to one of the bombers, we were gutted that we had been too late to prevent the attack.

Our journey north started to drag as intelligence reached us that there were no targets for us to work on. Scottish police had secured the scene at the airport and we knew our bosses would now be busy trying to wrestle the investigation off them.

As we settled down, my phone went. The team raised their eyebrows in hopeful expectation but it was more disappointment for us. The bomb factory had been found, but there were no further members of the cell for us to follow.

'That doesn't mean you can drink though. We stay teetotal until we're back in London.' I didn't want anyone having to step forward in embarrassment if the job broke in the small hours. But in my heart I knew it was over, and while I was of course delighted that we had the men in custody with no serious injury to any member of the public, I couldn't help but feel pissed off that all our efforts had been in vain.

Again we waited and waited. Playing cards, swimming, playing cards. We called other teams and much banter ensued about the quality of each other's accommodation.

After another twenty-four hours we were formally stood down for the evening and given the green light to 'Have a few beers, but don't go over the top.' This was good advice. There was the story about the county surveillance team who had been released during Operation Overt. Off they went to enjoy a night out in London. Halfway through their session they got the call. Can you come back? 'Shorry,' came the response, 'it'sh too late.' Not their fault, but there was no way I was going to risk putting my team in that position.

In the end there were no further developments. We were disappointed but as Danny said miserably when I gave him the news: 'It ain't like the movies, is it?'

Two young, highly educated professionals had put the

devices together but lady luck was not with them that weekend. The bomb disposal experts found that one of the devices left in central London failed to explode thanks to a loose wire in the mobile phone detonator while the other failed to detonate because there wasn't enough oxygen in the car.[70]

Unless you can arrest the terrorists before they get to execution stage, your chances of averting bloodshed and death simply come down to luck and London had had a very lucky escape indeed.

One of the terrorists, 28-year-old Kafeel Ahmed, died from the 90 per cent burns he received in the Glasgow attack. British-born Bilal Talal Samad Abdullah, twenty-six, of Iraqi descent, was found guilty of conspiracy to murder. He was sentenced to life imprisonment with a minimum term of thirty-two years in jail.

It was reported that Abdullah was motivated by avenging the death of a friend killed in the Iraq War by a Shia death squad, hatred against the West over Palestine, and that he had been radicalized by the teachings of al-Qaeda and Abu Musab al-Zarqawi, a militant Islamist from Jordan.

Al-Zarqawi, who was a leading insurgent in Iraq, was responsible for the organization of numerous beheadings, bombings and suicide attacks aimed at US soldiers until the US Air Force dropped a bomb on his safe house in June 2006.

During his own testimony, Abdullah said his motivation had been triggered by the destruction of Iraq, first through economic and medical sanctions, the rise in childhood leukaemia, which he blamed on depleted-uranium armour-piercing shells used in the 1991 Gulf War, and for the destruction of Iraq's infrastructure during the American and British 2003 invasion of Iraq.

The son of two doctors, Kafeel Ahmed was an Indian Muslim born in Bangalore, India, and raised in Saudi Arabia. Before he left his native Bangalore for the UK, he entrusted his mother with a compact disc he said contained some important information on his 'project'. Analysis of the disc revealed that it contained speeches by Osama bin Laden, propaganda against the United States and Britain, some jihadist literature and material on the plight of Muslims in Iraq, Afghanistan and Chechnya. There were also graphic depictions of actual torture in Chechnya, hundreds of bomb designs downloaded from the Internet as well as evidence that he used the Bangalore-based political platform Discover Islam for the purposes of terrorist recruitment.[71]

Much was made in the media about the fact that these men were highly educated; Ahmed was an engineer studying for a PhD in computational fluid dynamics while Abdullah was a doctor working for the NHS in Scotland. Not typical terrorists, they argued. But it shouldn't really be all that surprising. After all, Osama bin Laden's top deputy, Ayman al-Zawahiri, is a doctor. Computer-science student Omar Khyam was convicted for a 2004 plot to blow up a London nightclub and a shopping mall with fertilizer bombs. Khalid Sheikh Mohammed, who planned 9/11 and other attacks, has a degree in mechanical engineering. And London's universities were always providing us with a stream of intelligent and highly qualified terrorist suspects.

For me, the amazing and truly wonderful thing about the Haymarket bombings was the fact that although luck played a significant part, the bombers were also defeated by the good old British public. The first bomb was found and reported by an off-duty fireman and the first 999 call came from a passing ambulance crew who noticed vapour coming from the car. The second bomb had been reported by the team that had clamped it.

When the men attacked Glasgow Airport, John Smeaton piled in without question, saying later, in his distinct Glaswegian accent: 'Me and other folk were just tryin' tae get the boot in and some other guy banjoed [punched] him.' He had this warning for future terrorists: 'You're nae hitting the polis [police], mate, there's nae chance . . . Glasgow does nae accept this; if you come tae Glasgow, we'll set about ye.'

That's the spirit, old boy.

He was later quoted (some TV channels felt obliged to run subtitles during his interviews) as saying: 'I'm just an ordinary guy – I like my Xbox 360, trout fishing – and all I did was what anyone else would do. An airport worker has an obligation to the public. It wasn't really a choice. I don't understand some of these responses. As far as I'm concerned a human being is just a human being.'

It perhaps wasn't surprising that Smeaton was turned into a bit of a cult hero, with tribute websites set up in his name.[72] The people of Britain are proud of the fact that we won't sit idly by when under attack, and rightly so.

And of course there was the bravery of the policemen and women closest to the scenes, the PCs that had been on foot patrol who started to move the public away from the bombs, the policeman who fully believed he was risking his life to save others by removing the 'suicide belt' from the hospital and taking it to a place of safety (it was later found to be harmless). The public and the front-line emergency service workers defeated the terrorists after they'd slipped under our radar. So, while it had been a desperately frustrating mission for the SST, I took great heart from this.

The last word went (as usual) to Danny. We were driving back to London, tired and fed up, when a grin started to appear on his face. Soon he was shaking with laughter.

'All right,' George said finally, 'I'll bite. What is it, Danny?'

'If those bombers were after seventy-two virgins,' he said, 'then why did they go to Glasgow?'

THIRTY

FAREWELL, SPECIAL BRANCH

Khost is just across the border from North Waziristan, the lawless Pakistani tribal area from where al-Qaeda and the Taliban routinely launch attacks on NATO positions in Afghanistan.[73] It is home to Forward Operating Base Chapman, one of the most secretive and highly guarded locations in Afghanistan. In recent years it had evolved into a major counter-terrorism hub of the CIA's paramilitary Special Activities Division, used for joint operation with Special Forces and Afghan allies, and was a housing compound for American intelligence officers. It was where the CIA received intel about the location of al-Qaeda leaders and passed the coordinates on to the drone pilots.

On the late afternoon of 30 December 2009, one of the CIA's double agents, a Jordanian man, arrived at the base by car, having been driven from the Pakistani border. He was admitted through the multiple layers of security to meet with the CIA's base chief, along with several CIA officers and his handler, Al Shareef Ali bin Zeid, from Jordan's General

Intelligence department, who also happened to be first cousin to King Abdullah II of Jordan.

The CIA had come to trust the agent, and the Jordanian spy agency vouched for him. He had already provided useful intelligence over several weeks of undercover work in the region and he was seen as the agency's best hope of tracking down the al-Qaeda leadership.

On this occasion he was about to deliver intelligence relating to the location of al-Qaeda leader Ayman al-Zawahiri. The CIA considered that this would be one of the most important meetings with an agent since they'd been in Afghanistan. They'd even flown in a special debriefer from Kabul and were planning to call President Obama as soon as the meeting was over.

As the men and women gathered to meet the informant, he detonated a bomb, which had been hidden under his clothing, killing nine and seriously wounding six others. The chief of the base and his Jordanian handler were among them.[74]

Tragically, the security director of the base, an Afghan named Arghawan, survived the blast but was shot in the head by an American soldier who assumed he was part of the bomb plot. The attack was the worst committed against the CIA for twenty-five years and it effectively shut the base.

On 9 January 2010, a Pakistani television network showed a video that had been released by the Tehrik-i-Taliban. It showed the Khost suicide bomber – the supposed CIA double agent – a man called Humam Khalil Abu-Mulal al-Balawi, vowing to avenge the death of Baitullah Mehsud: 'We will never forget the blood of our emir, Baitullah Mehsud. We will always demand revenge for him inside America and outside,' he said. Sitting next to him was Hakimullah Mehsud, the man who replaced Baitullah Mehsud as the chief of the Tehrik-i-Taliban (they were from the same tribe, but not the same family).[75]

Humam Khalil Abu-Mulal al-Balawi, thirty-two, was a doctor and an al-Qaeda sympathizer from the town of Zarqa, the hometown of Jordanian Abu Musab al-Zarqawi. He was married and had two daughters. Jordanian intelligence had recruited him more than a year ago because of his strong links with extremist groups. It was thought that he had been successfully turned into a double agent loyal to the United States and to Jordan. Al-Balawi was told that if he travelled to Pakistan and infiltrated radical groups there his slate would be wiped clean and his family left alone. The CIA took over the management of al-Balawi from the Jordanians sometime in the second half of 2009.[76]

This was an incredibly sophisticated attack in which al-Qaeda, in an effort to fool the Americans, had sacrificed several of its warriors to the drones so that the CIA would trust al-Balawi. Indeed, according to US officials, Forward Operating Base Chapman implemented less stringent security measures than other military bases to help build trust with informants. Al-Balawi wasn't searched because of his high worth and because they saw him as a friend.

The Taliban and al-Qaeda in Pakistan and Afghanistan remain as hard to find as ever. The terrorists and the CIA appear to be locked intractably in a constant war in which the most valuable weapon, apart from the Hellfire missile and the suicide bomber, is intelligence.

The problem is that although the drones can seriously disrupt the Taliban and al-Qaeda by taking out a leader, there remains no shortage of volunteers to step forward to replace them. It's like trying to kill bees one by one without destroying the hive. Al-Qaeda's hives, particularly in Waziristan, are so well established that it doesn't seem likely that they'll ever be taken out.

Under pressure from the United States, Pakistan waged a major offensive in Waziristan at the end of 2009. Their methods were far more haphazard than the Americans had hoped, however, and the army ended up displacing hundreds of thousands of people as well as destroying thousands of homes, schools and offices. Although billions of dollars has been put aside to rebuild the area, much remains to be done and accusations of corruption and mismanagement abound. Although the Taliban and al-Qaeda were successfully evicted, they're now able to recruit from those who have been displaced.

Al-Qaeda continues to exact terrible vengeance on anyone who dares side with the government. Despite the offensive, beheaded bodies still regularly turn up in public places in Waziristan, with notes identifying them as ISI or CIA spies.

I'm not saying that what we're trying to do in places like Afghanistan and Iraq is wrong. Our armed forces are doing an amazing job in very difficult circumstances and battles are being won as well as hearts and minds. The problem is of course that peace is never going to be achieved easily and, as we've seen, it only takes a few hundred terrorists to bring a country to the brink. We can stabilize the region and must do so for our own safety here in the UK.

One thing remains clear: the 'new' terrorism we've seen since 2001 is not going to stop anytime soon. There's no shortage of new recruits, and here in the UK, as one of the principal allies in the 'War on Terror', we can expect to see many more young terrorists turning up in our cities, determined to wreak havoc on the West, for some time to come.

'OW!' I rubbed my head. Being six foot five does have its disadvantages, especially when you're on board a warship with low doorways. It was also bobbing up and down on the Thames – oh yes, and being a bit drunk didn't help either; it made it very easy to miss the 'Mind Your Head' signs.

I staggered out onto deck and into the evening sunshine. I was on HMS *Belfast*, one of London's great institutions and most popular tourist attractions. After having taken part in some of the Second World War's greatest missions, from Operation Overlord to the Battle of the North Cape, she's sat unmoving in her moorings on the Thames since 1971.

I could hardly believe how long it was since I'd walked through the doors of Tintagel House as one of the last ever Special Branch officers. Where had the time gone? Days like today had been all too few over the past two months, it was a rare occasion to take stock and reflect on all that S-squad had seen and done, from hunting assassins, suicide bombers, radical students and mysterious foreign agents – as well as sitting in cars and vans for days on end.

I'd learned so much and had changed as an officer and a person. I felt I now understood our enemies and I was well-versed in the complicated world that Special Branch – which had finally just been absorbed into SO15 – operated in. I knew I still had a great deal to learn but I now felt 100 per cent confident I was in the right job.

Next to me Theresa was, like nearly everyone else of the hundred-plus people on board, wearing the good old Special Branch tie.

'All right, Harry?' she said, handing me another glass of red wine.

It was a gorgeous summer's evening. 'Yeah, not bad, thanks,' I said, still rubbing my head. 'I'm going to be sorry to see Terry go, though.'

'He never struck me as the retiring kind.'

I shrugged. Roaring laughter came from above and we looked up. The upper deck was packed full of happy cops. 'Already?' Theresa said. 'They only opened the bar an hour ago.'

There were very few people who hadn't responded to the invitation; those that couldn't attend were operational or, like the wonderful DC who wore flip-flops to the Cabinet Office, out of the country.

Jenny and Raj were deep in conversation and I could see Danny talking to a detective inspector who'd just turned very red in the face. No doubt Danny had just come out with yet another corker that would have ended anyone else's career.

When Terry turned up a few minutes later, almost everyone was well-oiled and he got a much-deserved rapturous welcome as the crowd erupted into spontaneous applause, whistles and cheers.

Ten minutes after that, I'd grown a good-sized bump on my head but, being on my fifth glass of wine, I wasn't going to feel it for some time yet.

Someone tapped my shoulder and I turned to see Terry beaming back at me. He grabbed my hand and shook it firmly. He didn't let go.

'That was very funny the other day,' he said with a chuckle, 'I didn't find it until I was on the packed train home and when I read it I couldn't stop laughing. In fact I don't think I've ever laughed so much in all the years I've travelled to work on that train.'

What on earth was he talking about? I stared at him in bewilderment and after a couple of seconds it was clear to me that I wasn't going to be able to laugh this one off, so I decided to confess.

'Terry, I'm so sorry but I haven't got a clue what you're talking about.'

'Why, what you wrote about me in the book, of course.'

Aha, the fog finally cleared. Along with the rest of the SST, I'd taken Terry out for a farewell lunch. He'd brought a book with him that he was planning to read at his seaside retreat that weekend.

After a few glasses of wine, I decided that it would be a good idea to write a message inside, pretending it was from someone else. I'd written: 'I'm delighted to learn that you're retiring. Things will be much easier now. All the best, Osama bin Laden.'

Perhaps it wasn't in exactly the best taste but the sentiment was right. Terry was a real one of a kind and one of the very last true Special Branch officers. This was my way of telling him as much.

'Harry, I don't think I'm going to be missed *that* much,' Terry told me, 'but the thought is much appreciated. We've got a fine squad of young and experienced officers and they're more than capable of running things without me shouting at them every five minutes.'

'Thanks, Terry,' I said, recalling our first-ever meeting. 'I think what I should have written in that book was "*Regnum Defende et Servo Populus*".'

★

Towards the end of the evening, I moved away from the main crowd and strolled to the stern. I just managed to catch the last traces of a gorgeous multi-coloured sunset that bathed London in a soft warm pink light. It was truly amazing. The city was as busy as ever: cars, buses, taxis and pedestrians hurried across the bridges, every available outdoor chair and table of the nearby riverside bars was occupied with people living their lives to the full.

To think there are people out there who want to blow up that cafe, bus or street and kill those people – well, it's all the motivation we need to never tire of what we do. I'm so happy to be in the position I am so that I can be part of the team that stops that from happening.

I turned and looked back across the rest of the boat. It was packed full of men and women who stood in the terrorists' way. I was pleased to see that the 'jingle-janglers' had faded with the creation of SO15; now (apart from the SB ties, which were just for tonight) you couldn't tell anyone apart. We were all part of the Counter Terrorism Command and all of us would do anything to stop the extremists from succeeding. Then there were all the international agencies across the world with which we shared total cooperation. Add to that the will-ingness of the public to help us in the fight and I think then, as long as we stay alert, we will, in the long run, always defeat those who want to destroy us.

To an extent, we already had. There hadn't been one suc-cessful attack in the UK during the past year – although the terrorists had come close. A huge part of that success was down to the public, through people who'd called Crimestop-pers, people who'd allowed us to invade their homes with little explanation, people who'd appeared as witnesses and those brave souls who'd literally tackled the terrorists head-on.

I remembered after 7/7 the reaction of many people travelling the following day, myself among them. The proud defiance; the refusal to concede anything to the terrorists. London is the greatest city in the world and its citizens, who are from every corner of the globe, had done it proud.

As we know, Muslims were also murdered on 7/7. This is why we have to devote so much time and effort to supporting the Muslim community, a community that understandably has an ever-expanding list of perceived grievances, whether on British foreign policy, social and economic exclusion, or Islamophobia in the media and wider society.

Many feel alienated by the new anti-terrorist legislation, which is seen by some as having a disproportionate impact on Muslim communities. This can soon translate into a debilitating sense of victimhood, which is something that we still have to break. This task should not be left to the police alone. The responsibility belongs to us all. The threat to our nation remains grave and we desperately need the tools to prevent those who would kill any of us from doing so.

Terry was starting to say his goodbyes. It would take him another couple of hours at least; everybody wanted to shake his hand. He stopped for a long chat with the SST and roared with laughter at something Asad told him. He really was a legend, the man from the Branch who epitomized the essence of that famous department – a quintessential no-nonsense English gentleman.

Once Terry stepped off the ship and disappeared into the sunset, well that really would be the end of Special Branch. We were part of something else now, a new counter-terrorist force for the twenty-first century. Of course, the unrelenting fight against terror would continue with exactly the same unstoppable determination tomorrow morning.

REFERENCES

2. INTO THE WORLD OF SECRETS

1. Info about Special Branch departments can be found here: www.met.police.uk/foi/pdfs/other.../so12_introduction.pdf
2. For more about the creation of SO15, see p.96 of *The British War on Terror*, by Steve Hewitt, Continuum Books, 2008. See also pp.115–16, 322 of *The Terrorist Hunters*, by Andy Hayman, Bantam Press, 2009.

6. LITTLE BRITAIN

3. *The Predator War: What are the risks of the C.I.A.'s covert drone program?* by Jane Mayer, *New Yorker*, 26 Oct 2009.
http://www.newyorker.com/reporting/2009/10/26/091026fa_fact_mayer#ixzz0nJtjmVLu
4. For more on Rashid Rauf see: *Profile: Rashid Rauf: The mysterious adult life of a Birmingham baker's boy turned alleged al-Qaida terrorist*, by Ian Cobain and Matthew Weaver, *Guardian* 22 Nov 2008.
http://www.guardian.co.uk/world/2008/nov/22/rashid-rauf-profile

Rashid Rauf: the al-Qaida suspect caught, tortured and lost, by Ian Cobain and Richard Norton-Taylor, *Guardian*, 8 Sep 2009.

http://www.guardian.co.uk/uk/2009/sep/08/rashid-rauf-terrorism-torture-pakistan

Rashid Rauf: profile of a terror mastermind, by Andrew Alderson, *Daily Telegraph*, 22 Nov 2008.

http://www.telegraph.co.uk/news/worldnews/asia/pakistan/3500661/Rashid-Rauf-profile-of-a-terror-mastermind.html

Hunt for Rashid Rauf that ended with hellfire: A British terror suspect was killed by US forces in Pakistan yesterday. MPs want to know: did they tell Britain first?, *Sunday Times*, 23 Nov 2008.

http://www.timesonline.co.uk/tol/news/world/asia/article5213595.ece

5. *Profile: Omar Saeed Sheikh*, BBC News, 16 July 2002.
http://news.bbc.co.uk/1/hi/uk/1804710.stm

Omar Sheikh: The path from public school in London to Pakistan's death row, by Simon Jeffery, *Guardian*, 15 July 2002.
http://www.guardian.co.uk/world/2002/jul/15/pakistan.simonjeffery

7. WHAT TERRORISTS REALLY TALK ABOUT

6. *'Millennium bomber' gets 22 years*, BBC News, 27 July 2005.
http://news.bbc.co.uk/1/hi/world/americas/4722409.stm

The Terrorist Within, Chapter 11: The Ticking Bomb; Terrorist-training-camp graduate Ahmed Ressam turns to untrained friends for help in his plan to bomb the L.A. airport, *Seattle Times*, 1 July 2002.

'Foiling millennium attack was mostly luck', Lisa Myers, NBC

News Senior investigative correspondent, MSNBC, 29 April 2004.

http://www.msnbc.msn.com/id/4864792/

8. SPRINGING THE TRAP

7. *U.S.-born militant who fought for Al Qaeda is in custody*, by Sebastian Rotella and Josh Meyer, *Los Angeles Times*, 22 July 2009.

8. *Airline bomb plot: investigation 'one of biggest since WW2'*, by Duncan Gardham, Security Correspondent, *Daily Telegraph*, 8 Sep 2009.

http://www.telegraph.co.uk/news/uknews/terrorism-in-the-uk/6152185/Airline-bomb-plot-investigation-one-of-biggest-since-WW2.html

BBC News online Liquid bomb plot: What happened, 7 Sep 2009.

http://news.bbc.co.uk/1/hi/uk/8242479.stm

9. *Mass murder at 30,000 feet: Islamic extremists guilty of airline bomb plot*, *The Times*, 7 Sep 2009.

http://www.timesonline.co.uk/tol/news/uk/crime/article6824884.ece

Liquid bomb plot: three guilty of murder conspiracy, by Vikram Dodd, *Guardian*, 9 Sep 2008.

http://www.guardian.co.uk/uk/2008/sep/09/3

10. *Rashid Rauf: the al-Qaida suspect caught, tortured and lost*, by Ian Cobain and Richard Norton-Taylor, 8 Sep 2009.

http://www.guardian.co.uk/uk/2009/sep/08/rashid-rauf-terrorism-torture-pakistan

11. *Airstrike Kills Qaeda-Linked Militant in Pakistan*, *New York Times*, 23 Nov 2008.

10. DAYS OF THE JACKALS

12. *Contract killings in Australia: Research and public policy series no. 53*, by Jenny Mouzos and John Venditto. Canberra: Australian Institute of Criminology, June 2003.

13. Statistical Bulletin Criminal Justice Series CrJ/2003/9 Homicide in Scotland, 2002. See *Victims of homicide (1), by main motive and sex of main accused*, 1993–2002 Table 13. http://www.scotland.gov.uk/Publications/2003/11/18570/29572

14. *'Secret squad' tracks hitmen*, BBC News, 17 Sep 2003. *http://news.bbc.co.uk/1/hi/england/london/3117734.stm*

12. CLASSIFIED LOSSES

15. *A young American's journey into Al Qaeda; Bryant Neal Vinas of Long Island, N.Y., tells investigators how he trained and fought alongside terrorists*, by Sebastian Rotella and Josh Meyer, *Los Angeles Times*, 24 July 2009.
http://articles.latimes.com/2009/jul/24/nation/na-american-jihadi24. Retrieved 26 February 2010.

16. *Can Bin Laden Be Caught?* by Elaine Shannon, *Time* magazine, 22 Jan 2006.
http://www.time.com/time/magazine/article/0,9171,1151782-2,00.html#ixzz0nEpOiWpm

17. *Bryant Neal Vinas: An American in Al Qaeda*, by Claire Suddath, *Time* magazine, 24 July 2009.
http://www.time.com/time/nation/article/0,8599,1912512,00.html

18. *British intelligence cracks trans-Atlantic terrorist network*, by Duncan Gardham, *Daily Telegraph*, 9 Nov 2009.

http://www.telegraph.co.uk/news/uknews/6533021/British-intelligence-cracks-trans-Atlantic-terrorist-network.html

19. *GCHQ staff lost 35 laptop computers, report says*, by Richard Norton-Taylor, *Guardian*, March 2010.
www.guardian.co.uk/uk/.../gchq-mislaid-laptop-computers-report

20. *Police probe theft of MoD laptop*, BBC News, 19 Jan 2008
news.bbc.co.uk/2/hi/7197045.stm
http://www.independent.co.uk/news/uk/politics/exclusive-new-batch-of-terror-files-left-on-train-847451.html

21. *We've had 658 laptops stolen, MoD confesses*, *Daily Mail*, 18 July 2008.

22. *Cappuccino with an extra shot, please*, by Anthony France and Graeme Wilson, *Sun*, 4 Sep 2008.
http://www.thesun.co.uk/sol/homepage/news/article1645908.ece#ixzz0nFxIwm5B

23. *Security leak by senior Scotland Yard commander Bob Quick prompts arrests in suspected al-Qaida plot*, by Owen Bowcott and Vikram Dodd, *Guardian*, 8 April 2009 http://www.guardian.co.uk/politics/2009/apr/08/terror-raids-bob-quick-leak-met-police.

24. *Terror raids follow files blunder*, BBC News, 8 April 2009.
http://news.bbc.co.uk/1/hi/uk/7990719.stm.
Terror blunder: Met anti-terror chief's mistake, *Daily Telegraph*, 9 April 2009.
http://www.telegraph.co.uk/news/newstopics/politics/lawandorder/5127953/Terror-blunder-Met-anti-terror-chiefs-mistake.html.

25. *Police chief Bob Quick steps down over terror blunder*, *Guardian*, 9 April 2009.

http://www.guardian.co.uk/uk/2009/apr/09/bob-quick-terror-raids-leak. Retrieved 2009-04-11.

Police chief quits over blunder, BBC News, 9 April 2009. http://news.bbc.co.uk/1/hi/uk/7991307.stm.

14. DEBATES WITH A DIFFERENCE

26. *Freedom of thought is all we foment*, by Malcolm Grant, *The Times Higher Education Supplement*, 31 Dec 2009.
27. *BBC News – Profile: Umar Farouk Abdulmutallab*, 28 Dec 2009. news.bbc.co.uk/2/hi/8431530.stm
28. *How UCL Authorities Ignored Islamist Extremism, Proof of UCL President's systematic failure to tackle campus radicals*, by CSC Director Douglas Murray, The Centre for Social Cohesion, Press Briefing Pack, 5 Jan 2010.
29. *Profile: Jawad Akbar*, BBC News, 30 Apr 2007. news.bbc.co.uk/2/hi/uk_news/6149788.stm
    Man jailed over terror blueprints, BBC News, 17 July 2007. news.bbc.co.uk/2/hi/uk_news/6268934.stm
30. *Extremists target students claim*, BBC News, 16 Sep 2005. http://news.bbc.co.uk/1/hi/education/4252506.stm

15. TEENIE TERRORISTS

31. *Aabid Khan and his global jihad*, BBC News, 18 Aug 2008. news.bbc.co.uk/2/hi/uk_news/7549447.stm
32. *Anatomy of a Modern Homegrown Terror Cell: Aabid Khan et al.*, by Evan F. Kohlman, NEFA Senior Investigator September 2008
    http://www.globalterroralert.com/publications/501-anatomy-of-a-modern-homegrown-terror-cell.html

33. *'Model' pupil secretly studied ways of wiping out non-Muslims*, *Yorkshire Post*, 18 Aug 2008.
http://www.yorkshirepost.co.uk/news/Yorkshire-schoolboy-locked-up-on.4401314.jp

34. *Britain's youngest terrorist, Hammaad Munshi, faces jail after guilty verdict*, *The Times*, 18 Aug 2008.
http://www.timesonline.co.uk/tol/news/uk/crime/article 4558496.ece
Hammaad Munshi, schoolboy terrorist, given two-year sentence, *The Times*, 20 Sep 2008.
http://www.timesonline.co.uk/tol/news/uk/crime/article 4786555.ece

35. *Terror 'Mr Fixit' sentenced to 12 years*, by James Sturcke and agencies, *Guardian*, 19 Aug 2008.
www.guardian.co.uk/uk/2008/aug/19/uksecurity.ukcrime

17. WAITING FOR A BOMBER

36. *Taliban's income all termed illegal*, by Amjad Bashir Siddiqi, For CentralAsiaOnline.com, 16 April 2010.
http://www.centralasiaonline.com/cocoon/caii/xhtml/en_GB/features/caii/features/pakistan/2010/04/16/feature-02

37. *Terror plots and conspiracy theories: the hunt for Rashid Rauf*, *Independent*, 27 Sep 2008.
http://www.independent.co.uk/news/world/asia/terror-plots-and-conspiracy-theories-the-hunt-for-rashid-rauf-944064.html

38. *Taliban Commander Baitullah Mehsud*, by Alex Altman, *Time*, 3 Apr 2009.
http://www.time.com/time/world/article/0,8599,1889286,00.html

39. *Profile: Mullah Baradar – father of the roadside IED*, The Times, 17 Feb 2010.

   http://www.timesonline.co.uk/tol/news/world/asia/article7029075.ece

40. *Pakistan Takes On Taliban Leader Mehsud*, by Omar Waraich, Islamabad *Time* magazine, 16 June 2009.

   http://www.time.com/time/world/article/0,8599,1904905,00.html#ixzz0nJWwYdE0

   Was the Taliban's Captured No. 2 on the Outs with Mullah Omar? by Tim McGirk, Islamabad *Time* magazine, 23 Feb 2010.

   http://www.time.com/time/world/article/0,8599,1967291,00.html

18. DRAWING THE NET

41. *MI5 targets four Met police officers 'working as Al Qaeda spies'*, Daily Mail, 10 Mar 2008.

   http://www.dailymail.co.uk/news/article-528813/MI5-targets-Met-police-officers-working-Al-Qaeda-spies.html

42. Channel 4 poll reported in *Time* magazine: *Such Lovely Lads*, by Michael Elliott, *Time* magazine, 13 Aug 2006.

   http://www.time.com/time/magazine/article/0,9171,1226136-1,00.html#ixzz0nJachD3f

43. *CIA Places Blame for Bhutto Assassination: Hayden Cites Al-Qaeda, Pakistani Fighters*, by Joby Warrick, *Washington Post*, 18 Jan 2008.

   http://www.washingtonpost.com/wp-dyn/content/world/index.html

44. *The Predator War: What are the risks of the C.I.A.'s covert*

drone program? by Jane Mayer, *New Yorker*, 26 Oct 2009.
http://www.newyorker.com/reporting/2009/10/26/091026fa_fact_mayer#ixzz0nJtjmVLu

45. *Pakistan's arrest of Mullah Baradar: tactics or strategy?* Reuters, 17 Feb 2010.
http://blogs.reuters.com/pakistan/2010/02/17/pakistans-arrest-of-mullah-baradar-tactics-or-strategy/

20. STOLEN SECRETS

46. *Guilty plea in Met leak case*, by Andrew Hough, *Guardian*, 18 Jun 2007.
http://www.guardian.co.uk/media/2007/jun/18/sundaytimes.pressandpublishing
'Secrets leak' Met worker charged, BBC News, 17 May 2007.
http://news.bbc.co.uk/1/hi/uk/6663855.stm

47. *Scotland Yard man jailed for terror leak*, by Megan Levy and agencies, *Daily Telegraph*, 27 July 2007.
http://www.telegraph.co.uk/news/uknews/1558648/Scotland-Yard-man-jailed-for-terror-leak.html

22. SOLDIERS OF ALLAH

48. *Profiles: The terror gang members*, *Independent*, 26 Feb 2008.
http://www.independent.co.uk/news/uk/crime/profiles-the-terror-gang-members-787469.html
'Osama bin 'London's' years of terror training, by Duncan Gardham, *Daily Telegraph*, 26 Feb 2008.
http://www.telegraph.co.uk/news/uknews/1579916/Osama-bin-Londons-years-of-terror-training.html

23. THE GREAT CHINESE TAKEAWAY

49. *Top extremist recruiter is jailed*, BBC News Online, 26 Feb 2008.

    http://news.bbc.co.uk/1/hi/uk/7231492.stm

50. *Terrorists freed to live in bail hostels: Up to 20 convicted terrorists have been freed from prison to live in bail hostels normally used to house burglars, robbers and sex offenders*, by David Barrett, *Daily Telegraph*, 18 Jul 2009.

    http://www.telegraph.co.uk/news/newstopics/politics/lawandorder/5857850/Terrorists-freed-to-live-in-bail-hostels.html

    Back on the streets of Britain: 20 convicted Islamic terrorists freed from jail early, by Rebecca Camber, *Daily Mail*, 9 Sep 2009.

    http://www.dailymail.co.uk/news/article-1212247/Set-free-20-convicted-Islamic-terrorists-let-jail-early-roam-British-streets.html

    Five freed terrorists sent back to prison after breaching parole, by Niall Firth, *Daily Mail*, 1 Oct 2009.

    http://www.dailymail.co.uk/news/article-1217384/Five-freed-terrorists-sent-prison-breaching-parole.html#ixzz0nKCeJaUT

24. EAGLE EYE

51. *Photographers criminalised as police 'abuse' anti-terror laws: Fury as stop-and-search powers are used to block and confiscate legal pictures*, by Jonathan Brown, *Independent*, 6 Jan 2009.

    http://www.independent.co.uk/news/uk/home-news/photographers-criminalised-as-police-abuse-antiterror-laws-1228149.html

52. *Innocent photographer or terrorist?* by Tom Geoghegan, BBC News Magazine, 17 April 2008.
http://news.bbc.co.uk/1/hi/7351252.stm

25. THE MAN FROM YEMEN

53. *U.S. Embassy hit in Yemen, raising militancy concerns*, Shane Bauer, Christian Science Monitor, 18 Sep 2008.
http://www.csmonitor.com/2008/0918/p07s02-wome.html. Retrieved 18 September 2008.
Death toll in Yemen US embassy attack rises to 19. Associated Press via the *International Herald Tribune*, 21 Sep 2008.
http://www.iht.com/articles/ap/2008/09/21/news/ML-Yemen-US-Embassy.php.

54. *Inspired by bin Laden, Al-Qaida in Arabian Peninsula seeks to expand operations beyond Yemen*, by Sarah El Deeb, The Canadian Press, 29 Dec 2009.
http://www.google.com/hostednews/canadianpress/article/ALeqM5g1UTDynDE1FE3Zpk15QvuE3ihZzA

55. *Al-Qaeda group in Yemen gaining prominence*, Sudarsan Raghavan, *Washington Post*, 28 Dec 2009.

56. *Yemen identifies attackers in US embassy attack*, by Al-Haj, Ahmed, Associated Press, 1 Nov 2008.
http://ap.google.com/article/ALeqM5jyZ4yhVqAu5yqaNFXVY9748IMsNwD9465M980.
2 tourists dead in attack in Yemen, *International Herald Tribune*, 18 Jan 2008.

57. *New al-Qaida message urges Yemenis to fight gov't*, Associated Press, 19 Feb 2009.
http://www.google.com/hostednews/ap/article/ALeqM5jyZ4yhVqAu5yqaNFXVY9748IMsNwD96EKC980.

58. *British envoy to Yemen escapes suicide bombing*, *Bangkok Post*, 26 Apr 2010.
http://www.bangkokpost.com/news/world/175907/british-envoy-to-yemen-escapes-suicide-bombing

26. FAHRENHEIT 451

59. *Fanning the Flames* by Romesh Ratnesar, *Time Magazine*, 12 Feb 2006
http://www.time.com/time/magazine/article/0,9171,1158969-2,00.html

60. *Six killed, 24 injured in blast near Danish Embassy*, Associated Press of Pakistan. 2 Jun 2008.
http://www.app.com.pk/en_/index.php?option=com_content&task=view&id=40082&Itemid=1

61. *'My book honours the prophet Mohammed,' says author whose novel provoked fire-bomb attack on publisher*, by Tom Kelly and Lucy Ballinger, *Daily Mail*, 29 Sep 2008.
http://www.dailymail.co.uk/news/article-1063229/My-book-honours-prophet-Mohammed-says-author novel provoked-bomb-attack publisher.html#ixzz0nu6m W0I1

62. *Firebomb attack on book publisher: Firm had bought rights to a controversial novel about the Prophet Muhammad's child bride*, by Jamie Doward and Mark Townsend, *Observer*, 28 Sep 2008.
http://www.guardian.co.uk/uk/2008/sep/28/muhammad.book.attack

63. *Man guilty of inciting race hate at protest*, by Vikram Dodd, *Guardian*, 10 Nov 2006.
http://www.guardian.co.uk/uk/2006/nov/10/race.muhammadcartoons

64. *Three guilty of arson conspiracy*, Metropolitan Police Bulletin 0000001283, 15 May 2009
http://cms.met.police.uk/news/convictions/three_guilty_of_arson_conspiracy

65. *Why thugs must not be allowed to prevail*, by Luke Johnson, *Financial Times*, 29 Oct 2008.
http://www.ft.com/cms/s/0/f0cfbbc8-a559-11dd-b4f5-000077b07658.html?nclick_check=1
Plans to publish controversial novel about wife of Mohammed suspended after firebomb attack on publisher's home, by Richard Pendlebury, *Daily Mail*, 2 Oct 2008.
http://www.dailymail.co.uk/news/article-1064538/Novel-wife-Mohammed-suspended-bomb-attack-publishers-home.html#ixzz0ntvsKmj6

66. *Muslim extremists jailed for arson attack on Mohammed book publisher's home*, by Tom Kelly, *Daily Mail*, 8 July 2009.
http://www.dailymail.co.uk/news/article-1198111/If-choose-live-country-live-rules-says-judge-jails-Muslim-extremists-arson-attack-publishers-home.html#ixzz0ntuYSAhB

27. GETTING THERMOBARIC

67. *Firefighter 'found bomb in car'*, BBC News, 16 Oct 2008.
news.bbc.co.uk/2/hi/uk_news/7674350.stm

68. *Second car bomb found in London's West End*, by Duncan Gardham and Sally Peck, *Daily Telegraph*, 29 June 2007.
http://www.telegraph.co.uk/news/main.jhtml?xml=/news/2007/06/29/nbomb1029.xml.

29. GATE CRASHERS

69. *Blazing car crashes into airport*, BBC News, 30 June 2007.
http://news.bbc.co.uk/1/hi/scotland/6257194.stm
Flaming SUV rams U.K. airport; 2 arrests, Associated Press, 30
June 2007.
http://news.yahoo.com/s/ap/20070630/ap_on_re_eu/
britain_airport_crash_38
The baggage handler who tackled terrorists, by Simon Crerar, *The
Times*, 3 July 2007.
www.timesonline.co.uk/tol/news/uk/article2020607.ece
Britain under attack as bombers strike at airport, David Leppard,
The Times, 1 July 2007.
http://www.timesonline.co.uk/tol/news/uk/crime/
article2010062.ece
*Duo who attacked Glasgow airport 'were resigned to death', say
officers*, by Adam Fresco, *The Times*, 5 July 2007.
http://www.timesonline.co.uk/tol/news/uk/article2033389.
ece

70. *'Terror ringleader' is brilliant NHS doctor*, Daily Mail, 2 July 2007.
http://www.dailymail.co.uk/pages/live/articles/news/news.
html?in_article_id=465481&in_page_id=1770&ct=5.
Car bombing suspects: who are they? Sky News, 2 July 2007.
http://news.sky.com/skynews/article/0,,30000-
1273245,00.html.

71. *Glasgow Airport attack man dies*, BBC News, 2 Aug 2007.
http://news.bbc.co.uk/1/hi/scotland/glasgow_and_west/
6928854.stm
Doctor guilty of car bomb attacks, BBC News, 16 Dec 2008.
http://news.bbc.co.uk/1/hi/7773410.stm

Iraqi doctor's road to radicalism: Bilal Abdulla, by Dominic Casciani, BBC News, 16 Dec 2008.
http://news.bbc.co.uk/1/hi/uk/7784799.stm

72. *Baggage handler becomes web hero*, BBC News, 2 July 2007.
http://news.bbc.co.uk/1/hi/scotland/glasgow_and_west/62 62266.stm

30. FAREWELL, SPECIAL BRANCH

73. *The Afghan-Pakistan militant nexus*, BBC News, 1 Dec 2009.
http://news.bbc.co.uk/1/hi/7601748.stm

74. *The CIA Takes a Big Hit in the Afghan War*, by Bobby Ghosh, *Time* magazine, 1 Jan 2010.
http://www.time.com/time/world/article/0,8599,1950890, 00.html?iid=sphere-inline-bottom#ixzz0nKdeBCcE

75. *'Afghanistan CIA bomber' shown vowing revenge*, BBC News, 9 Jan 2010.
http://news.bbc.co.uk/2/hi/8449789.stm

76. *The CIA Double Cross: How Bad a Blow in Afghanistan?* by Joe Klein, *Time* magazine, 7 Jan 2010.
http://www.time.com/time/politics/article/0,8599,1952149, 00.html
The Khost CIA Bombing: Assessing the Damage in Afghanistan, by Robert Baer, 8 Jan 2010.
http://www.time.com/time/nation/article/0,8599,1952531, 00.html?iid=sphere-inline-bottom#ixzz0nKdAgpO3